For page-turning for[...] "chill to the bone" (F[...] these dazzling best[...]

SPIDER BONES

"A fine novel. . . . Reichs, who once again uses her own scientific knowledge to enhance a complex plot and continually developing characters, delivers a whopper of a final twist."

—*Publishers Weekly*

"Reading a new Tempe Brennan novel is like hooking up with old friends: you know you'll have a good time."

—*Booklist*

206 BONES

"With her usual blend of cutting-edge forensic science and a stubborn, compelling heroine, Reichs manages to juggle several story lines without losing an ounce of momentum."

—*Publishers Weekly* (starred review)

"The forensic procedures take center stage as they always do in this cleverly plotted and expertly maintained series."

—*The New York Times*

DEVIL BONES
#1 *New York Times* bestseller!

"Reichs keeps the roller coaster on track and speeding along, page after page."

—Jeffery Deaver, *New York Times* bestselling author of *Edge*

***Spider Bones* is also available from Simon & Schuster Audio and as an eBook**

"Her expertise is snappily and entertainingly delivered."

"I'm amazed by how seamlessly Reichs makes the transition from scientist to great storyteller. What's not to admire and envy?"

"The suspense is intense . . . and the forensic education is graduate level."

"*Devil Bones* is her best yet."

BONES TO ASHES

"We can't get enough."

BREAK NO BONES

"A rare treat. . . . Mesmerizing."

CROSS BONES

"A spirited rival to *The Da Vinci Code*. . . . Reichs is in top form."

MONDAY MOURNING

"The science is downright snazzy, the mystery plenty devious. . . ."

KATHY REICHS

SPIDER BONES

POCKET BOOKS

NEW YORK LONDON TORONTO SYDNEY

Pocket Books
A Division of Simon & Schuster, Inc.
1230 Avenue of the Americas
New York, NY 10020

This book is a work of fiction. Names, characters, places, and incidents either are products of the author's imagination or are used fictitiously. Any resemblance to actual events or locales or persons, living or dead, is entirely coincidental.

This Pocket Books paperback edition August 2011

POCKET and colophon are registered trademarks of Simon & Schuster, Inc.

For information about special discounts for bulk purchases, please contact Simon & Schuster Special Sales at 1-866-506-1949 or business@simonandschuster.com

The Simon & Schuster Speakers Bureau can bring authors to your live event. For more information or to book an event contact the Simon & Schuster Speakers Bureau at 1-866-248-3049 or visit our website at www.simonspeakers.com.

Cover design by John Vairo Jr.
Woman walking © Martin San/Getty Images.

Manufactured in the United States of America

10 9 8 7 6 5 4 3 2 1

ISBN 978-1-4516-4194-3
ISBN 978-1-4391-1279-3 (ebook)

For
Henry Charles Reichs
Born December 20, 2009

"Until They Are Home"

The motto of the Joint POW/MIA Accounting Command

ACKNOWLEDGMENTS

Spider Bones benefited greatly from the help and support of colleagues, friends, and family.

First and foremost I must thank those at the Joint POW/MIA Accounting Command (JPAC) and the Central Identification Laboratory (CIL). Robert Mann, PhD, D-ABFA, Director, Forensic Science Academy, patiently answered thousands of questions, some by text from Southeast Asia. William R. Belcher, PhD, D-ABFA, Forensic Anthropologist/Supervisor, and Wayne Perry, Lt. Col., USAF, Director of Public Affairs, hosted me on a thorough and congenial refresher tour of the facility. Andretta Schellinger, Archivist, J-2 Section, clarified the process of record keeping. Audrey Meehan, DNA specialist, enlightened me on DNA analysis JPAC style. Thomas D. Holland, PhD, D-ABFA, Scientific Director of the CIL, was a good sport about my invasion of his turf, both professional and literary.

Equally invaluable was the help of Kanthi De Alwis, MD, former Chief Medical Examiner for the City and County of Honolulu. Pamela A.

Cadiente, Investigator, provided details concerning the death investigation process in Hawaii.

Alain St-Marseille, Agent de liaison, Bureau du coroner, Module des Scènes de Crime S.Q., Service de l'Identité Judiciaire, Service de la Criminalistique; Mike Dulaney, Detective, Homicide Unit, Calgary Police Department; and Sergeant Harold (Chuck) Henson, Charlotte-Mecklenburg Police Department, helped with various policing and law enforcement queries.

Mike Warns answered some very odd questions. Frank and Julie Saul, Ken Kennedy, Tony Falsetti, and David Sweet gave input on gold inlays in teeth.

In the Belly of the Lizard, an unpublished manuscript by Miles Davis, provided insight into the United States involvement in the Vietnam War.

I appreciate the continued support of Chancellor Philip L. Dubois of the University of North Carolina–Charlotte.

I am grateful to my family for their patience and understanding. Extra credit to Paul Reichs for reading and commenting on the manuscript, and for sharing his experiences in Vietnam.

Deepest thanks to my agent, Jennifer Rudolph Walsh, and to my virtuoso editors, Nan Graham and Susan Sandon. I also want to acknowledge all those who work so very hard on my behalf, including: Katherine Monaghan, Paul Whitlatch, Rex Bonomelli, Simon Littlewood, Gillian Holmes, Rob Waddington, Glenn O'Neill, Briton Schey, Margaret Riley, Tracy Fisher, Michelle Feehan, Cathryn Summerhayes, and Raffaella De Angelis. I am also indebted to the

Canadian crew, especially to Kevin Hanson and Amy Cormier.

And, of course, I am grateful to my readers. Buckets of thanks for your e-mails, your visits to my Web site, and your presence at signings, author lunches, literary festivals, and other events. Most of all, thanks for reading my stories. I know your time is precious. I am honored that you choose to spend some of it with Tempe and me.

If I have forgotten to thank someone I am truly sorry. If this book contains errors they are my fault.

1

THE AIR SMELLED OF SUN-WARMED BARK AND apple buds raring to blossom and get on with life. Overhead, a million baby leaves danced in the breeze.

Fields spread outward from the orchard in which I stood, their newly turned soil rich and black. The Adirondacks crawled the horizon, gaudy bronze and green in the glorious sunlight.

A day made of diamonds.

The words winged at me from a war drama I'd watched on the classic-film channel. Van Johnson? No matter. The phrase was perfect for the early May afternoon.

I'm a Carolina girl, no fan of polar climes. Jonquils in February. Azaleas, dogwoods, Easter at the beach. Though I've worked years in the North, after each long, dark, tedious winter the beauty of Quebec spring still takes me by surprise.

The world was sparkling like a nine-carat rock.

A relentless buzzing dragged my gaze back to the corpse at my feet. According to SQ Agent

André Bandau, now maintaining as much distance as possible, the body came ashore around noon.

News telegraphs quickly. Though it was now barely three, flies crawled and swarmed in a frenzy of feeding. Or breeding. I was never sure which.

To my right, a tech was taking pictures. To my left, another was running yellow crime-scene tape around the stretch of shoreline on which the body lay. The jackets of both said *Service de l'identité judiciaire, Division des scènes de crime.* Quebec's version of CSI.

Ryan sat in a squad car behind me, talking to a man in a trucker cap. Lieutenant-détective Andrew Ryan, Section des crimes contre la personne, Sûreté du Québec. Sounds fancy. It's not.

In la Belle Province, crime is handled by local forces in major cities, by the provincial police out in the boonies. Ryan is a homicide detective with the latter, the SQ.

The body was spotted in a pond near the town of Hemmingford, forty-five miles south of Montreal. Hemmingford. Boonies. SQ. You get it.

But why Ryan, a homicide dick working out of the SQ's Montreal unit?

Since the deceased was plastic-wrapped and wearing a rock for a flipper, the local SQ post suspected foul play. Thus the bounce to Ryan.

And to me. Temperance Brennan, forensic anthropologist.

Working out of the Laboratoire de sciences judiciaires et de médecine légale in Montreal, I do the decomposed, mummified, mutilated, dis-

membered, and skeletal for the province, helping
the coroner with identification, cause of death,
and postmortem interval.

Immersion leaves a corpse in less than pristine
condition, so when Ryan caught the call about a
floater, he enlisted me.

Through the windshield I saw Ryan's passenger gesture with agitated hands. The man was
probably fifty, with gray stubble and features
that suggested a fondness for drink. Black and
red letters on his cap declared *I Love Canada*.
A maple leaf replaced the traditional heart icon.

Ryan nodded. Wrote something in what I
knew was a small notebook.

Refocusing on the corpse, I continued jotting
in my own spiral pad.

The body lay supine, encased in clear plastic,
with only the left lower leg outside and exposed.
Duct tape sealed the plastic under the chin and
around the left calf.

The exposed left foot wore a heavy biker boot.
Above its rim, a two-inch strip of flesh was the
color of oatmeal.

A length of yellow polypropylene rope looped
the boot roughly halfway up its laces. The rope's
other end was attached to a rock via an elaborate
network of knots.

The victim's head was wrapped separately, in
what looked like a plastic grocery bag. A black
tube protruded from one side of the bag, held in
place with more duct tape. The whole arrangement was secured by tape circling the neck and
the tube's point of exit.

What the flip?

When I dropped to a squat, the whining went mongo. Shiny green missiles bounced off my face and hair.

Up close, the smell of putrefaction was unmistakable. That was wrong, given the vic's packaging.

Waving off *Diptera,* I repositioned for a better view of the body's far side.

A dark mass pulsated in what I calculated was the right-thigh region. I shooed the swarm with one gloved hand.

And felt a wave of irritation.

The right lower was visible through a fresh cut in the plastic. Flies elbowed for position on the wrist and moved upward out of sight.

Sonofabitch.

Suppressing my annoyance, I shifted to the head.

Algae spread among the folds and creases of the bag covering the top and back of the skull. More slimed one side of the odd little tube.

I could discern murky features beneath the translucent shroud. A chin. The rim of an orbit. A nose, bent to one side. Bloating and discoloration suggested that visual identification would not be an option.

Rising, I swept my gaze toward the pond.

Nosed to the shore was a tiny aluminum skiff with a three-horsepower outboard engine. On the floor in back were a beer cooler, a tackle box, and a fishing rod.

Beside the skiff was a red canoe, beached and lying on its starboard side. *Navigator* was lettered in white below the port gunwale.

Polypropylene rope ran from a knot on the canoe's midship thwart to a rock on the ground. I noted that the knots on the rock resembled the one securing the victim's ankle weight.

Inside the canoe, a paddle lay lengthwise against the starboard hull. A canvas duffel was wedged below the stern seat. A knife and a roll of duct tape were snugged beside the duffel.

An engine hum joined the buzz of flies and the bustle and click of techs moving around me. I ignored it.

Five yards up the shoreline, a rusted red moped sat beneath a precociously flowering tree. The license plate was unreadable from where I stood. At least with my eyes.

Dual rearview mirrors. Kickstand. Raised trunk behind the seat. The thing reminded me of my freshman undergrad wheels. I'd loved that scooter.

Walking the area between the skiff and the moped, I saw a set of tire treads consistent with the pickup parked by the road, and one tread line consistent with the moped itself. No foot or boot prints. No cigarette butts, aluminum cans, condoms, or candy wrappers. No litter of any kind.

Moving back along the water, I continued recording observations. The engine sounds grew louder.

Mud-rimmed pond, shallow, no tides or chop. Apple trees within five feet of the bank. Ten yards to a gravel road accessing Highway 219.

Tires crunched. The engine sounds cut out. Car doors opened, slammed. Male voices spoke French.

Satisfied I'd learn nothing further from the scene, and wanting a word with the industrious Agent Bandau, I turned and walked toward the vehicles lining the road.

A black van had joined Ryan's Jeep, the blue crime-scene truck, the fisherman's pickup, and Bandau's SQ cruiser. Yellow letters on the van said *Bureau du coroner*.

I recognized the van's driver, an autopsy tech named Gilles Pomerleau. Riding shotgun was my new assistant, Roch Lauzon.

Exchanging bonjours, I assured Pomerleau and Lauzon the wait wouldn't be long. They crossed to view the corpse. Ryan remained in the cruiser with the unfortunate angler.

I approached Bandau, a gangly twentysomething with a wheat blond mustache and skin that looked like it really hated sun. Though it was hidden by his agent's cap, I envisioned pale hair going south at a rate that alarmed its young owner.

"What's with the plastic wrap?" Bandau asked in French, looking past me toward the corpse.

"Good question." I had no explanation.

"Male or female?"

"Yes," I said.

Bandau's face came around, winking my reflection off his aviator shades. My expression was not a happy one.

"I understand you were the first responder."

Bandau nodded, eyes unreadable behind the dark lenses.

"How'd that go?"

Bandau cocked his chin toward his cruiser.

"Local named Gripper found the vic. Claims he was fishing when he saw the canoe. He motored over to investigate, something snagged his propeller. Says he paddled in, saw his catch was a corpse, dialed nine-one-one on his cell. While waiting, he dragged the body ashore then retrieved the canoe."

"Thorough guy."

"Guess you could say that."

"Is he believable?" I asked.

Bandau shrugged. *Who knows?*

"What are his creds?"

"Lives on avenue Margaret with his wife. Works maintenance at the wildlife park."

Hemmingford is located in the Montérégie region, a hair from the Canada-U.S. border. The Montérégie is noted for apples, maple syrup, and Parc Safari, a combination drive-through nature preserve and amusement park.

When I first started commuting to Quebec, the media were following the story of a group of rhesus monkey escapees from the park. I had visions of the band belly-crawling south through the night to avoid border patrol, risking all for a green card and a better life. Twenty years later, the image still amuses me.

"Go on," I said.

"I caught the call around noon, drove out, secured the area."

"And printed the body." Chilly.

Sensing my disapproval, Bandau spread his feet and thumb-hooked his belt. "I thought it might speed the ID."

"You cut the plastic."

"I wore gloves." Defensive. "Look, I had the new camera, so I shot close-ups and transmitted the file electronically."

"You compromised the scene."

"What scene? The guy was bobbing in a pond."

"The flies will chip in to buy you a beer. Especially the ladies. They're ovipositing with glee as we speak."

"I was trying to help."

"You broke protocol."

Bandau's lips tightened.

"What happened with the prints?"

"I got ridge patterning on all five digits. Someone at the post sent the file to CPIC. From there it went into both NCIC and the New York State system."

CPIC is the Canadian Police Information Centre, a computerized index of criminal justice information. NCIC is the U.S. equivalent, the FBI's National Crime Information Center.

"Why send the prints south?"

"Being on the border, we get a lot of Americans coming through. And the scooter has a New York plate."

Not bad, Bandau.

Hearing a car door slam, we both turned.

Ryan was walking toward us. Released for the moment, Gripper was leaning on his pickup, looking uneasy.

Ryan nodded to Bandau, spoke to me.

"What do you think?"

"Guy's dead."

"Guy?"

"Based solely on size."

"How long?"

"Tough to say. Given this week's warm temperatures, and the shrink-wrap, I'd guess a day or two. There's some decomp, but not much." I cast a meaningful glance at Bandau. "That'll change now that the bugs have been issued a gate pass."

I told Ryan what Bandau had done.

"What kind of rookie move was that?"

Bandau's cheeks went raspberry.

"That's no way to make it up the chain, son."

Ryan turned back to me.

"Twenty-four to forty-eight hours tracks with the wit's account. Gripper says he comes out here on his days off, usually Tuesdays and Thursdays. Swears day before yesterday the pond was canoe and corpse free."

"Algae patterning suggests the body was floating with the head just at or below the waterline," I said.

Ryan nodded. "According to Gripper, the body was hanging head up in the water, with the booted foot attached to a rock lying on the bottom. He guesses the pond's about eight feet deep where he found the guy."

"Where was the canoe?"

"Beside the vic. Gripper says that's how the rope got tangled in his outboard."

Ryan spoke to Bandau. "Check for feedback on those prints."

"Yes, sir."

Ryan and I watched Bandau lope toward his cruiser.

"Probably DVRs cop shows," Ryan said.

"Not the right ones," I said.

Ryan glanced toward the body, back to me.

"What do you think?"

"Weird one," I said.

"Suicide? Accident? Murder?"

I spread my palms in a "who knows" gesture.

Ryan smiled. "That's why I bring you along."

"The vic probably kept the canoe at the pond and drove the moped back and forth."

"Back and forth from where?"

"Beats me."

"Yep. Can't do without you."

A wood thrush trilled overhead. Another answered. The cheerful exchange was in stark contrast to the grim conversation below.

As I glanced up, hurried footsteps startled the birds into flight.

"Got him." Bandau's aviators were now hanging by one bow from his pocket. "Cold hit in the States. Thirteen-point match."

Ryan's brows may have shot higher than mine.

"John Charles Lowery. Date of birth March twenty-first, nineteen fifty."

"Not bad, Bandau." This time I said it aloud.

"There's one problem."

Bandau's already deep frown lines deepened.

"John Charles Lowery died in 1968."

2

"HOW'S LOWERY A FLOATER TODAY IF HE clocked out four decades back?" Ryan voiced the question I'd been asking myself.

I had no answer.

We were heading north on 15. The coroner's van was somewhere behind us. Pomerleau and Lauzon would check their soggy passenger into the morgue, where he'd wait in a cooler until I unwrapped him in the morning.

"Maybe the hit was a mistake."

"Thirteen-point match?" My tone conveyed the skepticism I felt.

"Remember that lawyer in Oregon?"

Brandon Mayfield. The FBI linked him to the Madrid train bombing based on fingerprint evidence. Turned out the match was erroneous.

"That was a fluke," I said. "You think printing the body on-site will cause blowback?"

"On the good agent, yeah. A bonehead move, but probably little harm done."

"He meant well."

Ryan shook his head in disbelief.

For several miles, silence filled the Jeep. Ryan broke it.

"You going home?"

I nodded.

Minutes later we were arcing over the Saint Lawrence on the Champlain Bridge. Below us, the river flowed cold and dark. To one side, tiny gardens and lawns winked nascent green amid the condo and apartment towers on Île-des-Soeurs.

Back in the city, traffic moved like mud through a straw. The Jeep lurched and jerked as Ryan shifted between gas and brake.

Kind, yes. Witty, affirmative. Generous, absolutely. Patient, no way. Travel with Ryan was often a trial.

I checked my watch. Five ten.

Normally Ryan would have queried my dining plans by now. Suggested a restaurant. Tonight he didn't.

Supper with his daughter? Beers with the boys? A date?

Did I care?

I cracked my window. The smell of oily water drifted into the Jeep. Warm cement. Exhaust.

Yeah. I cared.

Would I ask?

No way. Since our breakup we'd established a bimodal new balance. Professional relations: same as always. Social relations: don't ask, don't tell.

My choice, really. Though Lutetia was once again history, getting dumped for Ryan's ex still hurt.

Once burned, twice shy.

And there *was* Charlie Hunt.

Snapshot image. Charlie on the rooftop deck of his uptown Charlotte brownstone. Cinnamon skin. Emerald eyes. Tall as his daddy, who'd played in the NBA.

Not bad.

I slid a glance toward Ryan.

Sandy hair. Turquoise eyes. Long and lean as his daddy in Nova Scotia.

Not bad either.

Truth be told, after decades of marriage, then a rocky postseparation readjustment, followed by going steady and an undeserved boot to the scrap heap, I was grooving on the nonmonogamy thing.

Except for two teensy details. Ryan hadn't shared my bed since the previous summer's split. Charlie Hunt had yet to gain access.

On dual levels it had been a long, cold winter.

The sound of Ryan's mobile broke into my musings.

I listened as he said a lot of *ouis*, asked a few questions. From the latter I assumed the call was about John Lowery.

Ryan spoke to me after disconnecting. "Bandau sent a query south. Turns out our boy died in combat in Vietnam."

"Are you using the *Sesame Street* theme as your ringtone?"

"'Keeping the clouds away,'" Ryan sang.

"Got some Big Bird sheets on your bed?"

"*Bien sûr, madame.*" Big wink. "Want to come check them out?"

"Lowery? Vietnam?"

"Ever hear of an outfit called JPAC?"

"Sure. I used to work with them. The Joint POW/MIA Accounting Command. Used to be called CILHI until two thousand three."

"Hallelujah. Alphabet soup."

" 'Now I've said my ABC's,' " I sang.

"Let's not push the metaphor," Ryan said.

"Central Identification Laboratory, Hawaii. JPAC resulted from the merger of CILHI and the Joint Task Force–Full Accounting Commission. JPAC's lab portion is now referred to as the CIL. It's the largest forensic anthropology laboratory in the world."

"Lowery didn't come through JPAC, but that's where his case has been bounced. What's your connection with the place?"

"Every positive JPAC ID has to be approved by a zillion reviewers, some of whom are civilian and external to the CIL. I served in that capacity for many years."

"Right. I forgot about those midwinter trips to Hawaii."

"Travel was required twice yearly for lab oversight."

"And a little surfing, my coconut princess?"

"I don't surf."

"How about I hang ten over to your place and we—"

"I rarely had time to set foot on a beach."

"Uh-huh."

"When was Lowery ID'd?" I asked.

"Bandau didn't say."

"If it was back in the sixties, things were totally different."

Ryan turned off rue Sainte-Catherine, drove half a block, and slid to the curb in front of a gray stone complex with elaborate bay windows fronting the sidewalk. Sadly, my unit is in back and derives no benefit from this architectural whimsy.

"You plan to do plastic man first thing tomorrow?"

"Yeah. Since there's a five-hour time difference, I'll phone the CIL tonight, see what I can learn about Lowery."

I felt Ryan's eyes on my back as I walked toward the door.

Quebec springs usually send a lot of work my way. Rivers and lakes thaw. The snow melts. Corpses emerge. Citizens abandon their sofas for the great outdoors. Some discover the corpses. Some join their ranks.

Because my May rotation to Montreal is usually a long one, Birdie accompanies me as a carry-on under the seat. Except during the flight, the little furball is pretty good company.

The cat was waiting inside the front door.

"Hey, Bird." I squatted to pet him.

Birdie sniffed my jeans, neck forward, chin up, nose sucking in quick little gulps.

"Good day today?"

Birdie moved off and sat with paws primly together.

"*Eau de decomp* not your scent?" I rose and tossed my purse onto the sideboard.

Bird raised and licked a paw.

My condo is small. L-shaped living-dining room and shotgun kitchen in front, two bedrooms and two baths in back. It's located at ground level, in one wing of a four-story U-shaped building. French doors give onto a tiny fenced yard from the living room. Opposite, through the dining room, another set opens onto a central courtyard.

Direct access to the lawn on one side and the garden on the other are what hooked me originally. More than a decade down the road, I'm still in the place.

Appetite intact despite the olfactory affront, Birdie padded behind me to the kitchen.

The condo's interior features earth tones and recycled furniture that I antiqued. Natural wood trim. Stone fireplace. Framed poster of a Jean Dubuffet. Vase full of shells to remind me of the Carolina shore.

My answering machine was blinking like a tripped-out turn signal.

I checked the messages.

My sister, Harry, in Houston, unhappy with her current dating arrangement.

My daughter, Katy, in Charlotte, hating her job, her social life, and the universe in general.

The *Gazette,* selling subscriptions.

Harry.

My neighbor Sparky complaining about Birdie. Again.

Harry.

Charlie Hunt. "Thinking of you."

Harry.

Deleting all, I headed for the shower.

Supper was linguini tossed with olive oil, spinach, mushrooms, and feta. Birdie licked the cheese from his pasta, then finished the crunchy brown pellets in his bowl.

After clearing the dishes, I dialed the CIL.

Five thousand miles from the tundra a phone was answered on the first ring. After identifying myself, I asked for Roger Merkel, the lab's scientific director.

Merkel was in Washington, D.C.

"Dr. Tandler?"

"Hold, please."

Daniel Tandler is assistant director of the CIL. Being the same age, he and I rose through the forensic ranks together, though always at different institutions. We met as undergrads, via the student association of the American Academy of Forensic Sciences. We'd even enjoyed a brief carnal romp way back at the misty dawn of creation. Good fun, bad timing. Enter Pete Petersons. I married, attended grad school at Northwestern, then joined the faculty first at Northern Illinois University, then at the University of North Carolina at Charlotte. Danny stuck with the University of Tennessee straight through, and upon completion of his doctorate, beelined to Hawaii.

The one that got away? Maybe. But, alas, too bad. Danny Tandler is now married and out of play.

Over the years Danny and I have provided mutual support through dissertation defenses, board exams, job interviews, and promotion reviews. When the CIL needed a new external consultant, Danny proposed my name. That was back in the early nineties. I served in that capacity for almost ten years.

The wait for Tandler was a wee bit longer than the one for the initial switchboard pickup.

"Tempe, me lass. How's it hanging?" A voice hinting of country and wide-open spaces.

"Good."

"Tell me you've reconsidered and are coming back on board."

"Not yet."

"It's eighty degrees right now. Wait, wait." Dramatic rustling. "OK. Got my shades on. The sun off the water was blinding my vision."

"You're inside a building on a military base."

"Palm fronds are gently kissing my window."

"Save it for winter. It's beautiful here now."

"To what do I owe this unexpected surprise?"

I told him about the pond, the plastic, and the fingerprint identification of the victim as Lowery.

"Why the packaging?"

"No idea."

"Bizarre. Let me see if I can pull Lowery's file."

It took a full ten minutes.

"Sorry. We've got an arrival ceremony starting in less than an hour. Most folks have already headed over to the hangar. For now I can give you the basics. Details will have to wait."

"I understand."

I did. An arrival ceremony is a solemn occasion honoring an unknown soldier, sailor, airman, or marine fallen far from home in the line of duty. Following recovery and transfer to U.S. soil, it is step one in the complicated path to repatriation.

I'd attended several arrival ceremonies during my tenure with JPAC. I envisioned the scene about to play out. The newly arrived aircraft. The servicemen and women standing at attention. The flag-draped transfer container. The solemn cross-base drive to the CIL lab.

"Private John Charles Lowery was an eighteen-year-old white male. Went in-country on June twenty-fourth, 1967." Danny's tone suggested he was skimming, picking out relevant facts. "Lowery went down in a Huey near Long Binh on January twenty-third, 1968." Pause. "Body was recovered several days later, ID'd, returned to family for burial."

"Burial where?"

"Your neck o' the woods. Lumberton, North Carolina."

"You're kidding."

I heard a voice in the background. Danny said something. The voice responded.

"Sorry, Tempe. I've got to go."

"No problem. I'll talk to you tomorrow. I should know more once I've examined our guy."

That's not how it went.

3

THE NEXT DAY I ROSE AT SEVEN. THIRTY MIN-utes later I was worming my Mazda through the Ville-Marie Tunnel. Again, the weather was splendid.

The Édifice Wilfrid-Derome is a looming T-shaped thirteen-story structure in the Hoche-laga-Maisonneuve district east of *centre-ville*. The Laboratoire de sciences judiciaires et de médecine légale occupies the building's top two floors. The Bureau du coroner is on eleven, the morgue is in the basement. The remaining acreage belongs to the SQ.

Yesiree. Ryan and I work just eight floors apart.

Though the morning staff meeting held no unpleasant surprise for the anthropologist, it had been an unusually busy Thursday. A workplace electrocution and a stabbing went to one pathol-ogist. A suspicious crib death and a fire victim went to another. Pierre LaManche, director of the LSJML's medico-legal section, assigned him-self an apparent suicide involving a teenage boy.

LaManche also assumed responsibility for

LSJML-49744, the case number assigned to John Lowery, but asked that I get the ball rolling. Since ID had been established via prints, once preliminaries were done, depending on body condition, either LaManche would perform a normal autopsy, or I would clean the bones and do a skeletal analysis.

By nine thirty I was downstairs in *salle d'autopsie* number 4, a unit specially outfitted for decomps, floaters, and other aromatics. I work there a lot.

Like its three counterparts, *salle* 4 has swinging doors leading to parallel morgue bays divided into refrigerated compartments. Small white cards mark the presence of temporary residents.

After locating the bay in which LSJML-49744 waited, I got the Nikon and checked its battery. Then I pulled the stainless steel handle.

The smell of putrefying flesh rode the whoosh of refrigerated air. Disengaging the foot brake, I pulled the gurney from its slot.

Pomerleau and Lauzon had dispensed with the usual body bag. Understandable, given Lowery's exotic outerwear.

I was shooting wide views when a door clicked open and footsteps squeaked across tile.

Seconds later Lisa Savard appeared.

Honey blond, with a ready smile and Dolly Parton jugs, Lisa is the darling of every straight homicide cop in Quebec. She's my favorite, too, for different reasons. The woman is the best autopsy tech in the province.

Wanting to improve her fluency, Lisa always speaks English to me.

"A strange one, yes?"

"Definitely."

Lisa studied Lowery a moment.

"Looks like a Ken doll still in the package. Radiology?"

"Yes, please."

While Lisa shot X-rays, I went through Lowery's dossier. So far it held little. The police incident sheet. The morgue intake form. Bandau's report of the NCIC hit. A fax showing an ancient fingerprint card.

I checked the source of the fax. NCIC.

Curious. If Lowery died in '68, why was he in the system? Were prints that old typically entered?

On impulse, I called the fingerprint section of Service de l'identité judiciaire. A Sergeant Boniface told me to come on up. Grabbing the file, I climbed the back stairs to the first floor.

Forty minutes later I descended, knowing a dizzying amount about tented arches, ulnar loops, and accidental whorls. Bottom line: though Boniface was uncertain why Lowery was in the FBI database, he had no doubt the match was legit.

Lowery now lay on a floor-bolted table in the center of *salle* 4. Flies crawled his plastic shroud and buzzed the air above it. A police photographer shot overviews from a ladder.

LaManche and Lisa were examining X-rays popped onto wall-mounted light boxes. I joined them as they moved along the row.

On each film, the skeleton glowed white within

the pale gray of the flesh. I noted nothing unusual in the skull or bones.

We were on the fifth plate when LaManche's gnarled finger tapped an object lying by Lowery's right foot. Radiopaque, the thing lay angled across the calcaneous.

"*Un couteau,*" Lisa said. A knife.

"*Oui,*" LaManche said.

I agreed.

The next prize appeared in a view of the thorax. Roughly eight centimeters long and two centimeters wide, the second object glowed as bright as the first.

"*Mais oui.*" LaManche nodded slowly, finally understanding. "*Oui.*" The nodding morphed to head shaking. "*Sacré bleu.*"

Great. The bizarre death now made sense to the chief. I still didn't get it.

I considered the shape on Lowery's chest. It wasn't another knife. Nor was it a watch, a belt buckle, or a piece of fishing paraphernalia. I hadn't a clue.

Crossing to the body, LaManche began dictating notes.

"Victim is enclosed in what appears to be a homemade bag constructed of a large plastic sheet doubled over and secured with duct tape. The bottom and all but the top ten centimeters of one side are sealed from the outside. The neck end and top ten centimeters of the side are sealed from the inside.

"The plastic has been freshly cut, exposing the right hand. Moderate insect activity is evident in the region of the cut."

As LaManche droned on with details, the photographer snapped away, repositioning the case identifier with each shot.

"It appears the victim entered the bag, then secured the plastic using one arm extended through the ten-centimeter side opening, which was later sealed from the inside."

LaManche gestured to Lisa to measure the ankle rope.

"The left foot is booted and attached to a rock by a twenty-centimeter length of polypropylene rope. It appears the victim secured the rope to the rock then to his ankle, which was left exterior to the plastic."

As Lisa ran her measuring tape, LaManche dictated dimensions. "The outer plastic envelope is one meter in width by two and a half meters in length and conforms closely to the body."

LaManche moved to the end of the table. Flies rose with a buzz of annoyance. Behind me, tiny bodies bounced off the light box.

"The head is wrapped separately. A breathing tube extends to the exterior, duct-taped to the bag."

Breathing tube?

I looked at the slime-covered cylinder. Was the plastic arrangement some sort of jerry-rigged diving gear?

"The bag's lower border is taped tightly around the neck."

On and on. Lisa measured. LaManche recorded lengths, positions, opening dimensions. Finally, he palpated the cranial setup.

"The breathing tube is displaced laterally and posteriorly from the region of the mouth."

I'm not sure why, maybe a vision of the tube popping from Lowery's mouth. A tube through which he intended to draw air.

Suddenly it clicked. The body wrapping. The ankle rock. The knife, meant for escape, but fallen far out of reach.

I felt like a dunce. The chief had it figured way before I did.

But underwater? I vowed to check the literature.

At that moment my mobile sounded.

Ryan.

Stripping off my gloves, I moved to the anteroom and clicked on.

"What's happening?"

"We're unwrapping Lowery."

"You sound pretty confident that's who it is."

I described my session with Boniface.

"Too early for cause of death?"

"I'm pretty sure LaManche is thinking autoerotic. The guy rigged himself up to get his rocks off."

"In a pond?" Ryan sounded skeptical.

"Anything's possible if you follow your dream."

"Worth sliding down for a peek?"

"Autoerotics usually are."

"In the meantime, I thought you'd want to know. The plate on the moped traced to one Morgan Shelby of Plattsburgh, New York. He and I just finished chatting.

"Shelby says he sold the scooter to a Hemmingford man named Jean Laurier. The transaction was, shall we say, informal."

"Cash, no paperwork, the bike goes north costing Laurier no cross-border tax."

"Bingo. According to Shelby, the purchaser promised to deal with registration and licensing in Quebec."

"But didn't."

"The sale took place only ten days ago."

"Jean Laurier. John Lowery."

"*Oui, madame.*"

"What's his story?"

"Bandau did some canvassing, found a few locals who knew the guy. One says Laurier's lived around Hemmingford for as long as he can remember."

"Since 1968?"

"The gentleman wasn't that specific."

"What did Laurier do?"

"Worked as a handyman, strictly freelance."

"Cash again?"

"*Oui, madame.* Laurier stayed pretty much off the grid. No voter registration or tax record. No social insurance number. Bandau's informants say the guy was a loner, weird but not threatening."

"Did you get an LSA?" Last known address.

"*Oui, madame.* Thought I'd toss the place tomorrow. You game?"

"I'm free."

"It's a date."

"It's not a date, Ryan."

"Then perhaps a little *après*-toss toss at my place?"

"I promised Birdie I'd make him deviled eggs."

"I also phoned the Lumberton PD." Ryan's

vowels went longer than Dixie. "Nice friendly boys down thataway."

"Uh-huh."

"Some Lowerys still live there. Guy I talked with actually remembered John, promised to go to the library and copy the kid's yearbook photo."

"Why were Lowery's prints in the system?"

"Because of some part-time job he held during high school. Nurse's aide? Orderly in a mental facility? Something like that."

"I'm impressed."

"I'm a detective. I detect. I'll be down when Lowery's face faxes in."

By noon, the plastic head bag and body wrap hung on drying racks in the hall. The breathing tube turned out to be a common snorkel. It had been photographed, swabbed, and sent upstairs for analysis.

So had a small piece of plastic found bow-tied around Lowery's penis. That would also be tested for bodily fluids.

Lowery lay supine on stainless steel, face distorted, scrotum bloated, gut swollen, and going green. But, overall, the guy was in pretty good shape. A skeletal analysis would not be needed.

"White male, fifty to sixty years old," LaManche dictated. "Black hair. Green eyes. Circumcised. No scars, piercings, or tattoos."

I helped Lisa maneuver the measuring rod.

"Approximately one hundred and seventy-five centimeters in height." Five foot nine.

Ryan arrived as LaManche was circling the

body, checking eyes, hands, scalp, and orifices. He handed me the Lumberton fax.

The image was so small and so blurry, it could have been anyone. But a few things were evident.

The boy had dark eyes, curving brows, and regular features. His black hair was worn side-parted and short.

"Victim shows no signs of external trauma." LaManche looked up. Nodded in greeting. "Detective."

After explaining its source, Ryan handed the fax to LaManche. He and Lisa studied it.

"Clean him, please," LaManche requested.

Lisa used a spray nozzle on Lowery's head. After toweling him dry and side-combing his hair, she positioned the printed image beside his right ear.

Eight eyes ping-ponged from the fax to the face and back.

Four decades of life and two days of death separated the man on the table from the boy in the photo. Though the nose was more bulbous, the jawline more slack, the pond victim had the same dark hair and eyes, the same Al Pacino brows.

Was the Hemmingford floater an older version of the kid from Lumberton?

I couldn't be sure.

"Think it's him?" I asked LaManche.

The chief gave one of his inexplicable French shrugs. *Who knows? Why ask me? What herb flavors the ragout you are making?*

I looked at Ryan. His eyes were glued to the man on the table.

No wonder. The sight was bizarre.

John Lowery had died wearing the following: a cotton soft-cup bra, Glamorise brand, color pink, size 44B; ladies' polyester hipster panties, Blush brand, color pink, size large; a cotton-polyester blend nurse's cap, one size fits all, white with blue stripe; one steel-toed boot, Harley-Davidson brand, side left, color black, size 10.

And that was just the wardrobe.

Lowery had taken two tools inside the plastic with him: a proctoscope, for sport I didn't want to envisage; a Swiss Army Knife, for escape when the party was over.

The proctoscope remained in a fabric sack suspended from his neck. The knife had ended up at his feet.

Bite marks on the snorkel's mouthpiece suggested this wasn't Lowery's first attempt at making subsurface solo whoopee. But somehow, this time, things went bad. Most likely scenario: the tube slipped from his mouth; the knife dropped from his hand.

The setting was unusual, but the chief's initial impression was most probably correct. Lowery's death would go down as accidental asphyxia associated with autoerotic activity.

John Charles Lowery died playing naughty nurse underwater in a self-made ziplock.

4

SATURDAY MORNING PRODUCED ANOTHER immaculate blue sky. Again meteorologists were promising eighty degrees.

Three spring beauties back-to-back. Perhaps a Montreal record.

LaManche called around nine. A courtesy, not required. I like that about him.

The chief's autopsy findings were as I expected. Other than slight atherosclerotic disease, Lowery had no preexisting medical conditions. No traumatic lesions. Some pulmonary edema. A blood alcohol level of 132mg/100 ml.

Cause of death was asphyxia due to oxygen deprivation. Manner was accidental, in the context of autoerotic activity.

By ten Ryan and I were zipping south toward Hemmingford. His mood was upbeat. A rocking Friday night? Light traffic? Too many doughnuts? I didn't pursue it.

I did ask the length of Laurier/Lowery's residence at the address to which we were heading. Ryan said a very long time.

Given that, I queried Laurier/Lowery's ability

to stay off the grid. Ryan relayed a complex story of lax rental agreements and changing proprietorship. Bottom line, when the last landlord died without heirs, Laurier/Lowery simply stayed on. Instead of paying rent, he paid taxes and utilities in the deceased owner's name. Or some such scheme.

The conversation turned to Jean Laurier/John Lowery's unfortunate demise. How could we resist?

"So Lowery got his kink on bundling in plastic, going deep, and beating off in a pond." Ryan's tone was tinged with distaste.

"Dressed as a nurse."

"Apparently he changed in the canoe. The duffel contained jeans, socks, sneakers, and a shirt."

"Must take good balancing skills."

"It also contained a flashlight."

"Suggesting he went to the pond at night."

"Wouldn't you?" Ryan shook his head. "I don't get it. What's the kick?"

Having no life, I'd done research the evening before, learned that the term *autoerotic* refers to any solitary sexual activity in which a prop, device, or apparatus is used to enhance sexual stimulation. I knew Ryan was fully aware of this.

"Most autoerotic activity takes place in the home," I said.

"Gee. Why would that be?"

"Death is usually due to the failure of a preestablished escape mechanism."

"Lowery probably lost his snorkel, then panicked and dropped the knife he was using to cut himself free."

"That's LaManche's take. And it's plausible.

Most autoerotic deaths are accidental. The person chokes or smothers, due to hanging, or the use of a ligature or plastic bag. Also in the mix are electrocution, foreign-body insertion, overdressing, or body wrapping."

"Body wrapping?"

"A plastic bag over the head is fairly common, body wrapping less so. Last night I read about a sixty-year-old man found rolled in fourteen sewn blankets, his penis wrapped in a plastic bag. A forty-six-year-old man was discovered wearing seven pairs of stockings, a dress, and ladies' undies cut to allow Mr. Happy a front-row seat. A twenty-three-year-old schoolteacher died sporting a plastic mackintosh, three cotton skirts, a raincoat, and a plastic—"

"I get the picture. But what's the point?"

"Heightened sexual excitement."

Two killer blues swung my way. "I can think of better routes to that end."

Oh, could he. I felt myself blush. Hated it. Focused on what I'd learned the night before.

"Autoerotic arousal derives from a limited number of mechanisms." I ticked points off on a hand. "One, direct stimulation of the erotic regions." My thumb moved to middle man. "Two, stimulation of the sexual centers of the central nervous system."

"As in strangulation or hanging."

"Or the use of a head covering. It's well known that cerebral hypoxia can heighten sexual pleasure."

My thumb went to ring man.

"Three, creation of fear and distress in the

context of a masochistic fantasy. Spice things up with electrocution or immersion, for example."

"Weenie-whacking submerged can't be all that common."

"There's actually a term for it. Aqua-eroticum. I found a few cases reported in the literature. One victim used an ankle rock, just like Lowery."

Ryan turned onto Highway 219. We passed the pond, and a few minutes later pulled to the shoulder beside a mailbox with the number 572 hand-painted on one side. An SQ cruiser was already there.

Ryan and I studied the house.

Laurier/Lowery's small bungalow was set back from the road and partially obscured by a thick stand of pine. Green frame. One story. Small storage shed attached on the right.

As we walked up the gravel drive, I noted freshly painted trim and neatly stacked wood. A large garden in back appeared recently plowed.

Catching movement through a window, I turned to Ryan. He saw it too.

"Bandau better not be pulling more of his Lone Ranger bullshit."

The outer door stood open, its frame gouged and splintered at the level of the knob. Ryan and I entered directly into a living room sparsely furnished with what looked like Salvation Army cast-offs. Bandau was in it. Hearing footsteps, he turned.

At Bandau's back was a desk holding a Mac-Book Pro that appeared fairly new. Its cover was open.

"Not jumping the gun again, are we, Agent?" Ryan's smile was icy.

"No, sir."

"You entered ahead of the warrant."

"Just securing the scene."

"Let's hope that's true."

Bandau offered nothing in defense or apology.

Ryan and I moved methodically, unsure what we were seeking.

In the kitchen cabinets were chipped tableware, cleaning products, supermarket shelf goods, and enough home-canned produce to outlast the next coming.

The refrigerator offered the normal array of condiments, dairy products, lunch meat, and bread. No caviar. No capers. No French bottled water.

A plate, glass, and utensils stood drying in a green plastic dish rack. A half-empty bottle of Scotch sat on one counter.

The bath, like the kitchen, was surprisingly clean. Over-the-counter meds and personal products in the medicine cabinet. Cheap shampoo and soap in the shower.

The bedroom was equally unremarkable. Double bed with gray wool blanket, pillow, no coverlet. Side table with lamp, clock radio, and lubricating eye drops. Wooden dresser containing boxers and tees, one striped tie, a half dozen pairs of rolled socks, all black.

The closet was the size of a mailbox. Jeans and shirts. Black polyester pants. One bad sports jacket, tan corduroy.

On the floor were two and a half pairs of boots, one pair of oxfords, and one pair of sandals, the kind with tire treads for soles.

The overhead shelf held stacked magazines.

Ryan pulled and scoped a couple. "Hell-o."

I read the titles. *Tit Man. Butt Man.*

"The guy's flexible," I said.

Ryan chose another. *Lollypop Girls.* The lead story was headlined *Park It in My Panties.* I tried to decipher that literary gem. Gave up. The request made no sense.

I looked at Ryan. His eyes were doing that scrunchy thing. I knew a panty suggestion was coming my way.

"Decorum, sir."

"Hither we yonder to fair computer?" Ryan asked demurely.

"Hither is not a verb."

"Let us forth, flaxen-haired maiden."

My eye roll may have attained a personal best.

"I yield to my lady's superior skills."

"Thank you."

"And to her unclean undies." Whispered.

Smacking Ryan's arm, I hithered to the desk.

Bandau continued staring out the window, feet wide, elbows winging, hands clasped behind his back.

"No phone," I said. "No cables. Did Laurier have an ISP account?"

"Meaning?"

"Internet Service Provider. Like Videotron or Bell."

"Not that I found record of."

The Mac whirred to life, asked for a password. I tried PASSWORD. 123456. ABCDEF. Various combinations of Jean and Laurier. Laurier's address and street name. All of the above jumbled, reversed.

No go.

LOWERY.

Nope.

YREWOL.

I took the initials JCR and converted them to number positions within the alphabet. 100318. Flipped the sequence. 813001. Reversed the initials to RCJ. 180310. Flipped that. 013081.

Still the little cursor defied me.

Picturing a phone, I tried the digits associated with the letters LOWERY, 569379.

I was in.

When the computer was fully booted, I checked a fan-shaped icon on the far right of the toolbar. Three stripes. I clicked on it.

"He pirated signal from the neighbors." I pointed to a network code name. Fife.

"Can he do that?"

"The Fifes probably use their phone number as their password. A lot of folks do. Laurier knew or looked it up. Or maybe he asked permission. Anyway, once the password is entered, the computer remembers and automatically selects that network. The Fifes can't be far away. The signal's weak but sufficient."

As Ryan jotted the name *Fife* in his spiral, I noted applications.

Standard Mac stuff. Numbers. Mail. Safari. iCal.

Laurier/Lowery had stored no spreadsheets or documents. He'd entered no contacts into the address book, no appointments into the calendar.

"He didn't use e-mail," I said. "Or iTunes, iPhoto, iMovie, iDVD."

"I see."

Another eye roll. "Let's check what he found amusing on the net."

I launched Safari and pulled up the browsing history.

In the past two weeks the user had researched mulch and fertilizer, corn hybrids, scuba diving, hypoxia, poison ivy, copper wire, roofing tiles, North American squirrels, Quebec dentists, and a variety of vitamins.

"A site called robesonian-dot-com was visited six times," I said.

Ryan leaned close. He smelled of male sweat and a "Don't worry, be happy, mon" cologne. Bay rum, I think.

The flaxen-haired maiden felt a tingle in her southern parts. She managed to stay focused.

Robesonian.com was an online newspaper for Lumberton, the county seat of Robeson County, North Carolina.

"Hot damn," Ryan said, close to my ear.

Back to the surfing log. In moments I'd spotted additional telling activity.

Laurier/Lowery had visited dozens of sites designed for and by American draft dodgers of the Vietnam era. CBC archive pieces. Coverage of a 2006 draft dodger reunion in Vancouver. A site devoted to an exile community in Toronto. A University of British Columbia page titled Vietnam War Resisters in Canada.

"That nails it." Ryan straightened. "Lowery left Lumberton for Canada to avoid service in Vietnam. He's been living the straight life as Jean Laurier ever since."

"Straight except for one quirk." I indicated several Web addresses. Love Yourself and Tell. Hard Soloing. Ramrod's Self-Bondage Page.

"Pick one," I said.

Ryan pointed.

Ramrod's blog featured two stories.

A Baptist minister was found dead, alone in his Arkansas home, wearing a wet suit, face mask, diving gloves, and slippers. Underneath the outerwear were a second rubberized suit with suspenders, rubberized male underwear, and bondage gear constructed of nylon and leather. The reverend's anus featured a condom-covered dildo.

A Kansas plumber hanged himself from a showerhead with his wife's leather belt. The gentleman survived to tell the tale. In vivid detail.

Ramrod's home page had a colorful sidebar encouraging visitors into his chat room. Ryan and I declined the invitation.

Shutting down the computer, I began casually rummaging in the desk. What more did we need? Jean Laurier of Hemmingford, Quebec, was clearly John Charles Lowery, a Vietnam draft dodger from Lumberton, North Carolina.

The top drawer was a jumble of rubber bands, paper clips, tape, pens, and pencils. The upper side drawer held lined tablets, envelopes, and two pairs of drugstore reading glasses.

I could hear Ryan behind me, lifting couch pillows and opening cabinets.

The lower side drawer contained computer paraphernalia, including headphones, keyboard brushes, cables, and AC adapter plugs. In closing it, I jostled a white corner into view from below a mouse pad.

Lifting the pad, I discovered a four-by-six white rectangle. On it were written a name and date. *Spider, April 7, 1967.*

I teased the thing free and flipped it.

The snapshot was black-and-white. Cracked and creased, it looked every bit of forty years old.

The subject was a teenage boy leaning against a fifties Chevy, ankles crossed, arms folded. He had dark hair and eyes, and heavy brows that curved the upper rims of his orbits. He wore jeans and a tee with rolled sleeves. His smile could have lighted the state of Montana.

"Check this out."

Ryan joined me. I handed him the picture.

"Looks like Lowery," Ryan said.

"The name *Spider* is written on the back."

Ryan studied the photo, then returned it to me.

I stared at Lowery's face. So young and unspoiled.

Other images flashed in my brain. Water-bloated features. Algae-slimed plastic. A soggy nurse's cap.

"We're done here," Ryan said.

"Take these?" My gesture took in the photo and the Mac.

Ryan's gaze went to Bandau, then to the gouged front door.

He nodded. "The warrant covers it."

I couldn't have known. But that photo would dog me for many days across many, many miles.

And nearly get me killed.

5

I AWOKE TO RAIN TICKING ON GLASS. THE
window shade was a dim gray rectangle in a
very dim room.

I checked the clock. Nine forty.

From atop the dresser, two unblinking yellow
eyes stared my way.

"Give me a break, Bird. It's Sunday."

The cat flicked his tail.

"And raining."

Flick.

"You can't be hungry."

Arriving back from Hemmingford, Ryan
and I had grabbed a quick bite at Hurley's Irish
Pub, then walked to my place. Thanks to Mr.
Soft Touch, the cat ended up the beneficiary of
my doggie-bagged cheesecake.

I know what you're thinking. Empty condo.
Barren winter. Spring awakening!

Didn't happen. Despite Ryan's bid to frolic,
the visit remained strictly tea and conversation, mostly about our kids and shared cockatiel, Charlie. Ryan took the couch. I sat in a wing
chair across the room.

I explained my concern about Katy's dissatisfaction with the concept of full-time employment. And about her recent fascination with a thirty-two-year-old drummer named Smooth.

Ryan talked of Lily's latest setback with heroin. His nineteen-year-old daughter was out of rehab, home with Lutetia, and attending counseling. Ryan was cautiously optimistic.

He left at seven to take Lily bowling.

I wondered.

Was Lily's fragile progress the reason for Ryan's recent good humor? Or was it springing from renewed contact with Mommy?

Whatever.

Ryan promised to deliver Charlie the following day, as per our long-standing arrangement. When I was in Montreal, the bird was mine.

When told of the cockatiel's upcoming arrival, Birdie was either thrilled or annoyed. Hard to read him sometimes.

After Ryan's departure I took a very long bath. Then Bird and I watched season-one episodes of *Arrested Development* on DVD. He found Buster hilarious.

In Montreal, the week's major paper comes out on Saturday. Not my preference, but there you have it.

I made coffee and an omeletlike cheesy scrambled egg thing, and began working through the previous day's *Gazette*.

A massive pothole had opened up on an elevated span of Highway 15 through the Turcot

Interchange. Two lanes were closed until further notice.

A forty-year-old man had snatched a kid in broad daylight and thrown him into the trunk of his car. The sleazeball now faced multiple charges, including abduction, abduction of a child under fourteen, and sexual assault.

Twelve stories reported on how the economy sucked.

I was reading a human interest piece about a hamster that saved a family of seven from a house fire when my mobile sounded.

Katy.

"Hey, sweetie."

"Hey, Mom."

We're Southerners. It's how we greet.

"You're up early."

"It's a gorgeous day. I'm going to Carmel to play tennis." Katy's lighthearted mood surprised me. Last time we'd talked she was in a funk.

"With Smooth?" I had trouble picturing the dreadlocks and do-rag on the country club courts.

"With Lija. Smooth's got a gig in Atlanta." Derisive snort. "His ass can stay there for all I care. Or Savannah, or Raleigh, or Kathmandu."

There is a God who answers our prayers.

"How's Lija?" I asked.

"Terrific."

Katy and Lija Feldman have been best friends since high school. A year back, following Katy's much-delayed college graduation, they'd decided to try rooming together. So far, so good.

"How's work?" I asked.

"Mind-numbing. I sort crap, Xerox crap,

research crap. Now and then I file crap at the courthouse. Those jaunts through the halls of justice really get the old adrenaline pumping." She laughed. "But at least I have a job. People are being dumped like nuclear waste."

Okeydokey.

"Where are you?"

"At the town house. Gawd. I hope we can stay here."

"Meaning?"

"Coop's returning from Afghanistan."

Coop was Katy's landlord and, from what I could tell, an on-again, off-again romantic interest. Hard to know. The man seemed perpetually out of the country.

"I thought Coop was in Haiti."

"Ancient news. His Peace Corps commitment ended two years ago. He was in the States ten months, now he's working for a group called the International Rescue Committee. They're headquartered in New York."

"How long has Coop been in Afghanistan?"

"Almost a year. Someplace called Helmand Province."

Was Coop's reappearance the reason for Katy's sunny mood? For Smooth's heave-ho?

"You sound happy about his homecoming." Discreet.

"Oh, yeah." The *Oh* lasted a good five beats. "Coop's awesome. And he's coming straight to me after he checks in at home."

"Really." My tone made it a question.

"Play your cards right, Mommy dearest, I might bring him by."

A blatant dodge, but since Katy was so excited, I decided to press on for details.

"What's this awesome gentleman's actual name?"

"Webster Aaron Cooperton. He's from Charleston."

"You met him at UVA?"

"Yep."

"How is it that young Mr. Cooperton holds deed to a town house in Charlotte?"

"He finished school here."

"Didn't like Charlottesville?"

"Wasn't invited back."

"I see."

"He's really nice. Loads of fun."

I had no doubt of that.

"And the town house?"

"His parents bought it for him when he transferred to UNCC. As an investment. They're beaucoup bucks up."

Thus Coop's freedom to hold morally admirable but woefully underpaid aid jobs.

Whatever. Shaggy musician out. Humanitarian in. Worked for me.

"You and Coop dated following his return from Haiti?"

"When we could. He was in New York a lot."

I paused, allowing Katy to get to the reason for her call. Turned out there was none.

"Well, Mommy-o. Have a good day."

Mommy-o?

Who was this strange woman posing as my daughter?

Ryan delivered Charlie around noon. Eager to

be off to Lily, he stayed only briefly. The door had barely closed when the bird fired off two of his bawdier quips.

"Fill your glass, park your ass!"

"Charlie."

"Cool your tool!"

Clearly, the cockatiel training CD had seen no play time in my absence.

Point of information: confiscated during a brothel raid several years back, Charlie became Ryan's Christmas gift to me. My little avian friend's repertoire is, shall we say, colorful.

Jean-Claude Hubert, the chief coroner, phoned at one o'clock. Hubert had located John Lowery's father, Plato Lowery, and informed him of the fingerprint ID on the body in Hemmingford. At first Plato was confused. Then shocked. Then skeptical.

The United States Army had also been brought into the loop.

"Now what?" I asked Hubert.

"Now we wait to see what Uncle Sam has to say."

At one thirty I headed to Marché Atwater, near the Lachine Canal in the Saint-Henri neighborhood. A ten-minute drive from my condo, the market there dates to 1933.

Inside the two-story art deco pavilion, shops and stalls offer cheese, wine, bread, meat, and fish. Outside, vendors hawk maple syrup, herbs, and produce. At Christmas, freshly cut trees fill the air with the scent of pine. In spring and summer, flowers turn the pavement into a riot of color.

When I first started shopping at Atwater, the neighborhood was blue-collar and definitely down-at-the-heels. Not so today. Since the reopening of the canal in 2002, upscale condos have replaced low- and modest-cost housing and the area has become a real estate hot spot.

Not sure I'm a fan of such gentrification. But parking is easier now.

Inside, I purchased meat and cheese. Outside, I bought produce, then flats of marigolds and petunias. Made of sterner stuff, I figured, their sort might survive my regime of horticultural neglect.

Back home, I planted the flowers around my postage stamp patio and in my little backyard. Rain was still falling. Hot damn. No need to water.

I was cleaning dirt from my nails when my cell phone sounded. 808 area code. Hawaii.

Toweling off, I clicked on.

"Dr. Tandler. To what do I owe this unexpected pleasure?" Though a Sunday call *was* unexpected, I had no doubt about the topic.

"What? I have to have a reason?"

"Yes."

Danny let out a long breath. "This Lowery thing is causing some concern on our end."

Sensing an edge of anxiety in Danny's voice, I waited.

"Yesterday Merkel got a call from Notter while driving home from the airport. You can imagine how getting tagged that soon after landing brightened his day."

JPAC employs more than four hundred people, both military and civilian. In addition to the

CIL, situated at Hickam Air Force Base, there are three permanent overseas detachments: in Bangkok, Thailand; Hanoi, Vietnam; and Vientiane, Laos; and another U.S. detachment at Camp Smith, in Hawaii. Each is commanded by a lieutenant colonel. The whole JPAC enchilada is under the command of an army major general. For now.

Danny referred to Brent Notter, deputy to the commander for public relations and legislative affairs, and Roger Merkel, scientific director and deputy to the commander for CIL operations. Merkel was Danny's direct superior.

"After hearing from the Quebec coroner yesterday, Plato Lowery contacted his congressman," Danny went on.

"Oh, boy," I said. "What's Lowery's juice?"

"Juice?"

"Danny, we both know phone inquiries aren't handled that fast. It's been only twenty-four hours since Plato Lowery was informed of the situation. He must have connections."

"According to Congressman O'Hare, John Lowery came from a family with a tradition of sending its boys into the military."

"So do a lot of kids."

"I checked. O'Hare has to run for reelection this year."

"So do a lot of kids."

"O'Hare and Notter were frat bros at Wake Forest."

"That'll do it."

"Go Kappa Sig." Danny was trying hard for casual. It wasn't working.

"Is Notter worried?" I asked.

"Lowery was pretty upset. Wants to know why some guy in Canada is questioning his son's proud record."

"Understandable."

"Why some Frenchie's calling his kid a deserter."

"I doubt the coroner used that term." Or provided details of the circumstances surrounding John Lowery's death. I kept that to myself.

"Congressman O'Hare has vowed to protect his constituent from a smear campaign by our neighbors to the north."

"He said that?"

"In a statement to the press."

"Why would O'Hare notify the media?"

"The guy's a showboater, jumps at every chance he sees to ingratiate himself to the voting public."

"But it's ridiculous. Why would the government of Canada pick John Lowery of Lumberton, North Carolina, as someone to smear?"

"Of course it's ridiculous. Merkel thinks O'Hare's probably in trouble over NAFTA. Lashing out at Canada might make him look good with the home folk."

That theory wasn't totally without merit. North Carolina was hit hard by the North American Free Trade Agreement, lost thousands of jobs in the textile and furniture industries. But the agreement had been signed in 1994.

"Lowery senior also demands to know, if John died in Quebec, who the hell's buried in his son's grave."

Understandable also.

"Notter wants to make sure the thing doesn't turn into a media nightmare."

"What's his plan?"

"You live in North Carolina."

"I do." Wary.

"Y'all speak the native lingo."

"Uh-huh."

"Notter wants you to go to Lumberton and dig up whoever is in that grave."

6

PLATO LOWERY WAS YOUNGER THAN I expected, early eighties at most. His hair was the kind that turns L.A. waiters into stars. Though white with age, it winged thick and glossy from a center part to swoop down over his ears.

But Lowery's eyes were what grabbed you, black as wormholes in space. His gaze seemed to laser straight into your soul.

Lowery watched as I called a halt to the digging. Others in the assembly: the backhoe operator; two cemetery workers; two coroner's assistants; a reporter from the *Robesonian*; another from WBTW; a Lumberton cop; an army lieutenant who looked all of sixteen.

It was Tuesday, May 11. Two days since my call from Danny.

Though the time was barely 10 a.m., the temperature already nudged ninety. Sun pounded the cemetery's psychedelically green lawn. The scent of moist earth and cut grass floated heavily on the air.

I squatted for a closer look at one side of the freshly opened grave.

Stratigraphy told the story.

The uppermost layer was a deep black-brown, the one below an anemic yellow-tan. Four feet down, the bucket's teeth had bitten into a third stratum. Like the topsoil, the dirt was rich with organic content.

I gestured the tractor back and the cemetery workers to action. Collecting their spades, the men hopped in and began shoveling dirt from the grave.

In minutes a coffin lid took shape. I noted no protective vault, only the remnants of a crushed burial liner. Bad news.

A vault, whether concrete, plastic, or metal, completely encloses a coffin. A burial liner covers only the top and sides and is less sturdy. Dirt is heavy. The absence of a vault boded ill for the integrity of a box forty years underground.

In an hour a casket stood free within the excavated grave. Though flattened at one end, it appeared largely intact.

While I shot pictures, one of the coroner's assistants drove the van graveside.

Under my direction, a plank was positioned beneath the bottom and chains were wrapped around the casket's head and foot ends. With the cemetery workers directing movement with their hands, the backhoe operator slowly raised the box up, swung left, and deposited it on the ground.

The coffin looked jarringly out of place on the emerald grass in the warm spring daylight. As I made notes and shot pictures, I thought of John Lowery's other sun-drenched resurrection far to the north.

And of the buoyant young man in the photo from Jean Laurier's desk drawer.

I'd read the entire IDPF that morning, the Individual Deceased Personnel File, including paperwork sent by the military back in 1968. DD Form 893, the Record of Identification Processing Anatomical Chart; DA Form 10–249, the Certificate of Death; DD Form 1384, the Transportation Control and Movement Document; DD Form 2775, the Record of Preparation and Disposition of Remains.

I understood the acronym TSN-RVN. Tan Son Nhut–Republic of Vietnam. Lowery's body had been identified and readied for transport at Tan Son Nhut, one of two U.S. military mortuaries in Vietnam.

The preparing official, H. Johnson, probably a GS-13 civilian identification officer, had listed John Lowery as the decedent on the DD 893, and provided Lowery's grade and service number. He'd checked both "decomposed" and "burned" for condition of the remains.

In the front and back body views, Johnson indicated that Lowery's head was severely injured, and that his lower arms and hands and both feet were missing. He diagrammed no scars or tattoos.

In the remarks section, Johnson stated that Lowery was found wearing army fatigues but no insignia, dog tags, or ID. Odd, but not unheard of. I'd handled one such case during my time consulting to the CIL. Since villagers had been caught looting bodies in the area, Johnson suggested these items had probably been stolen before Lowery's body was found.

A medical officer with an indecipherable scrawl had completed the DA 10-249, listing cause of death as "multiple trauma." Again, a common finding, particularly with victims of plane and chopper crashes.

Finally, a mortician named Dadko had signed the section titled Disposition of Remains. Dadko had also handled the DD 2775.

The DD 1384 listed Saigon as Lowery's point of exit from Vietnam, and Dover Air Force Base, Delaware, as his point of arrival onto home soil.

No form detailed the basis for the positive ID.

Who, I wondered, had we just raised from this grave?

Ordering the chains removed, I took a few final pictures. Then, with much grunting and sweating, the plank was lifted by joint effort of the cemetery workers, the cop, the backhoe operator, the army lieutenant, and one less-than-enthusiastic television journalist.

I glanced at Plato Lowery as the coffin was transferred to the coroner's van. Though his face remained rigid, his body jerked visibly at the sound of the slamming doors.

When the vehicle pulled away, I walked over to him.

"This must be very difficult." Banal, I know, but I'm lousy at small talk. No, that's being generous. When it comes to offering condolences, I totally suck.

Lowery's face remained a stone mask.

Behind me I could hear car doors closing and engines starting up. The journalists and the cop were heading out.

"I promise to do everything I can to sort this out," I said.

Still no response. Consistent. When we were introduced earlier, Lowery had neither spoken to me nor offered a hand to shake. Apparently I was one of the targets of his anger. For my role in Quebec? For intruding into his world to unearth his dead son?

I was about to try again when Lowery's eyes flicked to something over my shoulder. I turned.

The lieutenant was hurrying our way, a gangly man with close-cropped hair and olive skin. Guipani? Guipini? Undoubtedly he'd been sent from Fort Bragg to put the best possible spin on a bad situation.

"Dr. Brennan. Mr. Lowery, sir. I'm so pleased this went well." Sun glinted off bars on his shoulders and a plaque on one pocket. *D. Guipone.* "We're all pleased, of course."

A nervous smile revealed teeth that should have worn braces.

"The army knew that it would, of course. Go well."

Not a muscle fiber stirred in Lowery's face.

"My colleagues at the Central Identification Laboratory say Dr. Brennan is the best. That's how this will be handled, sir. Only the best. And total transparency, of course."

"Of course." Lowery's voice was gravel.

"Of course." Firm nod from Guipone.

"A horse is a horse."

"Sir?"

"Of course."

Guipone cast a confused glance my way.

"Of course," I said, deadpan as the old man.

Guipone was either too young or too dumb to realize he'd been made the butt of a joke.

"Well then." Again the snaggletoothed smile, directed at me. "What happens now?"

"This morning, using cemetery records and the grave marker, I established that this was, indeed, the plot assigned to John Lowery." I gestured toward the open grave. "Now, in the coroner's presence, I'll open the coffin, record the condition of the remains, then seal the body in a transport container. As soon as the army completes arrangements, the remains will be flown to JPAC for analysis."

"My son died a hero." Taut.

"Yes, sir. Of course, sir. We will get to the bottom of this."

Turning his back to Guipone, Lowery spoke to me. "I want to see him."

"I don't think that's a good idea." As gently as I could.

The ebony eyes bore into mine. Seconds passed. Then, "How do I know my son will be treated with the respect he deserves?"

Reaching out, I placed a hand on the old man's shoulder.

"My husband was a marine, Mr. Lowery. I am a mother. I understand the sacrifice made by the man in that coffin. And by those who loved him."

Lowery tipped his face to the sun and closed his eyes. Then, lowering his head, he turned and walked away.

* * *

Medical examiners are appointed. Most are physicians, preferably pathologists, ideally board-certified forensic pathologists.

Coroners are elected. Candidates can be mechanics, teachers, or unemployed pole dancers. Most are morticians or funeral home operators.

In 1965, the North Carolina General Assembly passed legislation allowing individual counties to abolish the office of coroner and to appoint medical doctors to investigate deaths within their borders.

Today North Carolina has a centralized death investigation system. County MEs are appointed for three-year terms by the chief medical examiner in Chapel Hill.

Sound progressive? Actually, the setup is not so hot.

In counties lacking willing or capable doctors, nonphysicians—sometimes registered nurses—still serve. Instead of coroners, they're now called "acting medical examiners."

And get this. On its Web site, the North Carolina Medical Examiner System describes itself as a network of doctors who *voluntarily* devote their time, energy, and medical expertise.

Read between the lines. Doctors or dog walkers, in North Carolina, MEs are paid zilch.

Robeson County's acting medical examiner was Silas Sugarman, owner and operator of Lumberton's oldest funeral home. By prearrangement, following exhumation the casket would go from the cemetery to Sugarman's facility.

I'd driven from Charlotte to Lumberton in my own car, departing as the first tendrils of dawn teased the Queen City awake. Though careful timing was required, I managed to shake Guipone and leave alone from the cemetery.

It wasn't just that I found the lieutenant annoying. I had a plan.

Over the years, I've driven countless times from Charlotte to the South Carolina beaches. The back route I favor involves a long stretch on Highway 74 and brings me close enough to Lumberton for a barbeque detour. That was my target today. Being already in Lumberton, it only made sense to score some "que."

I headed straight for Fuller's Old Fashioned BBQ. A bit of a diversion, but I wasn't due at the funeral home until two. And my stomach was broadcasting deprivation distress.

At one fifteen, most of the lunch crowd was gone. Ignoring the buffet, I ordered my usual. Barbecue pork, coleslaw, fries, and hush puppies. A tumbler of sweet tea the size of a silo.

OK. No smiley heart. But the owners, Fuller and Delora Locklear, know how to do pig.

Exiting the restaurant was like stepping into the molasses I'd left untouched on my table. The temperature inside my Mazda was 150.

After cranking the AC, I punched an address into my portable GPS and wound south toward Martin Luther King Drive. Within minutes the robotic voice was announcing arrival at my destination.

Sugarman's Funeral Home looked like Tara on steroids. Redbrick. White antebellum pillars and trim up and down. Elaborate drive-through portico in front.

The interior could only be described as rose. Rose carpet. Rose drapes. Rose floral wallpaper above the wainscoting and beadboard.

In the main lobby, a faux-colonial placard listed two temporary residents. Selma Irene Farrington awaited mourners in the Eternal Harmony Room. Lionel Peter Jones cooled his heels in Peace Ever After.

A young woman materialized as I was pondering the relative merits of harmony versus peace. When I requested directions to the owner's office, she led me past the Lilac Overflow Reposing Room and the Edgar Firefox Memorial Chapel.

Sugarman was seated at a massive oak desk with carved pineapples for feet. At least six-four and three hundred pounds, with greasy black hair and a crooked nose, he looked more mafioso than mortician.

Also present were the good lieutenant and a small, rat-faced man with short brown hair parted with surgical precision.

The trio was chuckling at some shared joke. Seeing me in the doorway, they fell silent and rose.

"Dr. Brennan. It is indeed an honor." Sugarman's voice was surprisingly high, his drawl as thick as the Fuller's molasses.

Sugarman introduced rat-face as his brother-in-law, Harold Beasley, sheriff of Robeson County. Beasley nodded, repositioned a toothpick from the right to the left side of his mouth. No comment, no question. Obviously he'd been prepped on my role in the day's activities.

"And you know the lieutenant."

"Yes." I resisted the impulse to add "of course."

Sugarman arranged his beefy features into an expression of appropriate solemnity. "Ma'am, gentlemen. We all understand the sad business the Lord has chosen to send our way. I propose we get to it without further ado."

Sugarman led us down a hall and through a door at the back of the facility. No name plaque. Everlasting Embalming? Perpetual Preparation?

The room was windowless, and maybe fifteen by twenty.

From the west wall, a door opened to the outside. Beside it, metal shelving held the usual array of instruments, chemicals, cosmetic supplies, plastic undies, and fluids whose purpose I didn't really want to know.

A deep sink jutted from the south wall. Aspirating and injection machines sat on a counter beside it. So did a crowbar and small electric saw.

Dressing and embalming tables had been snugged to the north wall. An open casket yawned ready inside an aluminum transport case on a gurney pushed up to them.

The exhumed coffin rested on the collapsible gurney on which it had ridden from the graveyard. Though fans did their best, the smell of mildew, moldy wood, and decomposing flesh permeated the small space.

Sugarman removed his jacket and rolled his sleeves. He and I donned gloves, aprons, and goggles. Beasley and Guipone watched from the doorway. Both looked like they'd rather be elsewhere. I hoped I was more discreet.

The old coffin was mahogany, with sculpted

corners and a domed top, now collapsed. Both swing bars and most of the hardware were gone. The metal that remained was eroded and discolored.

I made notes and took photos. Then I stepped back.

Sugarman raised both brows. I nodded.

Crossing to the gurney, the big man inserted one end of the crowbar and levered downward. Rotten wood cracked and flew.

Kicking aside splinters, Sugarman heaved again. And again. As fragments detached, I tossed them to the floor.

Finally, sweat rings darkening both armpits, Sugarman laid down his tool.

I stepped close.

Guipone and Beasley moved in beside us.

Breathing hard, Sugarman lifted what remained of the top half of the coffin lid.

Beasley's hand flew to his mouth.

"Sweet baby Jesus."

7

THE FUNERAL INDUSTRY CLAIMS ITS PROD-
ucts and services protect our dearly departed
from the ravages of time. Coffin manufacturers
offer vaults, gasket seals, and warranties on the
structural integrity of their caskets. Morticians
tout the permanence of embalming.

Nothing stops the inevitable.

Following death, aerobic bacteria begin acting on a corpse's exterior, while their anaerobic
brethren set to work in the gut. By excluding the
former, airtight coffins may actually accelerate,
not retard, action due to the latter. The result is
liquefaction and putrefied soup in the box.

A simple wooden coffin, on the other hand,
permits air passage, and thus, aerobic sport. The
outcome is rapid skeletonization.

With most exhumations it's anyone's guess
what lies under the hood. Bones? Goo? Some
time-hardened combo?

Burned body. Forty years. Compromised box.

With this one I'd had little doubt.

I was right.

The coffin held a skeleton covered with mold

and desiccated black muck. Below the pink-white outer crust, the bone surfaces looked dark and mottled.

"Dear God in heaven." Beasley's words came through a hand-shielded mouth.

Guipone swallowed audibly.

The remains had been casketed military-style. Though the traditional wool blanket shroud was now gone, rusted safety pins attested to its previous presence.

"May I see the file again?"

Sugarman retrieved a manila folder from the counter and handed it to me. This go-round I skipped the government forms in favor of the mortician's handwritten account.

"Regrettably, record keeping wasn't one of my daddy's strengths." Sugarman flashed what I'm sure he considered his "regrettable" smile. Probably practiced it in the mirror while knotting his somber black ties. "Such were the days."

Not everywhere, I thought.

Pvt. John Charles Lowery was killed in a helicopter crash in Vietnam. (See army forms.) The body was flown from Dover, Delaware, to the Charlotte, North Carolina, airport. On February 18, 1968, accompanied by Plato Lowery, I met and drove the body to Sugarman's Funeral Home in Lumberton, North Carolina.

At the request of Plato and Harriet Lowery, the deceased was transferred to a privately purchased casket and buried at the Gardens of Faith Cemetery on February 20,

1968 (Plot 9, Row 14, Grave 6). No additional services were requested.

Holland Sugarman
March 12, 1968

Note: Gravestone erected October 4, 1968.

Tossing aside Daddy's useless report, I began pulling remnants of decaying fabric from the casket and dropping them to the floor. Lining. Padding. Head pillow. Blanket shreds.

Sugarman helped. The sheriff and lieutenant watched mutely.

The smell of rot and mildew heightened.

Within minutes the skeleton lay fully exposed, naked but for its postmortem armor of mold and charred gunk. The skull was in pieces. Every tooth crown was gone. As indicated on ident official Johnson's diagram, the lower arms and hands and both feet were missing.

I evaluated the remains as best I could for compatibility with John Lowery's known biological profile.

A faucet dripped. Fluorescents hummed. Beasley and Guipone alternated shifting their feet.

Pelvic shape said the individual was clearly male. A pubic symphyseal face suggested an age range of eighteen to twenty-five. Skull fragmentation made accurate race assessment impossible.

With a gloved finger, I scraped at one cranial fragment. Below the outer crust, the cortical surface was black and flaky. Again, consistent with Johnson's report of body condition. The deceased had suffered a fiery event, either during or after death.

Besides the safety pins, the coffin contained one inclusion, an empty jelly jar with powder filming the bottom. No burial or dog tags, buttons, belt buckles, or insignia.

I made notes and took photos.

Finally, satisfied I'd missed nothing, I turned to Sugarman. The mortician donned new gloves, and together we maneuvered a blue plastic sheet beneath the bones. Then, gingerly, we lifted and transferred them to the new casket.

We all watched as Sugarman lowered and locked the coffin lid, then positioned the top of the transfer case. I helped twist the metal fasteners that held the thing shut.

Noticing the words *Head* and *Foot* stamped on the aluminum, I thought of the honor guard that would flag-drape the case, and of the respect with which it would be positioned in the plane and hearse.

It was five thirty when I finally washed my hands and signed the transfer paperwork.

We parted under the front portico. I thanked Sugarman. He thanked me. Guipone thanked all of us. If Beasley was appreciative, he kept it to himself.

Heat mirages shimmered above the parking lot. The asphalt felt soft under my sneakers.

Sensing movement, I glanced left. The driver's door on a blue Ford Ranger five slots down from my Mazda was opening. A tiny alarm sounded, but I kept walking.

A man got out of the pickup and tracked my

approach. Though his face was shadowed by the brim of a cap, I recognized the solid body and square shoulders. And the Atlanta Braves tee.

"Good afternoon, Mr. Lowery." When I was ten feet out. "Too early in the year for such a hot day."

"Yes, ma'am. "

"Could be a long summer."

"Yes, ma'am."

Above the coal black eyes, yellow letters double-arced the green silhouette of a landmass. *Korean War Veteran Forever Proud. 1950–1953.*

Though it was obvious Lowery had been waiting for me, he said nothing further.

Exhausted, dirty, and sweaty, I longed for soap and shampoo. And dinner. Under ideal conditions, the trip from Lumberton to Charlotte takes two hours. At that time of day I was looking at a minimum of three.

"Have you something to ask me, sir?"

"You gonna tell me what you saw in that coffin?"

"I'm sorry. I'm duty bound to keep my observations confidential for now."

I thought Lowery would leave. Instead he just stood there. Moments passed, then he nodded tautly, as though arriving at a difficult decision.

"I ain't much for words. Don't talk 'less I need to. Don't talk 'less I know who's on the other end of what I'm saying."

The old man wiped both palms on his jeans.

"O'Hare's using my troubles to get his name in the paper. Guipone's a moron. The army's got a dog in the fight. I ain't a churching man, so I can't ask the Lord who's upright and who ain't. I gotta go with my gut."

Lowery swallowed. His discomfort was painful to watch.

"I listened to what you said back at the cemetery. To what you said just now. My gut's telling me I can trust you."

"Thank you, sir."

"I'd appreciate you listening to what I got to say."

"Shall we talk in my car?"

As I wheep-wheeped my door locks and cranked the AC, Lowery retrieved something from the dashboard of his truck. When he dropped into my passenger seat, a wave of cheap cologne and stale sweat rolled my way.

Not pleasant, but it beat the odors I'd just left behind.

Lowery pressed a gilt-edged album to his chest. Eyes fixed on something outside the windshield, he drummed callused thumbs on its red leather cover.

Seconds passed. A full minute.

Finally, he spoke.

"My mama give me a cracker of a name. Plato. You can imagine the jokes."

"I hear you." I tapped my chest. "Temperance. People think I'm a movement to reinstate prohibition."

"So I picked good solid names for my boys."

"Hard to go wrong with John," I said, wondering at Lowery's use of the plural.

"John wasn't but five when he started collecting spiders. Lined 'em up in jars on his windowsill. Red ones, speckled ones, big hairy black ones. Got so his mama dreaded going into his room."

I didn't interrupt.

"Soon's he could read, John took to borrowing at the mobile library." The *i* in *mobile* was pronounced as in *spider*. "That's all he talked about. Spiders this and spiders that. What they ate, where they lived, how they made young 'uns. Librarian got him every book she could lay hands on. I wasn't working much, couldn't buy."

Lowery paused, gaze still on something outside the car, perhaps outside that moment in time.

"Folks took to calling him Spider. Nickname stuck like gum on a shoe. Before long, no one remembered nothing about John. Even his schoolteachers called him Spider."

Again, Lowery fell silent. I didn't push.

"Wasn't just spiders. John loved animals. Brought home all kinda strays. His mama let most of 'em stay."

Lowery turned toward me but kept his eyes lowered.

"Harriet. She passed five years back. Kidneys finally give out. Harriet was always poorly, even after the transplant."

"I'm so sorry."

"Spider offered his mama one of his very own kidneys. That's how generous that boy was." Lowery's voice dropped. "Didn't work out."

I didn't interrupt.

"Spider had a twin brother, Thomas. John and Tom. Good, solid names. Tom's passed, too.

Killed on a tractor in 2003. Losing both her boys just took the wind out of Harriet's sails."

"Grief has consequences not fully understood."

Lowery's eyes rose to mine. In them I saw the anguish of resurrected pain.

"You find a jar in that coffin, miss?"

"Yes, sir. I did."

"I put that there." He paused, perhaps embarrassed, perhaps regretting his disclosure. "Foolishness." With a tight shake of his head, Lowery turned away. "I went out and caught a spider and tucked it in with my boy."

"That was a very kind gesture, Mr. Lowery."

"*My* boy." Lowery thumped his chest so hard I jumped. "And he was growing into a fine young man." Lowery's jaw hardened, relaxed. "That's why I'm going on like this. I want you to think of Spider as a person when you're cutting him up."

"Mr. Lowery, I won't be the one—"

"His mama kept this."

When Lowery leaned my way, the cloaked BO was almost overwhelming. Opening the album, he slid it toward me.

Each page held four to six pictures. Black-and-whites with scallopy edges. Baby and school portraits. Three-by-five drugstore prints.

I leafed through the pages, asking about people, places, events. Lowery gave short, often single-word explanations. Christmas of 1954. 1961. 1964. A trip to Myrtle Beach. Harriet. Tom. The house on Red Oak. The trailer at the lake. Each image included a younger version of the boy I'd first seen in Jean Laurier's desk drawer.

One snapshot showed Plato and a woman I assumed was Harriet.

"Is this your wife?" I asked.

Plato provided uncharacteristic detail. "Harriet had real pretty eyes. One brown, one green as a loblolly pine. Damnedest thing."

The next Kodak moment caught Spider, Plato, and Harriet on a pier. All wore shorts and light summer shirts. Harriet looked like she'd seen way too much sun and way too little blocker. A stack of creases V'ed into her substantial cleavage.

The second to last picture captured Spider under a balloon arch with a girl in glasses and hair piled high on her head. He wore a boutonniered white jacket. She wore a pink satin formal and wrist corsage. Both looked stiff and uncomfortable.

The album's last entry was a formal portrait of a baseball team, twelve uniformed boys and two coaches, front row down on one knee, back row standing. A printed date identified the season as 1966–67.

Again, Plato's answer was unexpectedly long.

"This was took Spider's senior year, before he went off to the army. He weren't much for sports, but he give it a shot. Mostly rode the bench. That's him."

Lowery jabbed at a kid kneeling in the first row.

I was raising the album when Lowery yanked it sideways.

"Wait." He held the page out at arm's length, drew it in, then out again. This time the finger jab indicated one of the kids standing. "That there's Spider."

I understood the source of Lowery's confusion. Both boys had the same dark hair and eyes, the same heavy brows curving their orbits.

"Wow," I said. "They could be brothers."

"Cousins, down through Harriet's side. Folks used to confuse 'em. 'Cept Spider got the green eyes from his mama. Reggie's was dark like mine."

The image was too faded, the faces too small to note the difference.

"Thick as thieves, that pair," Plato went on. "Reggie's the one talked Spider into joining the team."

The old man took back and closed the album. There was another long, long silence before he spoke again.

"My daddy fought in France. I did my duty in Korea. Got three brothers was army, one navy. Their sons all joined up. Not bragging, just stating a fact."

"That's admirable, sir."

"Spider went off to Vietnam, come home in a box."

Lowery inhaled through his nose. Exhaled. Swallowed.

"I've always had faith in the military. Now—"

Abruptly, he reopened the album, yanked out the team photo, and thrust it at me.

"I'm trusting you to do right by my boy."

My estimate was low by over an hour. When I reached my town house in Charlotte, Gran's mantel clock was already bonging ten.

Bird cut me off at the door, radiating disapproval.

After apologizing and filling the cat's bowl, I stripped, chucked my clothes into the washer, and headed for the shower. While toweling off, I told him about my day in Lumberton.

I'd just slipped on pj's when something banged in the kitchen.

Puzzled, I hurried downstairs.

I was crossing the dining room when Katy slammed through the swinging door.

The look on my daughter's face froze the blood in my veins.

8

K ATY'S HAIR WAS BLOND CHAOS, HER EYES
wet and red. Mascara smeared her lower lids
and cheeks.

I rushed forward and drew my daughter to me.

"Sweetheart, what is it?"

Katy stood mute, shoulders hunched, fingers
curled into fists.

Urging her to the study and onto the couch, I
reengaged my embrace and began stroking her
back. She remained rigid, neither resisting nor
responding to my touch.

Seconds passed. A minute. Finally, chest heaving, her body collapsed into mine. Tears soon
dampened my pajama top.

My stomach knotted as memories kaleidoscoped in my brain. Childhood tragedies that
had elicited similar tears. The death of her kitten, Arthur. The relocation to Iowa of her middle
school best friend. The news that her father, Pete,
and I were separating.

But Katy was twenty-four now. What could
have happened to upset her so profoundly? Illness?
A clash at work? A crisis involving Lija? Pete?

As with those long-ago heartbreaks, my response was lightning, instinctual.

Fix it!

But I knew. There was nothing I could do.

Feeling helpless, I caressed my daughter's hair and made calming sounds.

Gran's clock ticked a steady metronome. I remembered her gnarled old hand on my small head, her voice soothing me through my own childhood misfortunes.

Outside, a dog barked. Others joined in. A horn honked.

At one point, Birdie appeared in the doorway. Sensing high emotion, or perhaps hungry or bored, he moved on.

Slowly, inevitably, Katy's sobs subsided and her breathing regained a normal rhythm. Pushing off from my chest, she sat up.

Normally perfect, my daughter's face set a new standard for makeup gone wild. Backhanding her nose, she dragged clumps of long blond hair from her face.

I plucked tissues from a box and handed them to her. She wiped her eyes, blew her nose, then tossed the wad to the floor.

"Coop's dead." Barely a whisper.

"Coop's coming home." Stupid, but it's what I said. I'd heard Katy's words, but my mind had locked down.

"Yeah." Fighting fresh tears. "In a box."

I offered more tissues, clasped Katy's hands. "What happened?"

"You haven't seen the news?"

"I was in Lumberton all day."

"Insurgents fired on their convoy. Coop was killed along with an Afghan driver and two women from England."

"Oh, my God. When?"

"Yesterday." She drew a tremulous breath. "I heard the story on CNN, never thought anything of it. They didn't give names, not of the dead people nor the organization they worked for. Then today, they identified the victims. I . . ."

Her lower lip trembled. She bit down hard.

"Oh, Katy," I said.

Sonofabitch, I thought.

But, yes, that's how it would work. Identities would be released only after notification of next of kin.

"Have you phoned Coop's family?"

"Yeah, right." She gave a derisive snort. "I got some uncle or cousin or something. Basically, he told me to kiss off."

"What did he say?"

"The guy hadn't a clue who I was, couldn't have cared less. Said the memorial service would be private. Thanks for calling. Go screw yourself."

"Where were they attacked?"

"Some road outside Kabul. Everyone in the convoy worked for the International Rescue Committee. They were taking Coop and one of the Brits to the airport."

To fly home. She couldn't say it.

"Two were injured in the second vehicle. All four in the lead car died on the spot." Katy swallowed. "Of multiple bullet wounds."

"Oh, sweetie. I am so, so sorry."

"They were aid workers!" It was almost a

shriek. "They dug wells and taught people how to boil water."

I squeezed Katy's hands. They trembled.

"The Taliban are claiming responsibility. They say Coop and his colleagues were spies. Spies! Can you believe it?"

Loathing battled sorrow inside me. And mounting fury. It was the Taliban's usual justification for murder. The victims were always spies or collaborators.

"The assholes described the International Rescue Committee as a hated ally of the foreign invader forces."

"I wish I knew what to say to you, sweetheart."

"The people in Coop's convoy were unarmed, Mom. Their vehicle was plastered with IRC stickers."

"I am so, so sorry." Exhausted by my trip to Lumberton, and wary of my own emotions should I unleash them, the response, though lame, was the best I could muster.

"Coop was no spy. He went to Afghanistan because he wanted to help people. It's totally wrong that he should die."

"War takes many blameless victims," I said.

"Coop volunteered." Fresh tears now flooded Katy's cheeks. "He didn't even have to be there."

"I know."

"Why him?"

I had no answer.

"Is Lija at home?" I asked gently, when several seconds had passed.

"She's in the mountains." Katy swiped a wadded tissue under each eye. "Banner Elk, I think."

"Does she know?"

"I left a message on her mobile."

"Stay with me tonight?"

Katy's shoulder shrug zinged straight to my heart. Since babyhood she'd used the gesture when deeply sad.

"I'll take that as a yes," I said.

For sixty ticks of Gran's clock we both sat lost in our separate thoughts.

When Katy spoke again her voice was jagged with anger.

"The fucking Taliban stinks." A bunched tissue ricocheted off the desk and landed on the rug.

The bitterness in my daughter's voice sent a chill up my spine. Encircling her shoulders, I drew her to me and rested my head against hers.

Together, we cried softly. She for her lost friend. I for my child whose pain I could not erase.

We opened and made up the sofa bed. While Katy showered, I took supermarket cookie dough from the freezer, placed it on a tray, and shoved it into the oven.

When Katy reappeared, the condo was rich with the sweet smell of baking. With exaggerated Martha Stewart grace, I offered milk and warm chocolate chips.

Reaching for a cookie, my daughter cocked a skeptical, and now spotless, brow. I admitted to using prepared frozen dough, but demanded credit for making the purchase. Katy almost smiled.

I was placing our glasses in the sink when the landline rang.

My eyes darted to the wall clock. Twelve fifteen a.m.

Annoyed, I snatched up the handset.

"First prize! An all-expense-paid trip to Hawaii!" Danny Tandler imitated a game show host.

"Do you know what time it is here?"

Wiggling good-bye fingers, Katy exited the kitchen.

"Travel time!"

"What?"

"Our lucky winner receives a coach-class seat by the loo and a low-budget room a zillion miles from the ocean."

"What are you talking about?"

"You charmed the shorts off Plato Lowery."

"He's a very nice gentleman."

"The very nice gentleman wants you and only you. And his congressman is turning the screws to make sure he gets it."

Based on our shared photo album moment, I was afraid something like this might unfold.

"O'Hare called again," I guessed.

"Yep. I don't know if Lowery phoned the good congressman or vice versa. O'Hare phoned Notter. Notter phoned Merkel. Ain't modern communication grand?"

"I can't come to Hawaii right now."

"Notter thinks otherwise."

"He'll get over it."

"What if we billet you on a really nice beach?"

"Danny."

"Why not?"

I told him about Coop.

"Jesus, I saw that story on the news. Katy's friend was the American?"

"Yes."

"Poor kid. Were they, you know, close?"

I didn't know. "Close enough."

"Give Katy a big hug for me. Wait. Better yet, bring her with you. A little Hawaiian sun could be just what she needs."

"Oh, Danny."

"Lowery is adamant that you accompany his son's body to Honolulu, and that you oversee the entire reanalysis."

"Have Notter talk him down."

"Not happening."

"Not my problem."

"When's the last time you took a vacation?"

"Christmas."

"Look, Tempe. We both know the guy you dug up today is not John Lowery."

"He went by Spider."

"Why?"

"Long story."

"This thing's going to skewer old Plato. Do it for him. And for Notter and Merkel. You may need a favor from us sometime."

I pictured tormented eyes beneath a Korean vet's cap.

A plastic-wrapped corpse.

A mold-crusted skeleton.

I had no urgent cases in North Carolina or Quebec. Maybe Danny was right. Maybe a trip to Hawaii would be therapeutic for Katy, and

Danny's point about my perhaps needing them in the future wasn't said entirely in jest. But would Katy go?

"When will action kick off at the CIL?" I asked.

"The remains are being transported on Friday. Lowery insists you travel with them."

"Adamantly."

"Adamantly."

"I'll ask Katy."

"Good girl."

"That's not a promise, Danny. Katy needs me right now. It's her call."

"I imagine she's pretty torn up."

"Very."

"Will she attend the kid's funeral?"

"The service will be open to close family only."

Silence hummed from the South Pacific to the southeastern seaboard. Danny broke it.

"I'll send flight information as soon as I have it."

9

I ROSE EARLY THE NEXT MORNING, BLITZED the Harris Teeter floral department, then returned home to download and print photos from the net. Armed and ready, I made a tippy-toe visit to my study-turned-guest-room.

Katy awoke to orchids and plumeria, a handmade lei, and a thumbtacked Hawaiian panorama.

She appeared in the kitchen shortly after ten, tousled and confused, holding a particularly dazzling shot of Maui's Kamaole I beach.

I asked how she felt. She shrugged, poured herself coffee.

I conveyed Danny Tandler's condolences. She slurped.

I launched my pitch. Snorkeling. Diving. Maybe a surfing lesson or two.

Katy listened, eyes on steam rising from her mug.

Interpreting shrugless silence as interest, I continued. Diamond Head. Waikiki. Lanikai Beach.

"So. What do you think, sweetie? Aloha?" I pantomimed a little hula.

"I guess."

Not exactly "Yippee!" But she was willing to go.

By noon, thanks to Charlie Hunt's intervention, the public defender's office had granted a "compassionate leave" for its very junior first-year researcher. Two weeks. Unpaid.

Fair enough.

After a lunch of tomato soup and tuna sandwiches, Katy and I dug out and organized scuba and snorkeling gear. At least I did. She mostly watched.

I made calls when Katy went home to pack. LaManche had no objection to my two-week absence from the LSJML in Montreal, provided I was reachable by phone. Pete agreed to take Birdie. My neighbor agreed to look after the town house. Tim Larabee, the Mecklenburg County medical examiner, asked that prior to my departure I examine a skull found off Sam Furr Road just north of Charlotte. I promised to do the analysis the following day.

Danny rang around six with flight information. Convinced of the righteousness of his plan, he'd gone ahead and booked a reservation for Katy.

Danny said he'd meet our plane, warned teasingly of a surprise. No amount of cajoling could wangle further information from him. Slightly uneasy, I disconnected.

Thursday night, after wrapping up with the Sam Furr skull, I treated Charlie Hunt to dinner. Partly because I missed him. Partly to thank him for scoring Katy her unearned vacation.

We met at Barrington's, a tiny bistro buried in a southeast Charlotte retail complex. Unlikely location. Pricey tab. Kick-ass food.

I had the tagliatelle. Charlie had the grouper. For dessert, we shared an order of bread pudding with white chocolate ice cream.

Afterward, leaning on my Mazda, I said *mahalo* to Charlie in a very big way. His response indicated eagerness to continue the thank-you at his place.

I was tempted. Very tempted.

But not yet.

To Charlie's dismay, we both went home solo.

Getting to Hawaii from North Carolina is easier now than back in the nineties when I consulted to the CIL. But the trip still takes half your life.

I rose at dawn on Friday and called Katy. She was up, but sounded groggy. Said she couldn't sleep and had spent all of Thursday and into the wee hours writing about Coop's death.

My daughter had begun blogging the previous winter. I'd visited her site, ChickWithThoughts. blogpost.com, and been surprised at the eloquence of her posts. And at the serious nature of the subject matter. Topics ranged from presidential politics, to ecoterrorism, to global economics. I'd been astounded at the number of people who read and participated in the discussions.

Flying US Airways from Charlotte via Phoenix, we arrived in Honolulu at two thirty in the afternoon. One gains five hours traveling west, so the outbound leg seemed deceptively painless.

But I knew from experience. The return would lay me low.

Though I hadn't been involved in the official transfer, I was aware of the young man riding below us in the cargo bay. Throughout the journey my thoughts had repeatedly drifted to him. Who was he? What was his story? How had he ended up in Spider Lowery's grave?

Katy slept through most of the flight. I tried writing reports, gave up. I'm lousy at working on planes. I blame it on altitude. It's really just lack of discipline.

The movie offerings were approved by censors for both sailors on shore leave and four-year-old Baptists, so I read, alternating between a Hawaiian travel book and a Stephen King novel.

During one of her brief waking periods, I explained the JPAC issue to Katy. No details. The last thing she needed was a reminder of the tragic cost of war. But Katy would be on her own while I was working at the CIL. She'd be curious about where I was and why.

Katy listened without interrupting, a response I found unsettling. Normally my daughter would have posed a thousand questions and offered an equal number of opinions. I understood her listlessness. Though Katy kept it to herself, I'd overheard her rephoning the Coopertons before leaving my house on Thursday. Her side of the conversation indicated another rebuff.

As promised, Danny was waiting in baggage claim, cart at the ready. Upon spotting us, he beamed like a kid who'd just downed a Snickers.

Hugs all around.

While Danny and I collected the luggage, Katy went in search of a john. Danny took the opportunity to query my daughter's state of mind. I waggled a hand. So-so.

I asked about the remains from Lumberton. He said that Silas Sugarman had delivered the transport container to the Charlotte airport and that it was listed on the manifest of our flight.

I knew the drill. The transport container would be off-loaded and taken to the cargo area, where it would be met by personnel from Borthwick, a local Oahu mortuary. With paperwork completed, the coffin would travel by hearse to Hickam and enter the CIL through a rear door. An accession number would be assigned, and the remains would await processing.

The Avis line moved at the pace of sludge. When I reached the counter, the agent could find no trace of my reservation. After much sighing and head-shaking, a car was finally located, a red Chevrolet Cobalt about the size of my purse.

Danny helped load our suitcases. Then, refusing to divulge any clue concerning our hotel, he insisted I follow his Honda.

In the past, when consulting to the CIL, I was always billeted in a moderately priced hotel on Waikiki Beach. That meant traveling roughly southeast into town.

Danny's route surprised me. He looped north on the H-1, then cut east on the H-3 toward Kaneohe.

We'd barely cleared the airport when Katy slumped against the window and fell asleep. My little navigator. It would be up to me to keep

Danny in sight. Challenging, since the guy had a foot twice the atomic weight of lead.

Twenty minutes out, Danny merged onto Highway 630, Mokapu Boulevard, then turned south on Kalaheo. Eventually we passed Kailua Beach Park.

As my internal GPS engaged, I felt a buzz of excitement. Danny knew that my favorite stretch of Oahu sand was Lanikai Beach. Lanikai lies just south of Kailua. Was that where Danny was going? Was that his surprise?

Forget it, a pessimist neuron scoffed. *You're traveling on the military dime.*

Anything's possible, an optimist fired back.

Once over the bridge at Kailua, it was like driving in Charlotte. At every little jog, the street name changed. Lihiwai. Kawailoa. Alala. Mokulua.

Hawaiian. You gotta love it.

Finally, Danny pulled into an opening barely visible between towering hedges. I followed.

The driveway led through an expanse of lawn to a two-story stucco home with a lanai bordering three sides. Beyond the house I could see more grass, white sand, and the glittering turquoise of Kailua Bay.

Danny pulled to a stop, got out, and walked toward my car. I lowered my window.

"Home sweet home." He swept a theatrical arm.

"We're staying here?" I admit. It was almost a squeal.

A grin split Danny's face from ear to ear.

Katy sat up and squinted through the windshield.

"How did you pull this off?" I asked.

"Danny has his ways." Tapping one temple.

I curled my fingers in a "give me more" gesture.

"The place belongs to a retired colonel. He's gone a month, visiting his kids on the mainland, and feels more secure with someone in residence."

Katy climbed from the car and walked toward the house.

"Shall we see if accommodations are up to madam's high standards?"

Ignoring the faux-British accent, I got out and followed Danny to the front door.

Things were definitely up to standard. A standard about which, given my profession, I had only heard rumors.

The decor was Hawaiian plantation meets modern tech. Arched windows and doorways. Carved woodwork. Luxurious greenery. Stone and Brazilian cherry floors.

The dining and living areas had vaulted wood ceilings and sliding glass doors leading to lanais overlooking a pool. Beyond the pool, thirty yards of lawn swept down to a row of coconut palms and the beach.

The kitchen had every appliance patented in the new millennium and enough stainless steel to outfit an OR. A bedroom and bath, a powder room, a small gym, and an office rounded out the first floor.

Each of the three upstairs suites had a bath with walk-in shower, Jacuzzi, and an acre of marble. King beds. Flat-screen TVs. Ceiling fans. Heart-stopping floor-to-ceiling ocean views.

As Danny gave the tour, Katy trailed mutely behind.

"Which room did you like?" I queried when we'd finished.

"The green one's OK."

"It's yours," I said.

"Now what?" I asked when Katy had gone to the car for her luggage.

Danny looked at his watch.

"It's Friday, now almost five. The lab will be emptier than a politician's heart."

I couldn't help smiling at Danny's metaphor.

"I've unearthed some info on Lowery. It's not much. Forty-plus years is a long time. How about I brief you, then you and Katy relax over the weekend? Monday morning, we'll meet at the CIL and start the analysis."

While I was disappointed at the two-day delay, Danny was right. It was almost 10 p.m. East Coast time and I'd been up since 5 a.m. I'd slept little on the plane and was probably beyond my capacity for critical thought. More important, I didn't want to leave Katy alone right away.

"Sounds like a plan," I said.

Danny offered to carry my things from the car. I told him I could handle my own suitcase and laptop. He proceeded to get them anyway.

While Danny collected my belongings, I checked the refrigerator. It was packed. Soft drinks. Juice. Cheese. Yogurt. Hummus. Fruit and veggies. Bagels and cream cheese. Trays of pre-packaged sushi.

I opened a few cupboards. Same deal.

The generosity was so Danny. Time and again,

when I'd been down, he'd sent a silly gift to make me smile. When I'd been buoyant, pleased over some small victory or accomplishment, he'd sent a silly gift to enhance my happiness.

When Danny returned, I thanked him and offered to pay for the groceries. He asked for a brew but declined the dinero.

We argued. Danny finally provided a figure. Knowing it was low, I doubled the amount and wrote a check. Then we both settled into lounge chairs on the lanai.

"Spider's story isn't going to please his old man."

Danny downed a slug of Corona and began.

"In December of 1967, while stationed in Vietnam, Private John 'Spider' Lowery took unauthorized absence from his unit."

"He just split?"

"Apparently. Six weeks later he was arrested by MPs at the home of a Vietnamese hooker on the outskirts of Saigon."

"They were ranching?" I used the Vietnam-era term for shacking up.

Danny nodded. "Long story short, Lowery landed in the Long Binh jail, a military stockade on the road between Bien Hoa and Saigon. Eventually he was offered early release from the slammer if he rejoined his unit and went back to duty."

"Was that standard practice?"

Another nod. "The war was in overdrive and the military needed as many bodies in action as possible, so if the offense was only UA the military would deal."

1968. The Tet Offensive. The Battle of Hue.

I'd been a kid at the time, but association with JPAC had familiarized me with details.

In January of 1968, hoping to spark a national uprising, the North Vietnamese Army, or NVA, and the National Front for the Liberation of South Vietnam, or Vietcong, broke the traditional Lunar New Year truce and launched the Tet Offensive. Over 100 cities were attacked. So were Westmoreland's headquarters and the U.S. embassy in Saigon.

During this urban offensive, the combined Vietcong and NVA troops captured Hue. The marines then counterattacked and took the former capital back, inch by bloody inch.

"Spider was released from Long Binh on January 23, 1968, and boarded a Huey to be returned to his unit," Danny continued. "The passenger manifest listed four crew and Private Lowery. Shortly after takeoff, the Huey crashed and burned with the loss of all on board.

"Three crew members were recovered and identified the next day. Two warrant officers who were the pilot and copilot, and a sergeant who was the crew chief. A fourth badly burned body was discovered near the crash scene several days later. The body was wearing army fatigues but no insignia."

"Wasn't that odd?"

"Not given the fact that Lowery was fresh out of jail." Danny took another pull on his beer. "The burned body was sent to the Tan Son Nhut mortuary, where forensic analysis showed that the victim fit Lowery's profile, including age, sex, race, and height."

"What about the fourth crew member?"

Danny shook his head. "A Spec 2 maintenance guy. They ruled him out. Not sure why."

"Were his remains ever found?"

"I'll have to ask." More beer. "Following identification and processing, Lowery's remains were shipped from Tan Son Nhut to Lumberton, North Carolina, for burial. End of story."

"Apparently not," I said.

"Apparently not." Danny set down his empty bottle and rose. "You and Katy have a nice weekend."

Despite Katy's anguish, we did.

10

KATY WAS STILL SLEEPING WHEN I SET OUT
Monday morning. Her day would be a repeat
of both Saturday and Sunday. Reading by the
ocean, later by the pool. A bit of snorkeling. A
run on the beach. A long nap.

Hawaii hugs the equator, so island weather
varies little. Sunny, highs in the eighties, maybe
a blink-of-the-eye afternoon shower. In a word,
perfect.

That descriptor does not apply to Honolulu's
rush-hour traffic.

Creep and lurch. Creep and lurch.

In addition to JPAC, Hickam Air Force Base
is home to the Fifteenth Airlift Wing and sixty-
seven partner units, including Pacific Air Forces
Headquarters and the Hawaii Air National
Guard. As with most military compounds, outsiders don't just stroll in.

Queuing at the gate took a full ten minutes.
When I finally reached the front of the line, an
exceedingly spit-and-polished young man saluted
me into an office manned by orange-vested security personnel.

Danny had left credentials. Once the car registration and safety-check paperwork were scanned, I was quickly cleared.

After skirting the military airport, I looped the traffic circle and drove past the air wing headquarters. The building's bullet holes, still visible from the December 7, 1941, attack that pushed the U.S. into World War II, are pointed out to every first-time visitor to the base.

Eventually I made a right, wound past aircraft hangars, turned left, and pulled into a small parking lot. Building 45. The military coins such poetic names.

I dialed Danny on my mobile. He answered and said he'd be right out.

While waiting, I thought about the charge of those working inside the nondescript brown building. About the raison d'être of JPAC.

From 1959 until 1975, North Vietnam, supported by its Communist allies in the south, battled the government and armed forces of South Vietnam, supported by the United States and other members of SEATO, the Southeast Asia Treaty Organization. At its peak, the war kicked the crap out of Vietnam, Laos, and Cambodia.

Here's how the conflict played out.

While the lightly armed Vietcong fought a hit-and-run guerrilla war, the NVA employed more conventional tactics, often committing large-sized units to battle. The U.S. relied on its usual trifecta of ground forces, heavy artillery, and gonzo airpower.

The human toll was enormous: 3 to 4 million Vietnamese from both sides; 1.5 to 2 million Laotians and Cambodians; 58,159 Americans.

Eighteen hundred of those Americans never came home and were not accounted for.

Thus the CIL, later JPAC.

Here come the acronyms.

The Central Identification Laboratory, Thailand, CIL-THAI for short, was founded in 1973 to locate American military personnel missing in Southeast Asia. Three years later the lab was moved to Honolulu, its mission expanded. The Central Identification Laboratory, Hawaii, CILHI, would henceforth search for, recover, and identify Americans missing from all previous conflicts. Today, in addition to Vietnam, that total includes 120 soldiers from the Cold War, 8,100 from the Korean War, and 78,000 from World War II.

Fast-forward almost two decades from the founding of CILHI.

In 1992, the Joint Task Force–Full Accounting, JTF-FA, was established to ensure the fullest possible resolution of questions surrounding Americans missing in Southeast Asia. Another decade and the Department of Defense, DOD, decided that accounting efforts would best be served by a single entity. Thus, in 2003, the two organizations were merged to form the Joint POW/MIA Accounting Command, JPAC.

As with its predecessor, JPAC's mission is to find American war dead and bring them home. Core operations involve the pursuit of leads, the recovery of remains and artifacts, and the identification of individual soldiers, sailors, airmen, and marines.

Every investigation begins with paper. JPAC historians and analysts gather correspondence, maps, photographs, unit histories, and medical and personnel records. JPAC's research and intelligence section backgrounds history.

Most investigations also utilize sources outside JPAC, including the national archives and record depositories maintained by the U.S. and foreign governments. Veterans, civilian historians, private citizens, families of missing Americans, and amateur researchers also routinely provide information.

Ultimately, JPAC experts combine everything into a "loss incident case file." At any given time, approximately 700 active files are under investigation at the CIL.

Danny emerged wearing a pink aloha shirt and baggy brown pants. Behind the thick lenses, his eyes blinked in the sunlight.

We entered building 45 through a back door and followed a corridor past the general's staff offices into the main lobby. On the walls, wood-mounted brass plaques named the fallen ID'd through JPAC efforts.

Danny swiped his badge at a pair of glass doors and we entered the CIL public area. To the left, a long glass wall provided a view of the main lab. Before it, a folding table held skulls, bones, and military equipment used for demonstration purposes.

Straight ahead a hallway led to offices, a copy center, a small kitchen, a conference room, and an autopsy area used for artifact cleaning and analysis. Ahead and to the right, a counter was manned by a young man in army fatigues. Above his shaved head, analogue clocks indicated the hour in five time zones.

The offices of senior JPAC personnel ringed the perimeter. Only two doors stood open.

Roger Merkel is tall, slightly stooped, and balding. Well north of fifty, his face is tanned and scoured with lines from years in the sun.

Merkel was at his desk. Seeing us, he rose and hugged me so tightly my eyes teared, momentarily blurring my view of his office.

Stepping back, I marveled, as usual, at Merkel's orderliness. Files and papers sat in neatly squared stacks. Books, photos, and mementos hung and stood in perfect formation.

After a few words with Merkel, Danny and I went in search of coffee. Gus Dimitriadus, a CIL anthropologist, was leaving the kitchen as we entered.

Though similar in age to Danny and me, Dimitriadus is someone with whom I've never felt a connection. He's attractive enough, good hair, good eyes, but the guy acts like he lives on embalming fluid.

Gus Dimitriadus never laughs. Ever. Frankly, I've never liked him much.

Apparently others share my view. For as long as I've known him, Dimitriadus has lived alone in a small apartment near Waikiki Beach.

Dimitriadus looked up from the fax he was skimming. Seeing me, his perpetually dour face went stiff. With a nod, he continued down the hall.

Surprised, I turned to Danny. "What the hell?"

"Come on. You two have never been soul mates."

"But we've always been cordial."

"Don't worry about it."

Danny busied himself setting up mugs, dispensing coffee that resembled liquid asphalt.

I tried to think how long it had been since I'd seen Dimitriadus. Twelve years at least. He'd been deployed on missions the last few times I'd been to the CIL.

"Is Dimitriadus still peeved over the Kingston-Washington fiasco?"

Bernard Kingston died along with three others from a skimmer boat on the Mekong River in '67. Thirty years later, four partial skeletons arrived at the CIL.

Long story. Short version, locals buried the seamen when they washed ashore, told their story in '95, hoping for cash.

Dimitriadus caught the files. On review, I bonged his report, suspecting that two of the IDs had been reversed. Turned out I was right.

"Is that it?" I pressed.

Danny nodded.

"Jesus, that was ages ago."

"What can I tell you?" Danny proffered a mug. "The guy's a grudge holder."

We passed no one else on the way to Danny's office.

"Seems quiet." I remembered a lot more hustle and bustle.

"A lot of folks are out in the field."

Danny referred to workers away on recovery missions.

Quick primer on JPAC operations.

Once a loss incident case file has been opened and a likely body location has been pinpointed, an investigative team, or IT, is deployed to the scene. Could be anywhere—a rice paddy in Southeast Asia, a cliffside in Papua New Guinea, a mountaintop in the Himalayas, an underwater trench off the coast of Tunisia.

An IT is composed of ten to fourteen people, led by a team leader and a forensic anthropologist, the former responsible for the overall safety and success of the mission, the latter for the actual excavation. Other members include a team sergeant, linguist, medic, life-support technician, forensic photographer, and explosive ordnance disposal technician. Additional experts patch in as needed—mountaineering specialists, divers, and such.

Recovery sites range from a few square meters, as with single burials, to areas larger than football fields, as with aircraft crashes. The anthropologist kicks things off by laying out a grid with stakes and string, then, one by one, individual sections are dug. All soil is hand-sifted to maximize retrieval of the tiniest skeletal bits or fragments of associated artifacts. Depending on circumstances, a handful or a hundred local workers may be hired for a project.

Once everything's back at the CIL, the lab rats gear up, examining bones, teeth, and material evidence and correlating all findings with historical records.

The anthropologist constructs as complete a biological profile as possible, analyzes trauma, and describes pathological conditions such as arthritis or old healed fractures. The odontologist compares recovered dentition to X-rays, handwritten charts, and treatment notes in ante-mortem records. Each collects a sample for mito-chondrial DNA testing.

Material evidence varies from case to case. Air-craft data plates. Ordnance or weapons. Packs, mess kits, uniforms. Life-support equipment. Per-sonal effects, such as rings, watches, or combs. Every shred, splinter, and chip is scrutinized.

As you can imagine, all this research, recovery, and analysis is labor-intensive, and an identifica-tion may take years for completion. If mtDNA is obtained from the bones or teeth, the search for family reference samples can add more time to the process.

Even then it's not over. Every positive ID requires review at multiple levels, including exter-nal study by independent experts. That's where I came in. For years I evaluated dossiers, dissect-ing the overlapping lines of evidence relevant to a particular set of remains.

Seems like beaucoup bother and bucks, you say? Trust me. The effort and expense pay off. On average, JPAC identifies six individuals each month. To date, more than 1,400 military per-sonnel have been returned to their families. The gratitude of relatives is incalculable.

Bottom line, our troops know: should they march off to war, one way or another, we're bringing them home.

"How many recovery missions are deployed each year?" No longer affiliated with JPAC, I hadn't a sense of current numbers.

"At least ten in Southeast Asia, maybe five associated with the Korean War." Danny twisted his lips in thought. "Ten others wherever, you know, for World War Two cases, or the Cold War. Teams are always coming or going."

Danny's office was the polar opposite of Merkel's. Papers and books lay scattered about, files threatened to topple from unsteady stacks. Mementos lay tossed where they'd landed coming through the door. A signed softball. A kite. A photo of Danny digging on a mountain.

The desk held a similar array of memorabilia. A Micronesian sculpture made of what looked like pig tusks. A painted coconut. A miniature skeleton with Danny's face glued to the skull. A stuffed lizard whose species was a mystery to me.

Danny cleared files from a chair so that I could sit. Before my arrival, he'd laid out Spider Lowery's file. Though familiar with the contents, we started there.

Working through the documents reminded me how much time I'd spent squinting at smeared carbon copies of forms, faded message traffic, and illegible script. Spider's record review took an hour.

"You've been swabbed?"

Danny referred to the DNA sampling required of anyone entering the lab. No big deal, a Q-tip swipe of the inner cheek. Specimens are kept on file should contamination become an issue with an ID.

I nodded.

We crossed to the glass wall and Danny placed his badge over the sensor. The door clicked. We entered and wove through a maze of tables, some empty, some holding bones, toward a man in a red sweater seated at a desk at the back of the room.

The Lumberton remains had been accessioned as 2010-37. Danny presented his badge and requested the case by number.

Red Sweater rose and pressed a button. Floor-to-ceiling shelving opened and he disappeared down a row. Moments later he reappeared with a long, white cardboard box.

I knew the routine. The remains would be assigned a specific table where they would be allowed to remain for thirty days. The transaction would be entered into the computer tracking system, and the location of the bones would be diagrammed on a blackboard on one wall of the room.

Danny swiped his badge, collected the box, and moved to the designated table. I followed.

We both gloved, then Danny gestured me the honors.

I lifted the cover.

The remains were as I remembered, skull shattered, lower arms and hands and both feet missing, cortical surfaces darkly mottled and covered by pink-white mold and charred muck.

Working silently, Danny and I reassembled what was left of the man so long buried in North Carolina. Skull. Torso. Arms. Legs.

When the skeleton was arranged anatomically, we ran inventory, with Danny naming bones and me recording. Though I'd done a preliminary assessment at Sugarman's, his would be the analysis of record.

Inventory finished, he went through the same

steps I'd followed at the funeral home. With the same findings.

The remains were those of a male who died between the ages of eighteen and twenty-five. Race remained elusive.

"Nothing to exclude Spider Lowery," Danny said.

"And nothing to positively ID him."

"Teeth are out."

"We might spot root fragments when we X-ray. Or we could compare alveolar configurations." I referred to the shape of the tooth sockets.

Danny shook his head. "The Form 603 is strictly narrative."

Danny meant Lowery's military dental record, typically containing diagrams called odontograms, X-rays, and information about the patient's care, identity of dentist, when, where, et cetera.

"Why no X-rays?" I asked. "Wasn't every soldier given a dental exam at induction?"

"Theoretically, yes. If not at his or her induction center, maybe in boot camp, maybe in-country, at Bien Hoa Air Base, for example. But it didn't always happen."

"You're suggesting Lowery slipped through the cracks?"

"Maybe. Here's another possibility. Troops reporting to a new duty station often carried their own records with them. It helped with in-processing if medical and dental information arrived at the same time as the soldier."

I saw where Danny was going. "But that didn't always happen either."

"No. Sometimes paperwork caught up later. Maybe Lowery's records arrived in Vietnam after he was killed and his body was shipped home."

"Any way to tell from the file if X-rays ever existed?"

"Not really. Say a soldier had a periapical or a bitewing done. The X-rays might have been attached to the folder using a two-hole punch. Or they might have been placed into a small manila envelope and added to the file loose. Either way, the films could be lost or misplaced."

Sudden ominous thought. "Or deliberately removed?"

Something flicked in Danny's eyes, vanished before I could read it.

"Meaning?" he asked.

"I don't know," I said.

"I suppose." Danny lifted and gently scraped at a skull fragment, much as I'd done at Sugarman's. "Fire damage."

"Consistent with the reported chopper crash," I said. "As are the missing hands and feet and the cranial fractures."

"The biological profile, the trauma, the timing, the body recovery location. It all fits. Thus the ID at Tan Son Nhut back in '68."

"Johnson, Dadko, and some writing-challenged medical officer shipped this guy home as Spider Lowery."

"Weickmann."

"What?"

"The medical officer's name was Weickmann."

"You could read that scrawl?"

"Years of practice."

"Whatever. Prints from my Quebec floater say they were wrong."

"Nam was exploding in '68. The system was overwhelmed."

Indeed.

Early in the war, a single facility processed all Americans killed in Southeast Asia. When fatalities soared in the spring of '67, it became apparent that the *status* could no longer be *quo*. Cramped and located in a congested part of the base, the Tan Son Nhut mortuary was inefficient, inadequate, and a hazard to health.

As a result, a second mortuary was opened at the Da Nang Air Base. Beginning in June 1967, remains recovered in the I Corps tactical zone went to Da Nang.

But the Tet Offensive shot numbers into the biosphere. In February 1968, the two mortuaries processed roughly three thousand sets of remains, a total greater than for any comparable period to that point.

The upshot was the construction of a modern twenty-table facility on a new patch of ground at Tan Son Nhut. The new facility became operational in August 1968.

Spider Lowery's Huey crashed at Long Binh in January of that year, shortly after Tet and eight months before the revamped Tan Son Nhut mortuary came online.

In the chaos of war, a mistake had been made.

At a little past one Danny and I took a break. Wanting to accomplish as much as possible that day, we passed up a nice lunch at the Officers Club or the Mamala Bay Golf Course in favor of a quick pizza at the BX. The food hole. There's a reason for the nickname.

While driving back to the CIL, I called Katy. To describe her as unhappy would be like saying Nixon was a bit bummed by the tapes.

By two fifteen Danny and I were back with 2010-37. For the next two hours we scraped desiccated flesh and fabric from bone, a job I find excruciatingly tedious. And the smell is revolting.

Adipocere is a waxlike substance formed by the hydrolysis of fat during decomposition. I'd about had it when a small chunk of the stuff dropped into the sink from the fragment of upper jaw I was scrubbing. I watched water eddy around it, swirling bits away and down into the drain.

I shifted my gaze to the newly exposed facial architecture. None of the cheekbone survived, and the zygomaxillary suture was unremarkable.

I rotated the fragment.

The upper palate was broad, its intersecting sutures largely unfused.

I inserted my probe into one of the empty tooth sockets. Another crumb of adipocere popped free. My eyes followed its flight path into the sink.

The original chunk had now been reduced by half. I was returning my attention to the maxilla when something caught my attention, more a glint of light than a visual impression.

Reaching down, I scooped the remainder of the original chunk onto my glove. When I poked, the thing split into two halves.

An object lay glistening in my glove.

11

"WHATCHA GOT?" DANNY NOTICED ME STARing at my palm.

I extended my hand.

Whipping off his glasses, Danny brought his nose to within inches of my find. Seconds passed.

"Flip her over."

I turned the thing with my probe. "Look familiar?"

"Nope."

"Think it's something?"

"Everything's something."

"Profound."

"Looks like metal. Where was it?"

"Enveloped in adipocere packing the basicranium, below the palate."

"Good eye."

"Thanks."

"M'lady's penchant for shiny things pays off. Let's scope it."

We did, at increasing powers of magnification.

The object was roughly five millimeters long by three millimeters wide by a millimeter or so thick, and appeared to be made of gold. Its shape was irregular, with a lopsided glob on one side and two tapering projections on the other.

"Looks like a duck with a wide-open beak."

The image didn't work for me.

I rotated the thing ninety degrees. Danny took another turn squinting through the eyepiece.

"Now it's a mushroom with two pointy stems."

I looked. "I can see that. Any idea what it is?"

"Not really."

"A chip from a filling or crown?"

"Ehhh." Danny scrunched his face.

"What? Ehhh?"

"Looks too thin and too flat."

Danny's eyes flicked to the wall clock. Mine followed.

Five forty-five. I hadn't noticed the lab grow quiet. Or realized we were now alone.

"Quitting time?" I asked, knowing the answer.

Though Danny had been married almost twenty years now, he and his wife still coochie-cooed like newlyweds. At times I found their giddy-gooey-bliss act irritating as hell. Mostly I envied them.

"Quitting time." Sheepish grin. Or horny. Or hungry. "Aggie's making Salisbury steak."

Danny sealed the mushroom-duck thing inside a baggy. Back in his office, he locked it in a desk drawer.

"Tomorrow we can pick Craig's brain." Craig Brooks was one of the three CIL dentists.

After removing our lab coats we headed out, Danny toward beef and gravy in Waipio, I toward gloom in Lanikai Beach.

* * *

Katy was on a lounge chair by the pool. I took a moment to observe her through the sliding glass door.

Katy wasn't listening to her iPod, talking on her cell phone, surfing or blogging with her laptop. No book or magazine lay in her lap. Dressed in the same tank and drawstring pants she'd worn the night before, she simply sat staring out to sea.

In a word, she looked miserable.

Again I was swept by a feeling of helplessness. I knew only time would ease my daughter's pain, and that a week had yet to pass since news of Coop's death. I also knew the delivery of that news had been cold and impersonal.

Still.

Steeling myself, I exited to the lanai.

"How you doing, tough stuff?" A childhood endearment.

"Ready for the play-offs." Flat.

"Where did you go today?" Dropping into the chair beside Katy's.

"Nowhere."

"What did you do?"

"Nothing."

"Got any thoughts on dinner?"

"I'm not hungry."

"You have to eat."

"No I don't."

Score one for Katy.

"I'm sure there's something in the kitchen that I could throw together. Danny bought out the market."

"Whatever."

"Or I could drive into Kailua for more sushi."

"Look, Mom. I know you mean well. But the thought of food revolts me right now."

You have to eat. I didn't say it.

"Anything I can do to perk you up? A little Groucho?" I raised my brows and flicked an imaginary cigar.

"Just let me be."

"I feel so bad."

"Not bad enough to stay home."

It felt like a slap. My expression must have said so.

"I'm sorry." Katy's hand fluttered to her mouth, froze, as though uncertain of the purpose of its trip. "I didn't mean that."

"I know."

"It's just . . ." Her fingers curled. "I feel such rage and there's nowhere to point it." Her fist pounded one knee. "At dumb-ass Coop for going to Afghanistan? At the Taliban for gunning him down? At God for letting it happen? At myself for giving a shit?"

Katy swiveled toward me. Though dry-eyed, her face was pallid and tight.

"I know anger and self-pity are pointless and counterproductive and self-destructive and blah blah blah. And I'm really trying to pull out of my funk. I am. It's just that, right now, life sucks."

"I understand."

"Do you? Have you ever had someone just blasted off the face of the earth? Someone you really cared about?"

I had. My best friend, Gabby. Cops I'd worked with and cared about. Eddie Rinaldi in Charlotte. Ryan's partner, Jean Bertrand. I didn't say it.

"Look, Mom. I know you've come here to do a job. And I know Coop's death is not your fault. But you're gone all day, then you get back all sunshine and Hallmark compassion." She threw up both hands. "I don't know. You're in the zone so you take the hit."

"I've taken worse."

Wan smile.

Turning from me, Katy fidgeted with the tie at her waist, finger twisting and retwisting the string.

Overhead, palm fronds clicked in the breeze. Down at the shore, gulls cawed.

Katy was right. I'd dragged her thousands of miles, then dumped her in a place she knew nothing about. Yes, she was twenty-four, a big girl. But right now she needed me.

The familiar old dilemma knotted my gut. How to balance motherhood and job?

My mind flailed for solutions.

Work alternating days at the CIL? Half days?

Impossible. I'd come to Honolulu at JPAC expense. And Plato Lowery was anxious for an answer.

Take Katy to the CIL with me?

Definitely a bad idea.

I started to speak. "Maybe I could—"

"No, Mom. You have to go to work. I shouldn't have said what I did."

"It helps to stay busy." Gently.

I braced for incoming. Didn't happen.

"Yes," Katy said. "It does."

Suggestions leaped to mind.

No! yipped a wise sector of gray cells. *Give her time. Space.*

Rising, I hugged Katy's shoulders. Then I went inside, changed to shorts, and strolled down to the beach.

The sun rode low, streaking the horizon and ocean tangerine and pink. The sand felt warm and soft underfoot, the breeze feathery on my skin.

Walking the water's edge, childhood memories popped into my brain. Summers at Pawleys Island. My sister, Harry. Gran. My mother, Katherine Daessee Lee.

Daisy.

Triggered by the setting and my recent encounter with Katy, synapses fired images and emotions.

My mother's eyes, green like my own. Sometimes radiant. Sometimes cool, refusing to engage.

A child's confusion.

Which mother today?

A woman driven by social pretension? The newest spa, the trendiest restaurant, the charity event receiving current social column ink.

A woman in seclusion? Shades drawn, bedroom door locked, sobbing or silence within.

How I hated Daisy's frantic party mode. How I hated her withdrawal into her lilac-scented cell.

Gradually, closed doors and distant eyes became the norm.

As a child I'd loved my mother fiercely. As an adult I'd finally posed the raw question to myself: Did my mother ever love me?

And I'd faced the answer.

I didn't know.

My mother loved my baby brother, Kevin. And

my father, Michael Terrence Brennan. I was eight when both died, one of leukemia, one drunk at the wheel. The dual tragedies changed everything.

But did they? Or had Daisy always been mad?

Same answer. I didn't know.

I wanted a closeness with my daughter that I'd been denied with my mother. No matter the irrationality of Katy's behavior or the unreasonableness of her need, I'd be there for her.

But how?

The cadence of the waves triggered no revelations.

Katy was gone from the lanai when I arrived back at the house. She appeared as I was washing my feet at the outdoor shower.

"You're right. Moping is stupid."

I waited.

"Tomorrow I'll go parasailing."

"Sounds good." It didn't. I preferred Katy safely grounded, not dangling a hundred feet in the air.

"Or I'll sign up for one of those helicopter rides over a volcano."

"Mm." I turned off the faucet.

"Listen, Mom. I really am grateful for this trip. Hawaii is awesome."

"And I'm grateful you're here."

"I took a dozen shrimp from the freezer."

"Fire up the barbie?" Delivered in my very best Aussie.

"Aye, mate."

Katie raised a palm. I high-fived it.

One dozen turned into two.

12

Birdie was chasing a very large dog along a very white beach. The dog wore an elaborate apparatus with lines rising to a bright red parachute high in the sky.

Katy dangled upside down from the chute, long blond hair waving in the wind. Sunlight glinted from tears on her cheeks.

A gull screeched.

The dog stopped.

Katy's chute deflated and she drifted earthward.

Fast. Too fast.

The gull's screeching morphed to a very loud buzzing.

I raised one semiconscious lid.

The room was dark. The bedside table was vibrating.

I fumbled for my BlackBerry and clicked on.

Don Ho was singing "Aloha 'Oe."

"How is my sweet rose of Maunawili?" A male voice. Not Don's.

Another twist to the dream?

No. My eyes were open. One managed to drag the clock face into focus.

"Do you know what time it is here?" Seemingly a frequent opener on calls to Hawaii.

"Seven."

"Redo the math, Ryan."

"Give me a hint."

"There's a five in the answer." Technically, two. The little green digits said 5:59.

"Oops. Sorry."

"Mm."

"That means I woke you."

"I had to get up anyway to answer the phone."

"That line is ancient."

"It's way too early for anything original."

"Thought you'd want to know. Floating Florence gave up some DNA."

"Floating Florence?"

"Nightingale? As in nurse? The Hemmingford corpse? Your lab pals did STR. Whatever that is."

"Short. Tandem. Repeat."

"Sorry. Too. Rarefied."

"Come on, Ryan. STR has been around since the nineties."

"So has cloning. Still no one gets it."

"It's standard for most forensic DNA labs."

Ryan was smart, genius at some things. Science was not one of them. Silence meant I was sailing right over his head.

Great. Biology 101 at dawn.

"Each DNA molecule is made up of two long chains of nucleotide units that unite down the middle like rungs on a ladder. Each nucleotide unit is composed of a sugar, a phosphate, and one of four bases, adenine, cytosine, guanine, or thymine. A, C, G, or T. It's the sequencing of the bases that's important. For example, one person can be CCTA at a certain position, while another is CGTA. With STR, four or five sequence repeats are analyzed."

"Why?"

"Shorter repeat sequences can suffer from problems during amplification. Also, some genetic disorders are associated with trinucleotide repeats. Huntington's disease, for example. Longer repeat sequences are more vulnerable to degradation. And they don't amplify by PCR as well as shorter sequences."

"Ten words or less, how does STR work?"

"Ten?"

"I'll go twenty, that's my top."

"First, you extract nuclear DNA from your sample. Next, you amplify specific polymorphic regions—"

"Flag on the field. Jargon violation."

"Regions on the genome where there is variability. You amplify, you know, make more copies. Then you determine how many repeats exist for the STR sequence in question."

I was oversimplifying for Ryan's benefit. It seemed to be working.

"Once you've got the genetic fingerprint from your suspect or unknown, in this case the Hemmingford floater, you compare it to that of a family member, right?" he asked.

"Even better, you compare a sample from your suspect or unknown to another sample taken from him or her before death. Extracted or saved baby teeth. Saliva from a toothbrush. Mucus on a tissue."

"So our next step is to swab Plato's cheek or find Spider's own snot."

"Nice."

"You said it."

"With much more élan."

"But similar connotation. Think Daddy will agree to open wide and say *ahh*?"

"I don't know," I said. "It's doubtful he's going to like the results."

"Very," Ryan agreed.

For several seconds empty air hummed across the line. Then Ryan asked about Katy.

"She's still pretty bummed," I said.

"You never mentioned a boyfriend. Did you know she was head over heels for the guy?"

"No."

Absence? Inattentiveness? Whatever the reason, my ignorance spoke of remoteness.

"She'll come around."

"Yes. How's Lily?"

"Attending group and keeping appointments with her psychologist. Her color's better and I think she's gained a little weight."

"Don't tell her that." An attempt at levity. It fell flat.

"The kid's saying all the right things. But I don't know." Ryan drew a deep breath, exhaled. "Sometimes I get the feeling she's just going through the motions. Telling me what she thinks I want to hear."

Not good. Ryan's instincts were usually dead-on.

"And she and her mother are like fire and ice. Lutetia's trying, but patience is not one of her strengths. Lutetia says something, Lily overreacts, Lutetia comes down hard, they both explode, and I end up dealing with the aftermath."

"Sounds like they need a break from each other."

"You've got that right. But I can't have Lily living with me. At this stage of rehab she needs someone around all the time. I'm away most days, often at night. You know."

I did.

Ping!

Bad plan.

It's perfect.

"Fly out here." Spoken before follow-up from the wiser brain cells.

"What?"

"Bring Lily to Hawaii. Katy's alone all day. They're close enough in age to be company for each other."

Twenty-four. Nineteen. From my perspective it looked like a match.

"You're nuts."

"You three can play tourist while I work. Then we'll party at night."

"I can't."

"You've banked, what, ninety years of unused vacation time? All it will cost you is a couple of tickets. There's plenty of room here."

I pressed on, though already I was questioning the wisdom of the whole idea.

"A change of climate could help. Lily was born in the Abacos. Maybe Hawaii will remind her of home."

"Lily's court agreement prohibits her leaving the province."

"Puh-leeze. She'd be with you, a sworn officer. Surely you know a judge who would bless that."

There was a very long pause.

"I'll call you back."

Danny wasn't there when I arrived at the CIL. But Dimitriadus was. With a frosty nod, he disappeared into his office.

Aloha to you, too, sunshine.

Donning a lab coat, I picked up where I'd left off with 2010-37. Under the tap, a fragment grudgingly yielded a suture, a squiggly line where the occipital bone had once met the left parietal bone at the back of the skull.

Oh?

I scraped gently with my toothbrush. Detail emerged.

Son of a gun.

Remembering the maxilla, I returned to the table.

Son of a gun.

I was back at the sink when Danny's laugh rang out, an unbridled soprano, infectious as typhoid.

Minutes later, Danny strode toward me. At his side was a giraffe of a man, tall and sinewy, with elephantine ears.

"Good to see you, Tempe." Craig Brooks, a CIL dentist, shot out a hand.

"Good to see you," I said as we shook.

"Danny claims you've discovered the Lost Dutchman mine."

"Hardly." Another girly giggle. "Tempe's find is the size of a mite."

"Let's check it out."

Craig spent a long time at the scope, positioning and repositioning our mushroom-duck thing, adjusting and readjusting the two snake lights. Finally he sat back.

"Danny Boy's right. The material is gold."

"Part of a filling or cap?" I asked.

"Nope."

"You're sure?"

"I've seen a lot of melted dental work, and this doesn't fit the pattern. There's some distortion due to heat exposure, but that's localized along the rounded edge. The rest of the shape looks original. And it doesn't track right for either a restoration or crown."

"How so?"

"First, it's far too thin. Second, one surface is smooth but has some rounded relief. The other surface is roughened but flat."

"So what is it?" I asked.

Craig raised and lowered his shoulders. "Beats me." He rose. "But I'll think about it."

When Craig had gone I told Danny I had something to show him. He asked if it could wait ten minutes. He needed to place a call before nine.

I was walking toward the sink when my mobile sounded. I checked the LCD screen, expecting Ryan's number. The line was local, but not the Lanikai Beach house.

Curious, I clicked on.

13

"A̲LOHA." WHEN IN ROME, RIGHT?

"Aloha. Dr. Temperance Brennan, please." The voice suggested years of unfiltered cigarettes. I was unsure if it was male or female.

"This is she."

"Hadley Perry here."

Great. A unisex name. Pulling back a chair beside 2010-37, I sat.

"ME." Medical examiner.

That Hadley Perry. Though we'd never met, I knew Perry by reputation. Chief medical examiner for the city and county of Honolulu for over two decades, the woman's antics were legendary and the press ate them up.

On one occasion Perry rolled blanket-covered bodies into her facility's parking lot to protest crowding at the morgue. Turned out the gurneys held inflatable dolls. Another time she issued death certificates for two state senators. Said their opposition to increased funding for her office was clear proof of brain death.

"Hope you don't mind me calling your private number."

"Of course not." Actually, I did. But curiosity ruled.

"I'm told you're the best forensic anthropologist in the Western Hemisphere."

A warning bell tinkled.

Danny and I have a history of practical jokes running back decades. Five days on his turf, and so far no prank.

OK, buckaroo. Bring it on.

"Yes, ma'am. That would be me."

A beat. Then, "I have a booger of a case. I'd like your help."

"A humpback with implants?"

"Sorry?"

"A transgender nene?"

"It's a homicide."

"A garroted gecko?" I was on a roll.

"I think the victim is young and male, but can't be sure. Few parts were recovered." Grim-toned. I had to admit. The woman was good.

"What parts? Gizzard? Wing?"

I was grinning at my own hilarity when Danny appeared.

"Nice try," I mouthed, pointing at the phone.

"What?"

"Hadley Perry," I mouthed again, rolling my eyes.

Danny looked genuinely confused.

"Please hold a second." I pressed the handset to my chest. "Gosh, there's a woman on the line claiming to be Hadley Perry."

"Must be Hadley Perry."

"It's not going to work."

"What are you talking about?"

"Payback for showing that slide at AAFS." I'd Photoshopped Danny's head onto an orang-utan wearing a Speedo and flippers. "I'm wise to you."

"I will get you. Take that to the bank. But adequate revenge will require time and intricate planning."

"Come on, Danny. It bombed."

"What bombed?"

"Your little farce."

"What farce?"

"Having a caller pretend to be the chief ME."

"Wrong guy." Danny placed spread fingers on his chest. "Perry scares the crap out of me."

I felt a tiny flame spark in my gut.

"Are you serious?"

"Totally."

Uh-oh.

"Are you still there, Dr. Perry?"

"Yes." Terse.

"We have a terrible connection. May I phone you back?"

She provided the number.

I clicked off and dialed.

"Aloha. Honolulu Medical Examiner."

"Dr. Brennan returning Dr. Perry's call." Face burning.

"Hold, please."

Perry picked up right away.

"I'm sorry. What I was hearing didn't make sense. Lord knows what was coming through on your end." Nervous laugh. "This phone jumbles sound when the signal gets weak." Dear God, I was rambling. "How can I help you?"

Perry repeated what she'd said earlier. Homicide, body parts, young male, help.

"Can't someone local assist you?"

"No."

I waited. She didn't elaborate.

"There are board-certified anthropologists at the CIL." I glanced at Danny. Though he was trying hard to look focused on 2010-37, I knew he was listening.

"And they often help me out, Dr. Brennan. This time I'm asking you."

"I'm in Honolulu for only a very short time."

"I know that."

Oh? I leaned back in my chair.

"Dr. Perry, I'm committed to resolving a situation at the CIL."

"That's military. They quit early. You can work with me after hours."

Choosing a long bone, Danny moved to the sink.

"Why me?"

"You're the best. You said so yourself."

"I was joking."

"I'm asking this as a personal favor."

Far down the line I heard a barely audible voice, like a ghost speaking in some parallel dimension.

Or a nameless victim crying out for justice.

I glanced at Danny. At 2010-37.

"I'll come by at five thirty," I said. "But only for an hour."

After disconnecting, I glanced at Danny. His shoulders had the tautness of someone who is angry or afraid.

"You overheard?"

"Enough."

"I assume the two of you don't get along."

"Let's just say Hadley Perry won't be dining at my house real soon. But that doesn't mean you shouldn't help her."

"Do you want to tell me?"

"I don't like her, it's mutual, we'll leave it at that."

Danny strode to the table. I followed. He added his freshly scrubbed tibia to the man from Lumberton.

For a moment we both stared at the half-cleaned skeleton.

"What did you want to show me?" Danny asked.

"It may be nothing." I scooped up the occipital fragment. "Look at the suture." I pointed to the squiggly line.

"Complex, with lots of accessories." Danny meant tiny islands of bone trapped within the suture.

I passed him the chunk of maxilla that had produced the mushroom-duck thing.

"Broad palate. Straight transverse suture, not bulging up over the midline." He viewed the bone face-on. "The zygomaxillary suture is angled, not S-shaped." He rotated it so the missing nose would have pointed skyward. "Cheekbones probably had some flare."

Danny's eyes rolled up to mine.

"You're thinking this guy might be Vietnamese?"

I shook my head. "You're right those traits

say Mongoloid ancestry. But others suggest Caucasoid. The high nasal bridge, the narrow nasal aperture, the moderately shaped skull, neither long and narrow nor short and broad."

"So, mixed race?"

"European-Asian or European–Native American."

"We had troops who would fit that bill. American Indians, Puerto Ricans, Mexicans, Filipinos. Not many, but they were over there fighting for us."

"What about the missing crew member? Did you learn if the fourth body was ever found?"

"Not yet."

"What was the man's name?"

"I'm still waiting for a response to my inquiry."

For the rest of that day we teased charred tissue and moldy fabric from bone.

By five a fully cleaned skeleton lay on the table.

The exposed bone produced no breakthrough moment.

Honolulu's medical examiner operates out of a curvilinear white structure on Iwilei Road just a short walk from Chinatown. Next door is the largest Salvation Army facility I have ever seen.

At precisely five thirty I pulled under an arch and into a small lot beside the building. Hadley Perry answered my buzz in person. The pictures I'd seen in the *Honolulu Advertiser* hardly prepared me.

Perry was a slim woman with disproportionately large breasts and a penchant for what Katy called "haute hooker" makeup. Her short black hair was gelled into spikes, several of which were fire engine red.

"Hadley Perry." She shot out a hand.

I offered mine.

Perry's grip could have molded forged steel.

"Thanks so much for coming."

"I'm not sure I can help." Wiggling my fingers to check for fractures.

"But you'll give it the old one-two, eh?" Perry launched a punch to my biceps that really hurt. "Let's have at it."

Good Lord. Who was this woman?

I followed Perry through double doors down a polished tile corridor, resisting the urge to massage my throbbing muscle. Bypassing a large, five-table autopsy room, we entered a small chamber not unlike *salle* 4 at the LSJML. Glass-fronted cabinets, side counter, dissecting scope, hanging scale.

The stainless steel gurney held a plastic-covered mound. Small and lumpy, the shape looked wrong for a human being.

Wordlessly, we both donned aprons and gloves.

Like a waiter presenting the table d'hôte, Perry whipped off the sheeting.

14

I SWALLOWED HARD.

The remains consisted of five amorphous lumps and an eighteen-inch segment of human lower limb. The skin was puckered and celery green, the underlying tissue gray and textured like pot roast.

Stepping to the table, I bent for a closer look.

The severed leg was sparsely populated with short, dark hairs. Bones were visible deep in the flesh, a partial femur up, a partial tibia and fibula below. All three shafts terminated in jagged spikes. Bones, skin, and muscle were scored by gouges, cuts, and parallel slashes.

"It's a knee, right?" Perry asked.

"Left. This came from the ocean?"

"Yeah. Check out the X-rays."

Perry crossed to a double-tiered illuminator, flipped two switches, and tapped a film lying on the box's horizontal surface. I joined her.

An object glowed white within a segment of flesh. Bean-sized, it looked like a cartoon whitecap.

"Shark tooth," I said.

"Yeah. There are others." A blue-lacquered nail jabbed two more films.

"You're thinking death by shark attack?"

Perry waggled a hand. *Maybe yes, maybe no.* "I see no hemorrhage in the tissue."

Dead hearts don't pump. Bleeding at a trauma site usually means the victim was alive when injured. No blood usually means the hit was taken postmortem.

"Could the absence of hemorrhage be explained by immersion in salt water?"

"Sure."

"So the dismemberment could have resulted from postmortem scavenging."

"I've seen it before."

I scanned the films, each taken at a different angle. Like the knee, three other hunks of flesh contained portions of skeleton.

"That's the pubic bone and a bit of ischium." I indicated a plate showing part of the pelvic front.

"Good for sex?"

"Not tonight."

"Hardy fucking har."

I braced for an arm punch. Didn't come.

"The V-shaped subpubic angle, blocky pubic body, and broad ischio-pubic ramus suggest male."

Perry nodded.

"That's a bit of iliac crest." I pointed to a section of the curving upper border of a left pelvic half. "It's only partially fused to the iliac blade. Assuming male gender, to be on the safe side, I'd say you're looking at an age of sixteen to twenty-four."

"Sonovafrigginbitch."

"That's a portion of proximal femoral shaft, from just below the head and neck. Left, like the knee and pelvis." I was pointing at a plate clipped to the light box's vertical surface. My finger moved to the one beside it. "And that's part of the left foot and ankle. Those are remnants of distal tibia, talus, and some smaller foot bones, I'd say the navicular and the third and second cuneiforms."

"Can you get height from them?"

I considered. "No. I could do a statistical regression off measurements taken from the partial leg bones, but the range would be almost uselessly broad."

"But you could say if the kid was very big or very small?"

"Yes. The muscle attachments suggest a robust build."

"What about race?"

"No way. The skin appears pale, but that could be the result of postmortem bleaching or skin sloughing due to immersion in salt water."

Human pigmentation is contained solely in the epidermis, the skin's outer layer. Lose the epidermis, we all look Scandinavian, a fact often misinterpreted by those unaccustomed to seeing bodies recovered from water.

Perry knew that. I knew that she knew that. The answer was strictly reflex. My attention was focused on the remains.

Returning to the table, I examined each mass in turn. Then, "Where was this found?" I waved a hand over the grisly assemblage.

"Come on, I'll loop you in."

Degloving, Perry led me back up the corridor. We encountered only one person, an elderly Hawaiian with a bucket and mop. The man dropped his eyes when we passed. Perry did not acknowledge his presence.

The chief ME's office looked like Danny Tandler's on uppers. Files and papers occupied every horizontal surface—desktop, coffee table, chair seats, windowsill, file cabinets, floor. Books, magazines, and reprints teetered in stacks. Open journals lay with spines cracking under the weight of overlying issues.

The window was covered with cheap metal blinds. The walls were hung with photos of an impressively large black dog, probably a Lab. Other decorative touches included a hanging skeleton, a pair of conch shells, now repositories for rubber bands and paper clips, several ashtrays from Vegas, a fake fern, and a collection of plastic action figures whose getups and weapons meant nothing to me.

Perry gestured to the single uncluttered chair.

I sat.

Circling the desk, my host dropped into one of those winged-meshy things designed for NASA missions to Mars.

"Nice pooch," I said. Actually, the dog looked scruffy and mean. But Southern ladies are bred to show interest in strangers. The mechanic, the receptionist, the dry-cleaning lady. Doesn't matter. Dixie daughters exude warmth to one and all.

Dr. Hadley Perry was not an exuder.

"Day before yesterday a couple of high schoolers were snorkeling in Halona Cove, between the Blowhole and Hanauma Bay. You know it?"

Setting for the famous Lancaster-Kerr kiss, Halona Cove was known to locals as From Here to Eternity Beach. The little inlet has soaring cliffs, killer waves, and very few tourists. Accessed only by a steep, rocky path, the spot is a favorite with local teens hoping to get more sand in their shorts than Deborah and Burt.

I nodded.

"Kids spotted something on the bottom, maybe twelve feet down, in one of the rock cuts. Brought it up, dimed nine-one-one when they realized their prize was a human knee.

"Cops called me. I ordered divers, went out there myself. The girl was still tossing chunks. The boyfriend was trying for macho, not pulling it off."

Perry worked a way too colorful nail on her blotter, brushed the flotsam with the back of one hand.

"Divers searched for over two hours. What you just saw is what they collected."

"Got any MPs fitting the profile?"

Perry lifted a printout and read.

"Anthony Simolini, date of birth December fourteenth, 1993. Haole."

"Meaning white."

"Sorry. Yeah. Brown hair, brown eyes, five-eleven, a hundred and eighty-five pounds. On February second of this year, at approximately ten p.m., Simolini left a Zippy's restaurant on the Kamehameha Highway in Pearl City. He was heading home but never showed. Kid's a high school senior, big-deal athlete. Friends and family say no way he's a runaway.

"Jason Black, date of birth August twenty-second, 1994. Blond hair, blue eyes, five-nine, a hundred and sixty pounds."

"Haole," I said.

"January twenty-seventh of this year, Black had a throw-down with his parents, stormed out of the home, vanished. Kid has a history of drug abuse, problems at school. Friends say he often talks about splitting for the mainland.

"Ethan Motohiro, date of birth May tenth, 1993. Asian, black hair, brown eyes, five-four, a hundred and twenty pounds. Last September Motohiro set off to circle the island by bike. A motorist saw him on the Kalanianaole Highway near the entrance to Makapu'u Point, probably on the seventh. That was the last sighting."

"Makapu'u Point is close to Halona Cove, right?"

"Yeah. Motohiro had a steady girlfriend, was an A student, planned on attending university."

"Not the pattern for a runaway. Also, he may be too small. I think this kid was pretty big."

Back to the printout.

"Isaac Kahunaaiole, date of birth July twenty-second, 1987. Native Hawaiian, black hair, brown eyes, six-three, two hundred and seventy-five pounds. Worked night security at the Ala Moana Shopping Center, lived at home with his parents and four of six siblings. December twenty-second, two years back, Kahunaaiole boarded a bus for Ala Moana. Never showed up.

Coworkers say he was cheerful, well liked, had a good work ethic."

"Maybe. Size sounds right."

"Four males sixteen to twenty-two. I suppose I could expand the age range. Or the time frame. I only went back two years."

"Given the amount of soft tissue, I doubt this kid has been dead that long."

Perry snorted. The sound was not pretty.

"A body drops deep enough, all rules about decomp fly out the window. Add sharks to the equation, forget it. I had a suicide once, a poet from Perth. People saw him jump off Makapu'u Point. Choppers got there within the hour. Sharks had already opened a soup kitchen. The guys in the chopper watched the bastards strip the body down to bone. A month later, I get a call. A fisherman found a segment of arm inside a shark belly."

"The dead poet?"

"Yep. Still wearing his engraved watch. In there with him I found seven corn husks, an alarm clock, a Cutty Sark bottle, and the hind leg of a dog."

Note to self: Research shark digestion.

"Hell, if this is murder, the kid could have been buried for a while. Or stashed in a freezer, then taken out and dumped."

"Have you queried missing boats and planes?"

"One body was never recovered following the *Ehime Maru* collision."

In 2001, a Los Angeles-class fast-track sub-marine, the USS *Greeneville,* struck a Japanese

fishing training boat, the *Ehime Maru,* just south
of Honolulu. Thirty-five students and crew went
down with the ship.

Later, the U.S. Navy raised the *Ehime Maru*
from a depth of two thousand feet with most
bodies still on board, and divers recovered additional victims. Thanks to the Honolulu ME, all
but one crew member were identified.

"Unlikely," I said.

"I agree," she said.

I looked at Perry. She looked at me. From the
hall, I heard the old man's mop clank his bucket
then smack the floor.

I glanced at my watch.

"Now what?" Perry ignored, or missed, the
obvious message.

"When you've done all you can, taken photos, collected samples, et cetera, clean the bones.
When they're ready, call me."

I rose.

Perry rose.

Pointedly, I gripped my briefcase in my right
hand and held my keys in my left. Sorry, no fingers available for cracking.

Approaching Kailua Beach, South Kalaheo Avenue doglegs, crosses a bridge over Kaelepulu
Stream as Lihiwai, and emerges on the other
bank as Kawailoa.

Ryan called as I was entering the bridge. He
wasted no time on chitchat.

"Plato Lowery is one obstinate bastard."

"Oh?"

"The old goat refuses to provide a DNA sample."

"Why?"

"Beats me."

"He gave no reason?"

"He says he doesn't need one."

Lowery was right. He didn't.

As my mind groped for ideas, my foot eased off the gas. Behind me, a car horn blared. So much for the aloha attitude.

"Are there any other relatives?" I asked. "I thought Plato mentioned a cousin."

"Not that we've found."

The horn sounded again. My eyes flicked to the rearview mirror. A big-ass SUV was right on my bumper.

"The Robeson County sheriff was present when I did the exhumation in Lumberton. His name is Beasley. Call him, see if has any suggestions."

"Worth a try." Ryan's tone conveyed little optimism.

I arrived home as the sun was flattening into the sea.

Katy's mood had improved buckets since the previous day. So had her appetite. In fact, she was starving. Buzz's Steakhouse was close, so we fired over there.

The Hawaiian gods were smiling. We scored a deck table and dined overlooking Kailua Beach. I ordered mahimahi. Katy chose teriyaki chicken.

As we ate, Katy described her day. She'd spent the morning in a helicopter, the afternoon sunning on Lanikai Beach.

Lots of blocker?

Yes, Mom.

Hat?

Hm.

Skin cancer. Wrinkles. Blah. Blah. Blah.

Eye roll.

"OK. Start at the beginning. How did you get to the chopper?"

"Took a bus. TheBus, it's called here. I like that. Direct."

"What did you see?"

"Downtown Honolulu, the harbor, some tower with a marketplace."

"The Aloha Tower at Pier 9. One of the premier landmarks of the state of Hawaii."

"The pilot mentioned that."

"Since the twenties, that lighthouse has guided ships at sea and welcomed visitors and immigrants to Honolulu."

"He mentioned that too. Compared it to the Statue of Liberty."

"Fair analogy. What Lady Liberty does for New York City, the Aloha Tower does for Honolulu. For four decades it was the tallest structure in Hawaii."

"The pilot also talked about shops and restaurants."

"The Aloha Tower Marketplace opened in 1994. But that's just one feature. The Hawaii Maritime Center is there, and the historic vessel *Falls of Clyde*. I read somewhere that Honolulu Harbor is the only harbor in the nation to combine a visitor attraction, retail and restaurant outlets, and working commercial harbor facilities in a single location."

"I think they do that in Baltimore. My earphones were pretty buzzy. I missed a lot of the commentary. We also flew over something called the Punchbowl."

The National Memorial Cemetery of the Pacific. A final resting place for American soldiers. I didn't say it.

"And we saw another lighthouse."

"At Makapu'u Point?"

"I think so. And Mount Olomana. Cool name. Easy to remember."

"That's over here, on the windward side of the island."

"The pilot said there was an awesome trail to the summit. I might try hiking it. And we overflew a place where some Hawaiian king won a battle to unite the islands. Didn't catch his name or who he was fighting. But I'm guessing he won."

"Nu'uanu Pali. Ready for some history?"

"Do I have a choice?"

"In 1795 King Kamehameha I sailed from his home island of Hawaii, leading an army of about ten thousand soldiers. After conquering the islands of Maui and Molokai, he moved on to Oahu. The defenders of Oahu, led by Kalanikupule, became trapped at Nu'uanu Pali. Kamehameha drove more than four hundred of them over the cliff to their deaths."

"Brutal."

"But effective."

"Will that be on the quiz?"

"Yes."

For dessert we shared an order of cocolatta, a vanilla bean ice cream–coconut creation that filled us with awe. Our waiter, Fabio, provided instruction on topping the concoction with juice squeezed from fresh limes.

Yeah. Fabio. Bleached hair, unbuttoned shirt, puka beads and all.

Driving home we laughed until our sides hurt.

15

WEDNESDAY I WAS BACK AT THE CIL BY NINE.

Danny was in his office, hunched over his desk. He spun a wheelie with his chair when I entered.

"Aloha." Beaming.

"You look like one of those obnoxious smiley-face logos."

I'd slept badly, awakened with bongos thumping in my head. The drive into Honolulu hadn't helped.

"I feel happy." Danny spread both arms and feet.

"And pretty, and witty, and gay?" Shoving aside journals, I dropped onto a love seat many years past its shelf life.

"Are we having a grumpy-pants day?"

"Headache."

"Did the ladies enjoy a hearty night out?"

"Katy downed the ten-gallon mai tai, not me." Rubbing circles on my temples. "What brings such glee into your world?"

"I finally got the poop on the Huey crash."

"The chopper transporting Spider Lowery from Long Binh?"

"The very one."

"And?"

"According to the REFNO, the fifth body was never recovered."

Danny used the shortened version of "reference number." REFNO files contain information on all military misadventures, including the names of those who died, those who survived, the location, the timing, the aircraft type, the artifacts recovered—all known facts concerning an incident.

"The missing crew member?"

"The maintenance specialist."

"Do you have a name?"

Danny's grin stretched so wide I thought his head might split and the top fall off, as in one of those Monty Python animation sequences. Maybe I was projecting.

Impatient, I gestured for more.

"Luis Alvarez."

It took a moment for the import to worm through my pain.

"The guy was Latino?"

"Presumably."

I shot upright. "Let me see."

Danny handed me a fax. "IDPF to follow shortly, I'm told."

The information was meager but telling.

"Spec 2 Luis Alvarez, maintenance specialist. Date of birth February twenty-eighth, 1948," I read.

"Alvarez was a month shy of twenty when the chopper went down."

"Five-nine, a hundred sixty-five pounds. Home of record, Bakersfield, California."

I looked up.

"Alvarez is listed KIA/BNR." Killed in action, body not recovered.

Danny nodded. "Here's my take. Lowery was just out of jail, so the mortuary staff at Tan Son Nhut assumed the victim wearing no uniform insignia was him. The profile fit, the location, it all made sense. But they blew it. The burned corpse was really Alvarez."

"If Alvarez was still MIA, why do you suppose they ruled him out?"

"You and I agree that 2010-37's racial architecture is a mixed bag. Given body condition, the guys at Tan Son Nhut probably missed what we saw. Or maybe someone with little knowledge of bone noted only the more Caucasoid craniofacial features. Either way, they concluded that the guy was white."

"Thus Lowery."

"I'll bet the farm Alvarez's records say Latino." I agreed.

"Dr. Brennan, I think we've done it."

"Dr. Tandler, I think we have."

"Oh, Cisco." Danny raised a palm.

"Oh, Pancho." I high-fived it.

We whooped. It hurt.

"Here's what I *don't* get." Danny began swiveling his chair from side to side. "Alvarez ends up buried in North Carolina. Lowery ends up diddling himself in Quebec. How's that roll?"

I had no explanation.

Seconds passed. Watching Danny loop back and forth started making me seasick.

I shifted my gaze to the desk. Remembered the gold whatsit locked in the drawer.

"Has Craig come up with any ideas on the duck-mushroom thing?"

"Not that he's shared."

"Now what?" I asked.

"Now we await the Alvarez file."

"And?"

"Reconstruct what's left of the skull."

That's what we did. *I* did. Danny was busy with a case review meeting most of the morning.

As I maneuvered and glued fragments, a maelstrom of emotions swirled inside me. If we were right about the mix-up back in '68, the Alvarez family would finally have closure. Plato would be forced to accept an altered reality.

So goes life. A positive for one, a negative for another.

Images elbowed for attention in my aching head. Plato leafing through photos in my car. Squinting in the sun at the Lumberton cemetery.

I wondered. I seemed to have his trust. Now, how to tell the old man that the grave at which he'd mourned all those years had never held his son?

I was squeezing Elmer's on a hunk of frontal when a thought blindsided me.

My hands froze.

Spider Lowery was from Lumberton, North Carolina. Robeson County.

No way.

I pictured Plato.

The faces in his album.

The boy in the snapshot in Jean Laurier's desk.

Way?

I returned to Danny's office and checked Spider's file.

Wherever a form queried race, a check marked the little box beside the word *white*. A handwritten note in the dental record described Lowery as "Cauc." Caucasian.

Yet.

I looked at the clock. Twelve forty.

I went to the kitchen and downed a yogurt and a granola bar. Popped a Diet Coke. Considered.

Returned to gluing.

Again and again I circled back to one simple truth.

People misrepresent when filling out forms. Men record themselves as taller. Women record themselves as slimmer, younger.

People lie.

One thirty.

Not too late.

I punched a number into my BlackBerry. Area code 910.

Twelve rings, then the line went dead.

Clicking off, I entered a different set of digits. Though the lab was cool, sweat now beaded my brow.

"Sugarman's Funeral Home," a syrupy voice purred.

"Silas Sugarman, please. Temperance Brennan calling."

"Hold, please."

"Dance of the Blessed Spirits" from *Orpheus and Eurydice*? Meant to be soothing, the music only agitated me further.

"Dr. Brennan. What a pleasure. You've returned from Hawaii?"

"I'm calling from Honolulu."

"How may I help you?"

"I'm in need of personal information on Spider Lowery."

"Perhaps you should talk to Spider's daddy."

"Plato isn't answering his phone."

"I'll do what I can." Apprehensive. "Within the bounds of ethical constraints, of course."

"Of course. Are the Lowerys Native American?"

Sugarman didn't reply for so long I thought he'd found my question offensive. Or an invasion of privacy.

"You mean Indian?"

"Yes, sir."

"Hell's bells, little lady, most folks in Robeson County have a papoose or two up the old family tree. My own great-grandma was Indian, God rest her soul."

"The Lowerys, sir?"

"Course they've got blood. Plato's half Lumbee, his wife too, come from up the road in Pembroke—"

Sugarman referred to the Lumbee, a Native American group taking its name from the Lumber River.

Descended mainly from Cheraw and related Siouan speakers, the Lumbee have occupied what is now Robeson County since the eighteenth century. They're the largest tribe in North Carolina, the largest east of the Mississippi River, and the ninth largest in the nation.

And perhaps the most disadvantaged.

The Lumbee were granted formal recognition as a tribe by North Carolina in 1885.

Three years later they started pressing claims with the federal government for similar recognition. To date, they'd met with limited success.

In 1956, Congress passed a bill acknowledging the Lumbee as Indian, but denying them full status as a tribe. As a result, they are ineligible for the financial support and Bureau of Indian Affairs program services provided to officially recognized groups.

All forty-seven thousand are pretty cheesed off.

"—don't take my meaning wrong."

"Of course not." I couldn't wait to get off the phone. "Thank you so much."

Danny was still in his case review meeting.

Damn. I was seriously jazzed.

Back to gluing fragments.

By the time Danny broke free I practically manhandled him into his office.

When I'd explained my misgivings, he checked Spider's file as I had done.

"Mongoloid features. Alvarez was undoubtedly Latino. Lowery had Native American blood. So probably we're back to square one. Your boy could be Lowery or Alvarez."

"Fingerprints say Lowery died in Quebec."

"Maybe the screwup belongs to the FBI, not to Tan Son Nhut."

"Maybe."

I thought for a moment.

"What if 2010-37 is neither?"

"Neither?"

"Alvarez or Lowery."

Danny's brows shot up.

"Was anyone else BNR from the region where the Huey went down?"

"I could do a REFNO search using geographic coordinates. What do you think?"

"I think you dazzle," I said.

"As do you."

"Me?"

"Don't forget." Danny winked. "I've seen you naked."

Heat flared across my face.

"How about I go back a month from the date 2010-37 was recovered?" Danny was once again all business.

"I should think that would do it, given the mortuary officer's description of decomp."

"Could take a while."

"I'll soldier on with the Elmer's."

Danny wasn't kidding. It was 4:45 when he finally reappeared. One look told me that something was up.

"You got a hit?" I asked.

"No. But I found this."

Danny waved a paper. I grabbed, but he held it beyond my reach.

"A decomposed body was recovered on August seventeenth, 1968, less than a quarter mile from the site of the January Huey crash. The remains were processed through Tan Son Nhut. White male, midtwenties to midthirties. The deceased came stateside as case number 1968-979."

"And?"

"There is no and."

"Was he identified?"

"No."

"Where are the bones?"

"Here."

Danny strode toward Red Sweater, who was sitting at his desk. I watched as he requested the case. Red Sweater disappeared into the movable shelving.

Time passed. A lot.

Red Sweater reappeared carrying what looked like a very old box. The color was different and the cardboard corners looked scraped and worn.

Danny accepted the box, swiped his badge, and rejoined me. Together we moved to the designated table.

Questions winged in my brain.

Was Luis Alvarez Latino, as his name implied?

Was 2010-37 Luis Alvarez?

Was 1968-979 Luis Alvarez? If so, why weren't Alvarez's remains ID'd back in August of '68?

If 1968-979 turned out to be Alvarez, then who was 2010-37? And how did this man end up designated as Spider Lowery and shipped to Lumberton, North Carolina?

The Lowerys had Native American blood. Could 2010-37 be Spider after all?

Clearly the body shipped from Long Binh and the body in the pond in Hemmingford could not both be Spider Lowery.

Danny lifted the cover on the box holding 1968-979.

We both leaned in.

Seconds passed.

Our eyes met.

Reflected mutual shock.

16

THE SKULL WAS NESTLED IN ONE CORNER, with the rest of the skeleton packed above and around it. Every element was dappled yellow and brown. Nothing special. Exposure to sunlight bleaches bone. Contact with soil and vegetation darkens it.

It wasn't the state of the remains that shocked us.

It was the object wedged behind an infolded flap of cardboard rimming the inside of the box.

"Is that a dog tag?" I asked.

"Yes."

"That shouldn't be in there."

"You think not?" Sarcasm not directed at me.

After wiggling the tag free, Danny whipped off his glasses, scrunched his eyes, and brought the small metal rectangle to his nose.

"Can you make out a name?" I asked.

"No." He thumbnail-scratched one side, flipped the tag, scratched the other.

"There's a thick accretion covering both surfaces. Let's try some water."

At the sink, Danny scrubbed the tag with a hard-bristle brush, then repeated the glasses-squinty-eye thing.

"If the raised lettering is abraded or squashed, usually I can dig out and read the indentation on the back. But this gunk's like cement. Let's give it a whirl in the sonicator."

Sonicators are used to clean jewelry, optical parts, coins, watches, dental, medical, electronic, and automotive equipment. The gizmos rely on ultrasound, usually in the 15–400 kHz range. No rocket science. Using liquid cleanser, you just shake the crap out of whatever is dirty.

Danny placed the tag in the stainless steel basket, added a vinegar-water solution, and closed the cover. Then he set the timer.

We were both staring at the thing, pointlessly, when a thought occurred to me.

"Who was the last person to examine this case?" I asked.

"Excellent question."

Danny crossed to Red Sweater. He was explaining what he wanted when my BlackBerry pinged an incoming text.

Katy.

Invasion!

Ants? A marching army?

Home shortly, I texted back.

Fast.

What?

This blows.

Great. A new crisis.

Problem?

Unbelievable.

???? I was clueless as to the basis of Katy's current discontent.

Vacation over, she replied.

???? I repeated.

A minute passed with no response.

What the hell?

I called Katy's cell.

Got voice mail.

Terrific. She'd turned off or was ignoring her phone.

I was clipping the BlackBerry onto my belt when Danny returned, his expression troubled.

"Dimitriadus," he said. "Back in 1998."

"Could Dimitriadus have missed seeing the tag?"

"It might have been jammed way up under the lip of the box. When the cardboard loosened with age, it could have slid into view." He didn't sound convinced.

Danny removed the tag from the sonicator and returned to the sink for another go with the brush.

Seconds passed. A full minute.

Scrub.

Glasses off.

Squint.

Glasses on.

Scrub.

Repeat.

Agitated by Katy's texting, I almost snatched the tag from his hand.

At last, the glasses came off and the myopic eyes narrowed.

"Holy shit."

Danny rarely used profanity.

"What?" I asked.

Danny read aloud.

"Let me see." I shot out a hand.

Danny yielded the tag.

He was right. The stamped info was easier to discern as an indentation.

I reversed the letters and digits in my mind.

> *John Charles Lowery*
> *477 38 5923*
> *A pos   Bapt*

Did Baptists commonly have A positive blood?

Inane, but that's the first question that formed in my mind.

"That's a Social Security number, right?"

Danny nodded. "The military made the switch from service numbers sometime in the sixties."

"This can't be *our* John Lowery." I knew as I said it that I was wrong. But what were the chances?

"Let's check."

We hurried to Danny's office.

Pulled Spider's file.

The SS number belonged to John Charles Lowery from Lumberton, North Carolina. Spider.

But Spider Lowery died in Quebec.

Forty years after crashing in Long Binh.

Sweet Mother Mary, could the situation possibly grow more confused?

"Shall we lay the guy out?" Danny's voice held little enthusiasm.

My eyes flicked to my watch.

Five fifty.

I was anxious to get home to Katy. And I

wanted to learn whether Ryan had found an alternate source of DNA for Spider.

"Let's do it first thing tomorrow."

"It's a date."

"You're on, big guy." I mimicked Danny's earlier wink. "But we both keep our clothes on."

I called out, explored.

Katy was not in the house.

At the pool.

On the lanai.

I found no note explaining her whereabouts.

I strolled down to the beach.

No Katy.

I was changing to shorts when a door slammed.

The cadence of conversation drifted to my room. Voices, one male, one female, not my daughter.

Had Katy made friends?

"Katy?"

"She's gone for a bike ride," the male voice called out.

Boing!

Katy's texts now made sense.

Had I asked her opinion?

I was half asleep, had acted on impulse.

Bonehead move, Brennan.

Had I given her a heads-up?

I'd had none myself.

Lame.

Slipping on sandals, I hurried downstairs.

Ryan's shirt featured turquoise bananas and lavender palms. His board shorts were apricot and had *Billabong* scrawled across the bum. Add flip-flops, Maui Jims, a "Hang Loose" cap, and a two-day stubble. You get the picture. *Miami Vice* meets *Hawaii Five-O.*

Lily held a string-handled shopping bag in each hand. By joint effort, her miniskirt and tube top covered maybe twenty inches of her torso. Ninety-inch wedge sandals, Lolita shades, maraschino lips.

Oh, boy.

"Aloha, *madame.*" Ryan crushed me with a bear hug. *"Comment ça va?"*

"I'm good." Freeing myself, I turned to Lily. "How was your flight?"

Lily shrugged one very bare shoulder.

"I hope it's OK that we just showed up," Ryan said.

"How did you find us?"

Ryan grinned and flashed his brows.

I knew his meaning. "You're a detective. You detect."

"Katy seemed a bit flustered at seeing us," Ryan said.

"I may have forgotten to mention your arrival."

Rolling mascara-laden eyes, Lily threw out one hip.

"Everything happened so last-minute, the judge granting permission, booking seats, racing to Dorval," Ryan said. "In all the rush, I forgot to charge my cell. Damned if it didn't die at the airport."

"They do that," Lily said.

"Did Katy get you settled?" I asked.

"She did. I'm down, Lily's in the spare bedroom up. This place is killer, by the way."

"Can I go?" Lily. Not whiny, but close.

Ryan looked an apology my way.

I glanced at my watch. Six thirty. "Katy should be back any minute." Please, God. "How about we meet at seven thirty and head out for dinner?"

"My treat," Ryan said.

"No way," I said.

"I insist," he said.

"Katy can hurt you," I said. "I think she checks the right-hand column, then orders the highest-priced item on the menu."

"That's why God gave us credit cards." Ryan smiled and tapped his back pocket.

The choice of restaurant involved stimulating dialogue. Lily wanted steak. Katy was avoiding red meat. Katy craved fish. Lily was over her quota on mercury. Katy suggested Thai. Too spicy. Lily proposed Indian. Katy wasn't in the mood.

We compromised on Japanese.

During dinner, neither Katy nor Lily was overtly rude, but icicles could have formed on our table. Back at Lanikai, each went straight to her room.

Ryan and I shared a drink on the lanai, Perrier for me, Big Wave Golden Ale for him.

Ryan apologized for Lily's insolence. She'd resisted making the trip. He'd insisted, gotten no support from Lutetia. He suspected a love interest, perhaps a man from Lily's drug rehab group. Or, worse, from her past as a user.

I explained that Katy was still dejected over Coop's death, but that she seemed to be on the mend.

We agreed that our daughters were champs at

the use of the sugar-coated dig. And that my sis-terhood-bonding therapy did not look promis-ing.

I brought Ryan up to speed on developments at the CIL. The Mongoloid craniofacial traits of 2010-37. Spider Lowery's Native American ancestry. Luis Alvarez, the maintenance special-ist who went down with Spider in '68. 1968-979, the decomposed body found near Long Binh eight months after the crash. Spider Lowery's dog tag in 1968-979's box.

Ryan filled me in on developments in Mon-treal. And Lumberton. Turned out my suggestion about Beasley, though a good one, was nonpro-ductive. The sheriff was cooperative but, to date, had offered nothing of value.

Listening to Ryan describe his exchange with the sheriff triggered a *Ping!* moment. A comment of Plato's during our scrapbook conversation.

"Ryan, listen. Spider's mother died of kidney failure five years ago. It's a long shot, but maybe the hospital where she was treated still has some samples on file, you know, a path slide or some-thing. And Spider had a brother who was killed a couple years before that."

"A long shot is better than no shot at all. I'll call first thing tomorrow, ask Beasley to poke around."

Ryan proposed taking Katy and Lily to Pearl Harbor the following day. I wished him luck.

At eleven, we too retired to our separate rooms.

Through my wall, I heard Lily talking on her cell.

17

THE SUNSHINE SISTERS WERE STILL SLEEPING when I entered the kitchen at eight the following morning. Ryan was lacing on Nikes for a run on the beach. The plan was that he and our daughters would spend the day at Pearl Harbor, visiting the USS *Arizona* monument and touring the USS *Missouri* battleship and the USS *Bowfin* submarine. I wished him luck in dealing with the dim and murky realm of female resentment. Then I was off to the CIL. I thought of the dog tag the whole drive. It just made no sense.

Dimitriadus was on my bumper as I turned in at JPAC. We crossed the lot together. In silence. I wondered how an examiner of unidentified bones could miss a dog tag in a box. Ten feet from the building, he accelerated his pace and shot inside, letting the door slam in my face.

Last night, Lily's cold shoulder. This morning, Dimitriadus. I was beginning to feel like the class pariah.

Danny was in his office.

"Dimitriadus is acting like I killed his puppy."

"Come in." Danny's smile faded. "Close the door."

Puzzled, I did.

"We're cutting Dimitriadus loose."

"Jesus. The guy's been here, what, twelve years? Why?"

"A number of reasons. Most recently, he failed his ABFA exam again." Danny referred to the American Board of Forensic Anthropology examination for certification, a credential essential for qualification in the field.

"The dog tag?"

"The decision was made before that came up, so no."

"What will he do?"

Danny spread both hands. Who knows?

"That info is for your ears only. So far only Dimitriadus, Merkel, you, and I know."

I nodded.

A beat passed.

"Today's *good* news is that J-2 has Alvarez's IDPF."

J-2, the joint command records section, has access to information on deceased personnel going back to World War I.

"I was just about to walk over and pick it up. Jackson asked about you. Come along, make the man's day."

"Corporal Jackson? The guy who convinced everyone the phone lines were scheduled for cleaning by a steam blast, and that all handsets had to be sealed in plastic bags for an hour?"

"It's Sergeant Jackson now."

"He's been here a long time."

"He's just been reassigned back, actually."

"I no longer have clearance to J-2."

"Follow me, little squaw."

Little squaw?

Danny and I took the corridor past the general's staff offices to a door at the back of the building and entered a large room furnished with cubicles containing desks, most occupied by civilians I knew to be analysts and historians. At the far end, a second door led to a secure area filled with movable shelving similar to that used for bone storage in the CIL lab. Instead of bones, these shelves held hundreds of small gray filing boxes, each identified by a sequence of numbers. The REFNOs.

At the counter, we chatted a moment with Sergeant Dix Jackson, a black man with mulberry splotches on his face and arms the size of sequoias. Needless to say, no one ever mentioned the splotches.

Jackson and I reminisced, each trying to top the other with recollections of practical jokes from the past. He won with a story involving Danny, a toilet stall, a burning bag, and buckets of water raining down from above.

Feigning annoyance, Danny filled out a request for the file on 1968-979, the unknown recovered near Long Binh in '68.

Jackson read the form. "When you need this, Doc?"

"Yesterday."

"You got it."

Danny signed for and scooped up Alvarez's IDPF.

We started to leave.

"And, Doc?"

We both turned.

"You feel the urge to do your business, relax. We got no fire drills scheduled this month."

Back in Danny's office, we cleared the love seat and coffee table. No banter. We were both very focused on learning everything we could about Spec 2 Alvarez.

Work space readied, we sat. Danny unwound the string, spread the file, and extracted the contents.

I swallowed.

Throughout my years consulting to CILHI, the photos always distressed me more than anything else. Alvarez's lay smack on top.

The old black-and-white showed a Latino-looking man in his army uniform. He had dark hair, dark eyes, and lashes that were wasted on a Y-chromosomer.

A second photo captured nine soldiers, hair sweat-pasted to their temples and brows. All wore fatigues with the sleeves rolled up. One sported a Tilley hat, fishing lure pinned to a rakishly flipped brim.

The name *Alvarez* was scrawled in faded blue ink across the chest of the third man from the right. Third *kid* from the right.

Alvarez wasn't big, wasn't small. Of the group, he alone wasn't looking at the camera. His face was turned, as though a momentary distraction had caught his attention.

What, I wondered? A bird in flight? A passing dog? Movement in the brush?

Had he been mildly curious? Startled? Afraid for his life?

"*¡Ay, caramba!*" Danny was looking at Alvarez's induction record. "The gentleman in question was Mexican-American."

"That fits our profile for 2010-37. Any medical or dental records?"

Danny viewed the stack side-on. "Yep. Let's save those for last."

Danny skimmed a sheet of blue-lined notebook paper, the kind kids use for middle school essays.

"A letter from Fernando Alvarez, Luis's father," he said. "You read Spanish?"

I nodded.

Danny handed me the paper.

The letter was written in a neat, almost feminine hand. No header indicated the recipient's name. The date was July 29, 1969. The English stopped after "Dear Sir."

The message was poignant in its simplicity.

I'd read many. Every single solitary one had touched me deeply.

"What's he say?" Danny asked. Knowing.

"My son was a hero. Find him."

Next came clippings from a Spanish-language newspaper. One announced Luis Alvarez's graduation from high school. The photo showed a younger version of the man in uniform. Mortarboard. Tassel. Somber grin.

One story announced Alvarez's departure for Vietnam. Another reported his status as MIA.

Danny picked up a telegram. I felt no need to read it. *We regret to inform you.* Maria and Fernando Alvarez were being notified that their son was missing.

Next came statements from witnesses who saw the Huey go down. A guard on his way from the Long Binh jail to his barracks. A motorist traveling the road to Saigon. A maintenance worker at the helicopter landing pad. One soldier had provided a hand-drawn map.

The file also contained a standard DD form recording the loss incident, and unclassified documents compiled by analysts attempting to determine what had happened to Alvarez.

An hour after leaving the J-2 shop, Danny and I turned to Luis Alvarez's medical and dental records.

Only to be disappointed.

Nothing in the antemorts positively linked the missing Spec 2 to the bones accessioned as 2010-37. Either Alvarez had enjoyed the best health on the planet or, like Lowery, his records were incomplete.

"Maria Alvarez died in 1987," I read aloud. "No other maternal relative provided a DNA sample."

"We probably won't get sequencing on 2010-37, anyway," Danny said.

I agreed. "Probably not."

"Nothing excludes Alvarez from being your Lumberton guy."

I agreed again. "No. Or he could be 1968-979."

I thought a moment.

"Think it would be worthwhile trying to track down the witnesses? Maybe one saw something that never made the files."

Danny returned to the statements. Read.

"The maintenance worker was a guy named Harlan Kramer from Abilene, Texas. Kramer was regular army. If he stayed in, it would be fairly easy to find him."

Danny made a note.

"Ready to hit it?" he asked.

I nodded.

Danny and I moved to the lab.

Though some bones were damaged by erosion, trauma, or animal scavenging, most of 1968-979's skeleton was in pretty good shape. While Danny opened an anthropology update file, I laid out my usual stick figure man.

Skull. Jaw. Arms. Legs. Sternum. Clavicles. Ribs. Vertebrae. Only the kneecaps and some hand and foot parts were missing.

Didn't matter. I knew straight off that 1968-979 was neither Spider Lowery nor Luis Alvarez. So did Danny.

"This dude was a tree-topper."

I nodded agreement. "Lowery and Alvarez were both five-nine. This man was much taller."

"What the hell is he doing with Spider Lowery's tag?"

I had no explanation.

"We've got dentition." Danny checked the jaw. "Two molars and a second bicuspid on the right. Two molars on the left." He rotated the skull to sit palate up. "Two molars on the right, two on the left, and a second bicuspid. Ten teeth. I'll get X-rays."

Feeling a vibration at my hip, I checked my BlackBerry.

"It's Katy."

"Take it. I'll do inventory."

"Hi, sweetie."

"I am so *outta* here. First flight I can get."

Great.

"Lily is a complete whack job."

"Where are you?" Anticipating a less than pleasant exchange, I put distance between myself and Danny.

"Pearl Harbor."

"What's the problem?"

"Where should I start? First, there's the trip into town. Ms. Head Case has to ride in front so she won't get sick. Guess who ends up stuffed in back? Then we get to the park and at least a million people are waiting in line. Guess who has to sit on a bench so her feet won't hurt? Big surprise, island girl! You're wearing heels that would kill the average pole dancer. Then—"

"Katy."

"—we have to eat at this totally gross ptomaine haven because Lily can't handle—"

"Katy."

"What?" Snapped.

"She's going through a rough patch."

"I'm not?"

"Is Lily really so bad?"

"She's a freak show. This was supposed to be our time together."

"I thought you'd enjoy Lily's company."

"Oh, yeah. The bitch is so cool I may vomit from sheer envy."

"I'm sorry. I should have asked your opinion before inviting them to join us."

"You think?"

Danny passed me holding the skull and jaw. I assumed he was going for X-rays.

"Where is Ryan?" I asked.

"Paying the bill."

"I'll call him."

I was answered by the silence of unspoken anger.

After a quick lunch, Danny and I constructed a biological profile for 1968-979.

Gender: male.

Race: white.

Age: twenty-seven to thirty-five years.

Height: six-one, plus or minus two inches.

Unique skeletal identifiers: possible healed fractures of the right mandibular ramus, right clavicle, and right scapula.

Unique dental identifiers: fragment of a restoration in the first upper left molar.

By three we'd taken X-rays and confirmed the dental work and the old jaw and shoulder trauma.

Danny was on the phone with J-2 when my BlackBerry buzzed again.

Hadley Perry.

The ME skipped all preliminaries.

"Divers found another hunk of leg."

"Where?"

"Halona Cove, lying on a coral ledge about twenty feet down."

I checked the time. Five thirty. I was living the movie *Groundhog Day*. New day, same scene.

"Have Tuesday's remains been cleaned?"

"Down to nice shiny bone."

"Have you contacted a shark expert?"

"The National Marine Fisheries Service has an office on Oahu. I called a guy I know over there. He's off-island, but a Dr. Dorcas Gearhart is coming by tomorrow at nine."

"I'll be there. But—"

"I know. You can't stay long."

18

THAT NIGHT WE OPTED FOR AN EVENING AT home. At least Ryan and I did. Lily and Katy added little but tension to the decision-making process.

Ryan purchased New York strips and tuna fillets, which he grilled to perfection. Amazingly, all dietary obstacles vanished. Both daughters downed bounty of land and sea, along with fingerling potatoes and spinach salad.

To describe the conversation as stiff would be like calling Ahmadinejad's reelection in Iran a tad contentious. Lily's favorite group was Cake. Katy found their music sophomoric. Katy loved classic blues, Etta James, Billie Holiday, T-Bone Walker. Lily said that crap put her to sleep. Lily wore Sung by Alfred Sung. Katy found the perfume overly sweet. Katy favored L'eau d'Issey by Issey Miyake. It made Lily sneeze. iPhone. BlackBerry. PC. Mac.

You get the picture.

Ryan and I insisted on courtesy. But one thing was apparent. Not only did our offspring have differing tastes and opinions, they were becoming masters at refining their expressions of contempt for each other.

After dinner I served fresh pineapple wedges. Ryan proposed another outing for the following afternoon. The Punchbowl or, perhaps inspired by my dessert, the Dole Plantation.

Katy said she preferred a day at Waikiki Beach. Lily wanted to go to Ala Moana. Katy said it was stupid to cross the whole frickin' Pacific just to go shopping. Lily said it was dumb to lie around getting sand up your butt. At that point open battle erupted.

Fortunately, I'd paid the extra insurance and listed Katy as a driver on my rental Cobalt. After much discussion, a compromise was reached. Katy would drop Lily at the mall, spend the afternoon at Waikiki, then collect Lily at a mutually agreed-upon time and location.

When the dishes were cleared, the combatants retreated to their rooms. Ryan and I went for a walk on the beach. I updated him on my two cases at the CIL, and on the one I was doing for the Honolulu ME.

"Hadley Perry?" he asked.

"You know her?"

"I do."

That surprised me. I didn't pursue it.

"Perry's got a shark expert lined up for tomorrow morning," I said.

"That should be different."

"From what?"

"Bones. Bugs."

"Quantum physics."

"That, too." Ryan paused. "Heard from Sheriff Beasley today."

"And?"

"Sometimes you impress me."

"Only sometimes?"

"Some times more than others."

"What did Beasley say?"

"You slipped in under the wire."

I waited for Ryan to elaborate. He didn't.

"Do you get perverse pleasure from messing with my mind?" I asked.

"I definitely get pleasure from messing with your—"

"Beasley?"

"Southeastern Regional Medical Center. Normally patient slides are kept five years."

"The hospital had something?" I couldn't believe it.

"*Oui, madame*. From Harriet Lowery's last admission. The material is winging its way to AFDIL as we speak." The Armed Forces DNA Identification Laboratory. "Or maybe it's already there. And I think a sample may have also gone to our DNA boys in Montreal."

"Hot damn."

"Hot damn."

The sand was cool underfoot. Waves pounded the shore. It felt glorious to be outside. To taste salt on my lips and feel wind in my hair.

To be with Ryan?

Yeah. OK. To be with Ryan.

He didn't reach for my hand. I didn't take his. Still. We both felt it. An enormous elephant plodding beside us up the beach.

"I wouldn't mind hearing what he has to say."

Lost in pachyderm reflection, I missed Ryan's meaning.

"What who has to say?"

"The shark guy."

"Why?"

"Who knows what may one day prove professionally useful?"

"You work in Quebec."

"Sharks are devilishly sly creatures."

Was Ryan's interest really in sharks? Or in the quirky but fetching Dr. Hadley Perry?

Whatever.

"Sure," I said. "Come along."

Dorcas Gearhart was in the lobby when we arrived at the ME's office. Ryan had erred. The shark guy turned out to be of my gender.

Gearhart had frizzy gray hair swept from her face by pink plastic barrettes, and wire-rimmed specs resting low on her nose. I guessed her height at five feet, her age at somewhere just south of sixty.

We exchanged alohas, names, shook hands. I wondered what comments Katy and Lily would have made on the good doctor's muumuu, sneakers, and cardigan sweater. I wondered what comments Katy and Lily had exchanged on their drive into the city.

While waiting for Perry, Ryan asked Gearhart how she'd gotten into the fish business.

Based on the woman's looks, I'd expected grandmotherly speech and deportment. Not even close.

"Fucking bad luck." Gearhart's laugh came from deep within her substantial girth. "Or good. Who knows? I applied for med school, got bonged. A prof I was sleeping with recommended the marine bio grad program. Seemed a better option than marrying and popping out kids."

"Why sharks?" Ryan didn't miss a beat.

"Some yank-off beat me out for the dolphin fellowship."

I was about to ask a question when Perry appeared. Today the hair spikes were emerald, the lids chartreuse.

More greetings, intros. I watched Ryan's face. Discreetly. Perry's. Neither gave a hint of past history.

Perry said she'd had the remains pulled from the cooler.

We trooped single file to the same autopsy room I'd visited on Tuesday.

A black plastic bag lay on a stainless steel cart. A small one.

Perry, Gearhart, and I gloved. Ryan watched.

Perry opened the bag, slid a glob of bone and tissue onto the cart.

The smell of salt and decaying flesh filled the room.

I lifted and inspected the soggy mass.

One glance told me I was holding a portion of human calf. I could see a fragment of fibula, the slender outer bone of the lower leg. The tibia, or shinbone, was in better shape. Its ankle end was recognizable within a mass of tangled tendons and rotting muscle.

Both bones were covered with shallow cuts, deep gouges, and long grooves. Both terminated in jagged spikes.

I looked up. To six expectant eyes.

"It's part of a human lower leg. Decomp is consistent with the remains we examined on Tuesday."

"So's the shark damage, right?" Perry.

Stepping to the cart, Gearhart nudged me not so gently aside. I moved back.

"Oh, yeah. This was shark."

"Can you tell what kind?" Perry asked.

"Got a magnifier?"

Perry produced a hand lens.

We all clustered around Gearhart. Her short stature worked in our favor.

"Look here, inside this groove." Gearhart positioned the glass. "See how fine and regularly spaced the striations are? That means the teeth were ridged, like a serrated knife. I'd say we're talking *Galeocerdo cuvier* or *Carcharodon carcharias*."

The collective lack of response was question enough.

"Tiger or white," Gearhart said.

I couldn't help it. A few beats of the *Jaws* theme thrummed in my head.

"White sharks are pretty rare in Hawaiian waters, so I'd put my money on tiger. Based on distance between the striations, I'd say this baby's probably twelve to fourteen feet long."

"Jesus." Ryan.

"Hell, that's nothing. I once met a twenty-two footer, up close and personal. That mother had to weigh nine hundred kilos."

Quick math. Nineteen hundred pounds. I hoped Gearhart was exaggerating.

"Do tiger sharks really deserve the nasty Hollywood image?" Ryan asked.

"Ooooh, yeah. Tigers are second only to whites in the number of recorded attacks on humans. And they're not what you'd call discriminating diners. These buggers'll eat anything, people, birds, sea turtles, plumbing parts. Generally tigers are sluggish, but tweak the old taste buds, they can really move. You see one, it's best to haul ass."

"Where might I see one?" I asked.

"They're mostly active at night—"

Yep. The opening scene from *Jaws*.

"—reason tigers encounter humans so often is that they like to enter shallow reefs, lagoons, harbors, places like that. To feed. Mostly after dusk."

Perry interrupted the nature lesson.

"Can you tell if the vic was alive when the shark bellied up?"

Gearhart played her lens over the remains.

"The random nature of the tooth marks suggests the leg was fleshed at the time of feeding. The tiger's pattern is to bite down then shake, allowing the serrated teeth to rip through the flesh. The jaw muscles are astounding. Strong enough to slice right through bone, or the shell of a tortoise."

I was really wishing Katy had gone to the mall with Lily.

"So you can't determine if the shark killed the kid or just scavenged on his body?" Perry pressed.

"Nope."

As Perry and Gearhart spoke I studied the leg.

"Can you tell if the kid was killed at Halona Cove, or elsewhere, then regurgitated there?"

"Nope."

I rotated the sad little hunk of flesh.

"Look, Doc." Perry's voice had an edge. "I have to consider whether this presents an issue of public safety. Do I need to close that beach?"

"In my opinion, no. Not based on a single isolated incident."

Using one finger, I retracted the flesh overlying the distal tibia.

My heart kicked to a tempo that matched the refrain in my head.

"Meaning?" Perry asked.

"You get more than one death, then maybe you've got a rogue."

"A rogue?"

"An opportunist. A shark who's developed a taste for people."

I looked up and met Ryan's eyes. His brows dipped on seeing my expression.

"Bad news," I said.

19

"THIS IS NOT THE SAME KID."

"What do you mean?" Perry strode to the cart.

"Look." I pointed to a triangular projection on the lower end of the tibia. "That's the medial malleolus, the bony lump you feel on the inside of your ankle. The malleolus articulates with the talus in the foot, and provides joint stability."

"So?"

I oriented the limb. "That's correct anatomical position."

Perry studied the short segment of calf. Then, "Sonofabitch."

"What?" Ryan and Gearhart asked as one.

"This is from a left leg," I said. "Parts of a left leg were also recovered on Tuesday, including a portion of medial malleolus."

"A freakin' duplication." Perry shook her head in disbelief.

Gearhart got it. "A human being does not have two left feet. This has to be from a different person."

I waited for Ryan to make a bad dancer joke. Mercifully, he didn't.

"Two shark vics from the same bay." Perry's voice sounded higher than normal.

"That could change the picture."

"You think?" Perry rounded on Gearhart. "So. Do I close that beach?"

"That's your call, Doc."

"Will this fucking fish strike again?"

Gearhart raised both brows and palms.

"Come on. Best guess."

Gearhart shifted a hip. Bit her lip. Sighed. "If the shark is feeding, not just scavenging, the bastard bloody well might."

Perry arm-wrapped her waist. Found the maneuver unsatisfactory. Dropped both hands. Turned to me.

"What can you tell me about this second vic?" Chin-cocking the cart.

"This individual is smaller than the first. Beyond that, zilch. There's not enough to work with."

Crossing to a wall phone, Perry punched buttons.

Seconds passed.

"Hope I didn't interrupt the poker game." Sharp.

I heard the buzz of a muffled response. Perry cut it off.

"Get me the Halona Cove bones. ASAP."

The handset hit the cradle with a loud crack.

Less than one minute later a bald young man rolled a cart through the door.

"Anything else, Dr. Perry?" Baldy avoided eye contact with his boss.

"Stay in touch."

Baldy bolted.

On the cart lay the following: proximal and distal portions of a left femur; a fragment of proximal left fibula; two fragments of left tibia, one proximal, the other distal, including the mangled malleolus; a portion of left pelvis extending from the pubic bone out into the blade; the talus, navicular, and third and second cuneiforms from a left foot.

Two large brown envelopes occupied the cart's lower shelf.

"Double-check," Perry ordered. "Be sure they're both lefts."

I did.

They were.

Despite the riotous hair and makeup, the ME's face looked pallid.

I could imagine the battle playing out in Perry's mind. The recession had slammed the Hawaiian economy. Air travel was down, and tourism was in the toilet. Close a beach due to shark attack, hotel bookings would vanish like early morning mist. Go the other way, lose a swimmer, mainlanders would opt for the Shenandoah or Disney World. The consequences would be worse than closing a beach.

Guess right, lose dollars. Guess wrong, lose lives as well as dollars.

And Perry had to act quickly.

My hunch? Honolulu's flamboyant ME would once again piss people off.

I was rotating the new hunk of leg when I noticed an irregularity centered in the shaft approximately five centimeters above the troublesome malleolus. By scraping back tissue, I was able to see that the defect was a hole with a raised outer rim, too perfectly round to be natural.

"This could be helpful," I said.

Perry snatched the magnifier and held it where I indicated.

"I'll be damned. You thinking surgical pin?"

I nodded.

"The placement makes sense. Too bad we don't have the calcaneous."

"Yes," I agreed.

"Someone going to educate us nonmedical mopes?" Ryan asked.

I kept my finger in place while Perry handed him the lens.

"That tiny hole?" he asked.

"That tiny hole."

Ryan passed the lens to Gearhart.

"Everyone familiar with traction?" I asked.

Gearhart nodded.

Ryan shrugged. Not really.

"In orthopedics, traction is used for the treatment of fractured bones and for the correction of orthopedic abnormalities," I explained for Ryan's benefit. "Traction aligns the broken ends by pulling a limb into a straight position. It also lessens pressure on the bone ends by relaxing the muscles."

Ryan snapped his fingers. "The old leg-in-the-air trick. Remember the scene in *Catch-22*? The guy's in traction, covered with plaster, never moves, never speaks—"

I shot a narrow-eyed warning.

Ryan's face went all innocent. What?

"My nephew got put in traction when he busted his leg." Gearhart was again peering through the lens. "They drilled a pin right into his femur."

"Once the hardware is inserted, pulleys and weights are attached to wires to provide the proper pull. Skeletal traction uses anywhere from twenty-five to forty pounds."

"How long does the pin remain in place?" Ryan now sounded overly proper.

"Weeks, maybe months. This one was removed years ago."

Gearhart jabbed at her glasses, which had slipped low on her nose. "What's your take, Doc?"

"I'd guess an unstable tibial shaft fracture. The distal tibia would have been pinned to the calcaneous."

"Which we don't have." Perry.

"Fractured how?" Gearhart asked.

"Skiing? Cycling? Car crash? Without more of the leg it's impossible to say."

"Space shuttle wipeout." Perry began pacing.

"Look," I said. "We still have potentially valuable information. The vic underwent treatment, was probably admitted as an in-patient somewhere. The cops or one of your investigators can check hospital records for distal tibia surgical implants."

Perry stopped. "Time frame?"

"What we're seeing is merely a scar, the result of bony remodeling at the pin site. The injury wasn't recent. I'd start at least five years back, work farther into the past from there. A more effective shortcut, if you get lucky, would be to run the names from your MP list through local hospitals for matches, or to contact family members for histories of leg fractures."

Perry gave a tight nod.

"You get any new leads on the first vic?" I asked.

"No, but we got some new MPs. Last January a college kid washed overboard from one of those Tall Ship things. We're checking that out. A soap salesman disappeared from a Waikiki Beach hotel last summer. Left all his belongings in the room. Could be a suicide, a drowning, a cut-and-run."

"How old?"

"Thirty-two."

I shook my head. "Not likely."

Perry waggled frustrated hands. "It's hard to keep the cops interested with thousands of tourists flowing through the islands each year. The medical angle might goose their effort. Or I could just pray for a benevolent god to save us the trouble with a DNA hit."

Collecting a scalpel from the counter, Perry oriented the leg so that the flesh covering the outer ankle was positioned faceup. We all watched her blade kiss muscle.

Stop abruptly.

Laying the implement aside, Perry shot out a hand.

"Gimme the lens."

Gearhart offered the magnifier. Perry grabbed it.

A few seconds of observation, then Perry strode to the sink and wet a sponge. Returning to the cart, she gently swabbed the tissue, wiping off any remaining epidermis.

"We may have us a tat."

Gearhart and I exchanged glances.

A tattoo, I mouthed.

Gearhart's mouth formed an O.

A bit more cleaning, then Perry gestured us forward with a back-flung arm.

We advanced as one, students gathering around Mr. Wizard.

Perry was magnifying a discoloration barely visible in the glob of flesh I'd retracted from the malleolus. I'd noticed the little blotch earlier, but, distracted by the realization that we had a second victim, I'd ignored it.

"I'll be damned," Ryan said.

Perry shot photos of the tattoo, then, with intersecting cuts of her scalpel, excised it. Using both palms, she spread and flattened the flap of skin on the stainless steel.

"Get the lights."

Ryan hit the wall switch.

The room went black.

I heard a drawer open, close. A click.

A blue beam hit the flap of flesh.

Under UV lighting, the tattoo sharpened. I could make out black and red swirls within a half-sickle form. A filigreed strip extended outward from the sickle's two sides.

"That's a traditional shark tooth pattern." Gearhart's voice came from somewhere to my left.

"You sure?" Perry asked. "We haven't got much here."

"Absolutely. I collect shark images. Paintings.

Prints. Tattoos. I've seen dozens of variations on this theme."

Perry made a grunting noise in her throat.

"Must be part of a *tapuvae,*" Gearhart said. "An ankle band. The only unusual elements are these three loopy things."

Gearhart indicated two backward C's with a U between them sticking up from the filigreed strip.

A full minute passed, then the lights came on.

Without asking if we'd seen enough, Perry peeled the specimen free and dropped it into a jar of formalin. The tissue looked ghostly pale floating in the clear liquid.

"There we have it, sports fans." Perry was marking the case number on the jar lid with a Sharpie. "Looks like Señor Shark ate a tattooee with a gimpy left leg."

Cold, I thought.

"The cops can work the hospitals and tat parlors while I query the MP families."

"You might try computer image enhancement," I said. "To tease more detail out of the design."

"Or high-contrast or infrared photography," Ryan added.

"Will do." Perry stripped off her gloves. "So. Not a bad morning's work. Given our vic is the size of a pork roast."

Toeing the lever on a bio-waste can, Perry tossed her gloves.

"*Mahalo,* Dr. Gearhart. I get you a set of photos, you'll write up your thoughts?"

"No problem."

Perry turned to me.

"You going to spend some time with the first kid?"

"Yes, I—"

To Ryan. "Come with me, champ. I'll buy you a Danish while I ponder whether to close that beach."

As the trio filed out, two Viking blues slid my way. Words snapped from my tongue before I could stop them.

"Think shark attack. Champ."

My testiness surprised me. Was I really feeling threatened by Hadley Perry?

It amused Ryan. The smile that whispered in his eyes only goosed my resentment.

A reexamination of the cleaned bones turned up nothing new.

Thirty minutes later, Ryan and I took our leave. I didn't bother to monitor his or Perry's face for hidden meaning.

We were on Iwilei Road when my BlackBerry buzzed.

Danny.

"You coming in today?"

"Just leaving the ME's office."

"Was Perry her usual delightful self?"

Feeling a reply was pointless, I offered none.

"Got some info on 1968-979."

"Good news or bad?"

"Yes."

I could sense Ryan listening.

"Katy has my car. Detective Ryan was kind enough to give me a ride."

I'd cleared with Danny that it was OK for Ryan to bunk at the Lanikai house. Knowing our history, he'd responded with a few lines of "Let's Get It On." Marvin Gaye he's not.

"The girls are over the cat phase?" Danny asked.

I'd also told Danny about the friction between Lily and Katy. At that moment, I didn't want to discuss it.

"Will Ryan have a problem getting past the gate?" I asked.

"Has *monsieur le détective* got plans for the day?"

"Why?"

"I'll sponsor him. He can hang here if he wants. We can bounce ideas off him. Fresh perspective, you know."

"Hold on."

Pressing the device to my chest, I queried Ryan's interest in visiting the CIL. To my surprise he gave an enthusiastic thumbs-up.

Good thing.

The idea-bouncing proved very useful.

20

OVERNIGHT, DANNY HAD HAD AN IDEA. THAT morning he'd been busy in the J-2 shop.

"Circle search." He smiled and leaned back, fingers laced on his chest.

Ryan and I regarded him blankly.

"Civilians." Danny's head wagged in mock disgust.

"You're a civilian," I pointed out.

"OK." His palms came up. "Slow and simple. First, I got a topo map and located the grid coordinates for Lowery's Huey crash. We all good so far?"

Ryan and I nodded.

"Then I had a J-2 analyst search to see how many troops went MIA within a fifteen-kilometer radius of those grid coordinates—air, ground, overwater, whatever. Next I had him narrow to losses occurring January twenty-third, 1967, through August seventeenth, 1968.

"From one year prior to the Huey crash up to the date 1968-979 was found," I said, for Ryan's benefit.

"Bingo." Danny arced an arm at folders

stacked on the love seat. "Those are the people who remain KIA/BNR."

Ryan looked to me for translation.

"Killed in action, body not recovered. How many?" I asked.

"Eighteen," Danny said. "I just signed the files out."

"On the phone you said you had new info on 1968-979."

"When the decomposed remains now designated 1968-979 went to Tan Son Nhut in '68, mortuary personnel found John Lowery's dog tag inside the body bag. But Lowery had already been identified months earlier and sent stateside."

"The burned body that ended up buried in North Carolina," Ryan said.

"Yes," I said. "Now exhumed and reaccessioned as 2010-37."

"Since the decomposed remains, 1968-979, couldn't, in the thinking of the military personnel, be Lowery, and they matched no one else reported MIA in that sector, they remained at Tan Son Nhut as an unknown until 1973. Then they went to CIL-THAI. In 1976 they came to Hawaii. They've been on our shelves here ever since."

A smile crawled Danny's lips.

"What?" I prompted.

"Except for one brief sabbatical. While at Tan Son Nhut, hair and tissue samples were retained and sealed in jars. In 2001, because of similarities to another file open at the time, those samples were pulled for DNA testing."

"Nuclear or mitochondrial?" I asked, referring to the two human genomes typically sequenced.

"Good old nuclear." Danny's grin spread. "The profile for 1968-937 is on file. We just need a relative for comparison."

I glanced at the folders. Four decades. Was a family out there somewhere, still hoping? Or had everyone long since given up and moved on with their lives?

"Let's do it," I said.

With guidance, Ryan quickly became adept at reading files. He found the perfect candidate two hours after lunch.

Alexander Emanuel Lapasa. Xander to friends and family.

Lapasa's folder was the slimmest of the lot.

Why? Xander Lapasa never served a day in the military.

But everything fit.

Alexander Emanuel Lapasa was a twenty-nine-year-old white male who stood six foot one and weighed two hundred pounds. Lapasa's mother reported him missing in March 1968, two months after Xander's weekly letters stopped arriving from Vietnam.

Ryan passed Danny a photo. He passed it to me.

The snapshot showed a tall young man from the waist up. His curly dark hair was tucked behind prominent ears. A mile-wide smile revealed straight white teeth.

Lapasa wore a striped shirt with the top buttons open, a knapsack over one shoulder. His arms elbowed out from hip-planted hands.

"Looks like he's got the world by the tail," Ryan said.

"Or believes he soon will," Danny said.

I returned the photo. Danny studied it a moment.

"Looks like Joseph Perrino," he said.

"Who?" Ryan and I asked.

"The actor? Appeared on *The Sopranos* now and then? Never mind."

"I didn't think civilians went to Nam in the sixties," Ryan said.

"Sure," Danny said. "Civilian employees of the army's post exchange system, aid workers, missionaries, journalists. Check the wall. Quite a few nonmilitary personnel are listed."

"Is there anything to indicate why Lapasa was in Nam?" I asked.

Ryan flipped a few pages, read.

"According to the mother, Theresa-Sophia Lapasa, Xander was, quote, pursuing business interests, unquote. That sound kosher?"

"Oh, yeah," Danny said. "There were plenty of opportunists in-country back then. Knowing the fighting would eventually end, some balls-to-the-wall entrepreneurs went over to establish position for the postwar boom. Several ran bars and restaurants in Saigon."

"Where was Lapasa from?" Not sure why I asked. Place of residence didn't really matter. Guess it was my way of personalizing.

Ryan shuffled pages. Read. Shuffled a few more. Then, *"Ke aloha nô!"*

Danny grinned. I resisted the impulse to roll my eyes.

"Lapasa was a home boy." Ryan had switched back to English. "Honolulu, Hawaii."

"Got an address?" I asked.

Ryan read out a street number on Kahala Avenue.

"Cha-ching!" I pantomimed a cash register. Or something.

Ryan looked at me.

"Kahala has some of the priciest real estate in Honolulu."

Danny's smile faltered, slowly faded. He looked down, then to his left, as though searching for an answer deep in his memory. Wordlessly, he jotted a note.

"Got antemorts?" I asked.

"Your bailiwick." Ryan handed me the folder.

The men watched as I leafed through papers.

There were multiple letters from Lapasa's mother to the army. A couple more photos. Statements from witnesses who'd seen or been with Lapasa before his disappearance. The last was dated January 2, 1968. Lapasa had rung in the New Year at Saigon's Rex Hotel with one Joseph Prudhomme, a member of the Civil Operations and Revolutionary Development Support Agency.

According to Prudhomme, Lapasa planned to travel to Bien Hoa and Long Binh during the month of January. I assumed that was the reason Lapasa came up in Danny's circle search.

At the very back of the folder was a manila file. I flipped through the contents. Charts. Narrative. A small brown envelope. I peeked inside and saw the little black squares I was hoping for.

"The dentals are here, including X-rays." I read the final page of the file. "Lapasa's last dental appointment was on April twelfth, 1965."

I backtracked. Skimmed.

"Theresa-Sophia Lapasa states in a letter dated November sixteenth, 1972, that medical records can be provided." I looked up. "Why wouldn't she just do it?"

"Makes it too real," Danny said.

I raised questioning brows.

"It's a form of denial. Sometimes families can't face the possibility that their loved one really is dead."

I read a few more of the letters Theresa-Sophia had written over the years.

"The old gal must have faced reality. In 2000, Mrs. Lapasa expressed her willingness to provide a DNA sample."

"Did she?"

I looked. Found no lab report. Shook my head.

We all went still, thinking the same sad thought. Had Theresa-Sophia Lapasa died never knowing what happened to her son?

Ryan spoke first.

"Lapasa wasn't military. How could he have been on that chopper?"

"Civilians hitched rides all the time," Danny said.

"And your CIL 1968—" Ryan circled a hand in the air.

"1968-979."

Ryan nodded. "1968-979 was found a quarter mile from the crash site, seven months later, too decomposed for visual ID or fingerprinting, wearing a dog tag but no insignia?"

"The mortuary affairs people at Tan Son Nhut assumed the body had been looted."

"Like 2010-37," I said.

Danny nodded. "Apparently it was a problem in that area."

"Why leave the dog tag?" Ryan asked. "You'd think that was a priority item for looters."

Good question, I thought.

"Who knows?" Danny said.

"I'm confused," Ryan said. "Spider Lowery was army. Wasn't Tan Son Nhut an air base?"

Danny crossed his arms. "Long or short version?"

"Short."

"First off, army personnel moved through air facilities all the time. That's how they got there. But beyond that, during the early years of U.S. involvement in Vietnam, death rates were low and mortuary services were provided by the air force. A civilian mortician was assigned TDY to Clark Air Force Base in the Philippines, and only preliminary preparation of remains took place in-country. At that time the mortuary at the Tan Son Nhut Air Base consisted of just two rooms." Danny had clearly given the briefing before.

"By sixty-three the TSN mortuary had a USAF civilian mortician, a U.S. Army graves registration NCO, and a couple of locals. As casualties escalated, the facility was expanded and an embalmer and more graves registration personnel were added.

"In 1966 the air force transferred operational control of the mortuary to the army and procedures changed. In previous wars, temporary cemeteries were established to hold bodies until hostilities ceased. Remains were later disinterred and returned to next of kin, or at the request of next of kin, relocated to permanent U.S. cemeteries overseas. Embalming was done at the cemetery.

"When the army took over in Nam, it phased in a concurrent return program. Remains were processed through collection points to the Tan Son Nhut mortuary or to Da Nang after that one was built. There they were identified, embalmed, and evacuated home. Processing took place in a matter of days, not months or years, as with the old temporary burial system."

"That's fast."

"In most cases a KIA was helicoptered from the battlefield to the nearest collection point in a matter of hours. Within a day the remains were at one of the two in-country mortuaries."

"I guess you had to move quickly in that climate."

"You've got that right. With so much heat and humidity, skin soon sloughed and corpses swelled and doubled in size. Especially during the monsoons. And scavenging bugs and animals moved in before a body even hit the ground. Thank God refrigeration was available at the collection points and at the mortuaries."

"But it didn't help 1968-979."

"Once you get inland from the coast, a lot of Vietnam is pure jungle," I said. "The dead weren't always found right away."

"And think about the timing," Danny added. "The revamped TSN mortuary only went online in August of sixty-eight, the month 1968-979 was found."

"Did you shoot dental X-rays for 1968-979?" I asked Danny.

He lifted a tiny brown envelope from his blotter. "Shall we?"

We were rising when my BlackBerry sounded.

As I answered, Ryan's mobile chirped the *Sesame Street* song.

21

"Hı, sweetie." I was following Danny toward a light box located against the left wall of the lab.

"Don't you *dare* sweetie me. I can't *believe* you made me do this."

Katy's tone was pure outrage.

"This vacation was supposed to be fun. Surfing? Diving? Aloha? Remember? Alo-*ha*! I'm a friggin' taxi service!"

I could hear traffic in the background. Something bluesy blasting from a radio.

"Where are you?"

"Heading home, that's where I am. After cooling my heels for so long I thought I'd qualify for old-age benefits."

I checked my watch. Four forty. Obviously the rendezvous had not gone well.

"Where is Lily?"

"No idea. Couldn't care less."

"You never connected?"

Behind me I sensed Ryan having essentially the same conversation.

"Oh, I found her. After sweltering in the car for almost an hour."

How does one simultaneously swelter and cool one's heels? I didn't ask.

"The AC went out?"

"That's not the point," Katy said.

I caught a snippet of Ryan's exchange.

"Katy, turn down the music."

The noise level dropped a microdecibel.

"Did you leave Lily at the mall?"

"Do you have any idea how long I waited? I got there on time, early even. No Lily. I circled, thinking I might have misunderstood her instructions. No Lily. I waited some more. An hour after she told me to be there, the little bitch comes strolling out. Laughing, not a care in the world. And get this. She's with some loser mall crawler thinks he's 50 Cent."

"You took off and left her?"

My gaze met Ryan's. I could hear shrill indignation buzzing through his handset.

"As far as I'm concerned, Miss Island Diva can spend the rest of her life shopping her little black ass off."

"Katy!"

"*Ex-cuuus-ay-moi!* Lily's a prima donna junkie and everyone coddles her. Ask me, she's heading for a smackdown."

"Are you finished?"

Silence.

"Here's what you will do."

More silence.

"Are you listening?"

"Like I have a choice."

I do not react well to histrionics. To me, drama queen displays are a waste of time and energy. My tone reinforced what my daughter already knew.

"Turn around. Go back to Ala Moana. Now."

"Traffic is sick. It will take me forever."

"You should have thought of that."

"You're down there, right?"

"Yes, I am."

"You could pick her up."

"Yes, I could." Weighty pause. "Go back. Get Lily. Drive her to Lanikai."

Ryan was laying parallel directives on his daughter.

"She won't—"

"She'll be there." Sharp. "Ryan and I will be home at five thirty. At which time we will all have a nice little chat."

I clicked off and looked at Ryan. He merely wagged his head.

Danny had 1968-979's X-rays arranged beside the X-rays we'd just taken from Xander Lapasa's file.

One glance told the story.

In both, a small white glob glowed in the first upper left molar. Though truncated on the post-mortem film, the glob that remained in the molar was nearly identical to the top half of the glob on the antemortem film.

"Looks like Illinois," I said.

"With everything south of Springfield broken off." Danny pointed his pen at one of the bite-wings. "And lookee here."

I did.

An opaque line crossed the right mandibular ramus, near the junction of the vertical and horizontal parts of the jaw.

Danny shot out a hip. I bumped it with mine.

Dorky, I know. But we like doing it.

"What?" Ryan asked.

"When we examined 1968-979 we saw what we thought were old fractures. One in the shoulder and one in the jaw." I tapped the jagged line. "That's a healed break."

"Nice," Ryan said. "What about the dental work?"

"It's a match," I said. "One of the dentists will have to verify, of course, but 1968-979 is undoubtedly Alexander Lapasa."

Hot damn. One down.

But other questions remained.

Was Lapasa on the Huey that crashed near Long Binh? If so, why?

Was Spider Lowery also aboard that chopper?

Why was Lapasa wearing Lowery's dog tag?

Why was the tag boxed with 1968-979's bones and not processed through proper channels?

If Lowery was on the Huey, how did he end up dead in Quebec?

If Lowery died in Quebec, as suggested by fingerprint evidence, who was 2010-37, the man I'd disinterred in North Carolina? Luis Alvarez? If so, who had screwed up?

Ryan and I have differing views on, well, most everything not work-related. Nevertheless, we're like atoms interacting in space, our mutual positive and negative fields attracting, drawing us together. Until Lutetia, of course.

Was the old current still humming below the surface? Was that the reason for my snappishness at the ME's office?

Maybe. But no way I'd test those waters with our daughters around.

That evening Ryan and I were in total agreement. Katy and Lily were being a double-barrel pain in the ass.

On the way to Lanikai, Ryan and I bought sushi, a foodstuff curiously approved by both sides of the warring home front. After much discussion, we opted for a policy shift. Since sanctioned separation had proved a disaster, we would now implement compulsory companionship.

That decision was wildly unpopular.

Dinner was eaten in glacial silence. Afterward, *Hawaii* was viewed from opposite sides of the living room. Kind of like a wedding. Groom's on the left, bride's on the right.

Katy liked Julie Andrews. Lily said Julie was lame but loved Max von Sydow. Katy thought Max was a pansy.

Ryan swore he spotted Bette Midler doing a walk-on as a ship's passenger.

I was skeptical: 1966? It would have been a very young Bette.

By eleven we were all in our rooms.

Maybe it was too much panko-crusted ahi. Or mango crab salad roll. That night I had one of the strangest dreams of my life.

When Katy was ten she attended equestrian camp. Her horse was a small chestnut with a white blaze and stockings, named Cherry Star.

In the dream I was riding Cherry Star bareback down a long white beach. I could sense the mare's muscles rippling beneath me, could feel the sun hot on my back.

Beside us, water stretched clear and still as far as I could see. Midnight green kelp floated and curled just below the surface.

Cherry Star's hooves kicked up spray as we galloped. Fat flecks burned my face like snowflakes in winter.

A tiny black speck appeared on the horizon. Grew. Took shape.

Katy, on horseback. On Cherry Star.

I waved. Katy did not wave back.

But I was on Cherry Star.

Confused, I looked down.

I was walking.

I looked up.

Cherry Star was thundering toward me. I watched her blaze grow bigger and bigger. Turn yellow. Gold. Sunlight shot from the shiny metal surface.

Blinded, I threw up a hand.

Surrounded by a halo of fragmented light, Cherry Star's shimmering blaze changed shape. A diamond. A half-moon. An inverted mushroom with a bifurcated stem.

Suddenly Cherry Star was on top of me. Her back held no rider. Her reins were dragging in the sand.

She'll step on them and break a tooth!

I lunged but couldn't grab the trailing leather straps.

I could smell the horse's sweat, hear the air rasping in and out of her nostrils.

Cherry Star threw back her head. Opened her mouth in a silent scream.

I saw amber teeth. Curled lips. Saliva foaming in glistening streams.

Heart hammering, I tried to run.

Every step sank me deeper into the sand.

The dream shifted.

I was treading water.

Using both arms, I rotated shoreward.

The land was very far off.

Kelp surrounded me.

I watched the green-black clumps slowly coalesce. The dark circle closed in.

Something brushed my foot.

I looked down.

Saw a snout. Membrane-hooded eyes. Cold. Primordial.

The shark stretched its jaws, revealing razor-sharp teeth.

I awoke, damp with perspiration, nails digging little crescents into my palms.

The sky was gray. A moisture-laden breeze wafted in from the window.

I checked the clock. Six forty-five.

The house was quiet.

I rolled onto my side. Pulled the quilt to my chin.

Much as I willed it, sleep would not return.

I tried every relaxation trick I knew, but my mind focused only on the dream.

My nighttime fantasies are typically not Freudian puzzlers.

Bareback on the horse? OK. Most of us know that one.

Katy? Fine. I was worried about her.

The gold blaze? The kelp? The shark?

At eight I gave up and went down to the kitchen.

Ryan had already cranked up the espresso machine. Good. The thing scared the crap out of me.

"Perry closed that beach." Ryan pointed to the local section of the *Honolulu Advertiser.* "Got to hand it to the lady. She's really something. And looking pretty good."

Only if you're sighting down a penis. This time I didn't say it.

I skimmed the article. It reported that Halona Cove was closed to swimmers until further notice, but offered no explanation.

Sipping coffee and crunching toast, Ryan and I formulated a plan.

First, we'd visit the Punchbowl. The girls might not be thrilled. Tough. It was Ryan's pick. And a good one. I'd been there.

The Punchbowl is an extinct volcanic tuff cone located smack in the city of Honolulu. The crater was formed when hot lava blasted through cracks in coral reefs extending to the foot of the Koolau Range.

Hot lava?

Relax. That eruption was 100,000 years ago.

There are various interpretations of the Punchbowl's Hawaiian name, Puowaina. Most translate it as something like Hill of Sacrifice. Supposedly, native Hawaiians used the place for human sacrifice to the gods. Legend has it taboo violators were also executed there. Later, Kamehameha the Great had cannons mounted at the crater's rim to salute distinguished arrivals and to kick off important celebrations.

In the 1930s, the Hawaii National Guard used the Punchbowl as a rifle range. Toward the end of World War II, tunnels were dug through the crater's rim to construct batteries to guard the island's harbors, Honolulu and Pearl.

In the late forties, needing a final resting place for World War II troops lying in temporary graves on the island of Guam, the U.S. Congress voted funds to establish the national cemetery. Eight hundred unknowns from the Korean War followed. In the mideighties, Vietnam casualties joined the mix.

Ernie Pyle is buried at the Punchbowl. So is Hawaii's first astronaut, Ellison Onizuka, killed on the *Challenger.*

After the Punchbowl, we'd drive up to the north shore, hit the beach, and try some of Hawaii's famous shave ice.

Finally, hours of camaraderie under their belts, Lily and Katy would stay home, together, and the grown-ups would enjoy a night on the town. We needed it.

Though our little band would not have been mistaken for the Brady Bunch, the day went reasonably well.

The adult night out proved pivotal.

22

RYAN CHOSE THE RESTAURANT. HIS CRITERIA? Proximity to Waikiki was the only thing I could come up with.

We ate at the Ha'aha'a Seafood and Steakhouse, the Hawaiian Walmart of dining establishments. My first misgivings came with the table.

We were seated in a dark corner, inches from a band whose repertoire was probably fixed right out of Moanalua High. I placed the graduation year at circa 1965.

My second clue came with the menu. Six of nine pages were devoted to drinks, most with names formed from incredibly bad puns. Son of a Beach Daiquiris. I Lava Party Bacardis. O'Lei Margaritas.

Ryan ordered a Kona beer and jerk mahimahi. I went with a virgin colada and cilantro shrimp.

The drink wasn't bad. Hard to mess up pineapple juice and coconut cream.

Ryan and I chatted while awaiting the food. Shouted, actually. Over such memorables as "My Waikiki Mermaid" and "Pearly Shells."

Ryan apologized for Lily. I apologized for Katy. He offered to relocate from the Lanikai house to a hotel. I told him that was unnecessary.

Overhead, a mirrored disco ball sent fragmented light spinning the room. Groovy.

"Not exactly the way to a girl's heart." Ryan's face went sapphire as a colored spot aimed at the stage lighted our table.

"Depends on the girl. Why *did* you pick this particular place?"

"Proud Seafood and Steakhouse. What could disappoint?"

"I'm pretty sure *ha'ahea* means proud." I'd seen the word in English and Hawaiian on a headstone at the Punchbowl. "I think *ha'aha'a* translates as humble."

"Oh."

The band picked up tempo. The lead singer crooned, "Oh, how she could yacki hacki wicki wacki woo."

Ryan's neon brows climbed his neon forehead.

Forty minutes after ordering, we were served by a waiter different from the one who had handled our drinks. This man had a leaping tiger tattooed the length of one biceps and a central incisor inlaid with what looked like a gold martini glass. His name badge said *Rico.*

"Careful." Rico lowered towel-held plates to our table. "These suckers are hot."

Doubtful. My shrimp were trapped in a pool of congealed grease.

"That it?" Rico asked.

Ryan ordered another beer.

"Enjoy the show."

Ryan and I nodded politely.

"It's hapa haole music."

"Didn't think it was the gospel hour."

Rico and I both frowned at Ryan.

"Really?" I flashed Rico my most disarming smile. "What is hapa haole music?"

Rico hitched one feline-enhanced shoulder.

"Sometimes the song's done traditional, you know, four-four time, but the words are in English, so that makes it half English, half Hawaiian. Sometimes the words are in Hawaiian but the beat is hyped, so that makes it hapa haole." He thought a moment. "Not all Hawaiian songs with haole words are hapa haole. Sometimes the words are Hawaiian and the music isn't."

All righty, then.

The cuisine lived up to my expectations.

As I chewed shrimp the texture of all-weather radials, the band played the inevitable "Tiny Bubbles."

"Did you know that Don Ho served in the air force?" Ryan asked.

"Yes," I said.

"Did you know that he had ten kids?" Ryan spoke between bites of incinerated fish.

"Impressive," I said.

"As am I."

"Indeed."

Ryan reached over and brushed my jawline. My pulse jumped as fire burned a path below his fingers.

"Have you thought about giving it another try?"

"It?" I swallowed.

"Us."

And Lutetia? Hadley Perry? I restrained myself by a thin, thin strand.

"Mm. Tell me more about Don Ho," I said, wanting safer ground.

Ryan settled back in his chair. "Ho started singing at a bar called Honey's out at Kaneohe. The joint belonged to his mother."

"Honey," I guessed.

"Yes, sugar lump?"

The quip hit like a hot poker to the heart. Buttercup. Sweet pea. Though I'd always chided Ryan for his goofy endearments, secretly I'd loved them. I wondered who else was being so honored.

"Honey's was a hangout for marines from the base out there," Ryan continued, oblivious to the emotions he'd triggered. "Ho moved the business to Waikiki back in the sixties."

"I thought he performed at a place called Duke's." My steady voice belied nothing.

"That was later. Then he hit the big time."

"And the rest is history."

"Hi Ho."

I gave up on the crustaceans and laid down my fork.

"Is Ho still alive?"

Ryan shook his head. "He died a couple years back."

At that moment, a sequence of unrelated events coincided on the great space-time continuum that forms reality as we perceive it.

As Rico placed a coaster on our table, a swirling light particle danced off his tooth. Glancing down, I noticed the coaster's sole design element, a cheesy male totem from another time.

Bang!

The previous night's dream flashed in my brain. A horse's white blaze gone gold. Equine teeth.

More images popped.

A maxillary fragment.

Crumbling adipocere circling a drain.

A lopsided gold sliver with two tapering points.

An open-beaked duck.

A pointy-stemmed mushroom.

Rico.

My hand flew to Ryan's wrist. "Ohmygod! I know what it is!"

"My arm?"

I released my grip.

"The gold thing Danny and I found. I found." I was totally psyched. "The fragment we thought was part of a dental restoration. Well, I did. Danny wasn't sure. But the dentist didn't think so. Craig Brooks. He was right. Well, he was wrong and right. It *was* dental but not a restor—"

Setting his fork on his plate, Ryan raised two calming hands. "Take a breath."

I did.

"Now. Slowly. In English. Or French. But comprehensible."

The band segued into a way-too-twangy rendition of "Hawaii Calls."

I reeled in my thoughts.

"I'll bet the bandstand the thing we found with 2010-37 is a broken dental inlay."

"Whose bandstand?"

"Look." I spun the coaster and pointed to the logo. "What's that?"

"A Playboy bunny."

"The whole Playboy shtick is passé now, but it was huge in the sixties. Did you notice Rico's tooth?"

"Shaken, not stirred."

I rolled my eyes, a gesture wasted in the dark.

"I had a North Carolina case in which the victim had a dental crown with a gold symbol shaped like a Playboy bunny. It's how we finally got him ID'd."

"Did he also have *Eat at Joe's* tattooed on his—"

"The crown was strictly decorative. I did research. I learned you can get them as full gold crowns with cutouts shaped like crosses, martini glasses, stars, half-moons—"

"The ever popular bunny."

"Yes. Or you can get what's called a sparkle. That's an acrylic crown that looks like a natural tooth with a gold shape affixed to the front."

"Are these little gems permanent?"

"You can do it either way. Rough-backed sparkles are permanently bonded to the tooth. Smooth-backed sparkles can be slipped on or off at will."

"For that special night-on-the-town look." Said with disdain.

"Different people, different tastes."

"J. Edgar loved marabou trim. Doesn't mean fluffy pumps will be filling my shoe rack."

I ignored that.

"The North Carolina guy was a migrant worker missing since 1969. He was Latino. My research suggested that the wearing of ornamental gold caps is popular among Hispanics. Some articles talked about the pre-Columbian roots of the custom."

"The Mayans also cut out people's hearts. Doesn't mean we should give that a whirl."

"That was the Aztecs."

Ryan started to comment. I cut him off.

"Spider Lowery's Huey went down with four crew members aboard. Three were recovered and ID'd straight off. The fourth, the maintenance specialist, was never found."

"I'm guessing he was Latino."

"Luis Alvarez. He was Mexican-American."

"Wouldn't gold hardware be mentioned in Alvarez's dental antemorts?"

"His file contains no dental or medical records. Besides, if Alvarez added the sparkle after his last checkup, that wouldn't be in his record."

"Or he might have removed the thing when reporting for duty."

"Exactly."

Rico appeared at our table.

Ryan requested the check.

Rico pulled out his pad. As he summed, I tried observing his tooth. No go. His lips were compressed with the effort of the complex math.

Finally a slip hit the table.

Ryan and I reached for it. Argued. Our usual ritual.

I won. Handed Rico my Visa.

Smirking at Ryan, Rico headed off.

"What about Spider Lowery?" Ryan asked.

"What about him?"

"Might he have slipped into something a little

more gold? He could have picked the thing up in Nam."

"He could have."

"Or he might have gotten the little doodad before shipping out, but removed it when he was around Mommy and Daddy."

"Another possibility."

"Is there anyone he might have told?" Ryan asked. "A buddy? A sibling?"

I remembered the photo session in my car.

"The brother's dead, but Plato said Spider was close to a cousin. They played on the same high school baseball team."

"The cousin still live in Lumberton?"

"I don't know."

"Might be worth a phone call. You know, cover all bases."

True.

The band launched into "If I Had a Hammer," the singer trying hard for Trini Lopez but missing badly.

"But Spider Lowery died in Quebec," I said.

"Or the FBI screwed up the prints. I'd say the first step is to establish that your gold duck-mushroom thingy is, in fact, a broken gold sparkle. Then go from there."

True again.

Rico returned with my card. I signed and added a tip. A big one, hoping for a smile.

Nope. With a mumbled "*Mahalo*," Rico was gone.

"Does Alvarez's file contain photos?" Ryan asked.

"Several."

"Any smiling shots?"

In my mind's eye I pictured the three black-and-whites.

A head-and-shoulders portrait of a uniformed young man.

A grainy reproduction of a high school gradu-ate.

Nine sweaty soldiers, one glancing away from the camera.

I looked at Ryan.

Suddenly I was in a frenzy to reexamine that snapshot.

23

SUNDAY DAWNED COOL AND RAINY. I AWOKE, noted conditions, and went back to sleep. Apparently, my cohorts reacted in a similar fashion. Or no one even raised a lid.

At nine thirty, muffled rattling sounds roused me again. Throwing on shorts and a tee, I descended to the kitchen.

Ryan was preparing French toast and bacon. The smell was orgasmic.

I rousted the ladies and the four of us shared another prickly meal. As we ate, the rain tapered off and the sun began gnawing holes through the clouds.

After breakfast, we went our separate ways, Ryan and Lily to view fish from a glass-bottom boat, Katy and I to snorkel and read on the beach.

I took my BlackBerry, figuring I could make calls from the sand. Knowing Danny was not an early riser, I put that one off. But I was anxious to talk to Plato Lowery.

As before, Plato did not answer his phone. Neither did Silas Sugarman.

Frustrated, I stared at my current screen saver,

a shot of Birdie sitting on Charlie's cage. The photo usually triggered a smile. Not this time.

The tiny digits told me it was six thirty p.m. East Coast time. I searched my brain for inspiration. Who might be available on a Sunday evening in Lumberton, North Carolina?

Idea. Why not? He'd proven useful before.

I got a number through Google. Punched it in.

"Robeson County Sheriff's Department." The voice was crisp, more New York than Dixie.

"Sheriff Beasley, please."

"Not in."

"Could you patch me through to him?"

"Not possible."

"This is Dr. Temperance Brennan. Could you give the sheriff my number and ask him to call me back? It's rather urgent."

"What is the nature of your complaint?"

"It's not a complaint. On May eleventh I conducted an exhumation in Lumberton. The sheriff was present. I need information concerning the disinterred remains."

"The sheriff is extraordinarily busy."

"As am I." The woman was starting to piss me off.

"Your number?"

I provided it.

During the pause that followed, a gull cried out. I hoped the sound didn't carry across the line.

"I'll transmit your request."

Click.

"Do that," I snapped to dead air.

Katy's head came up. I flapped a hand. She resumed reading her book.

Ten minutes later the phone rang.

"Sheriff Beasley." High and a bit rubbery, like Barney Fife.

"Thanks for returning my call. I apologize for intruding on your Sunday evening."

"Just watching the Braves get their sorry butts whupped."

"I'm calling concerning the individual buried at the Gardens of Faith Cemetery under the name John Charles Lowery."

"First that detective, now you. Spider's sure stirring up a hornet's nest of interest."

"Yes, sir. Did you know him?" I asked. "Personally?"

"We run up against each other from time to time."

"What can you tell me about him?"

"Spider was three grades behind me in school. After graduation, I went into law enforcement." Yep. Deputy Fife. "My rookie years I had to deal with a couple of his antics."

"Antics?"

"Actually, Spider wasn't so bad. It was that cousin of his. That was one rambunctious juvenile." A very long *i* in juvenile.

"And he was?"

"Reggie Cumbo. Boy had a sheet longer than my arm."

"Why was that, sir?"

"Kid was a dick."

I said nothing. Like many, Beasley felt compelled to fill the silence.

"Drunk and disorderly, mostly."

"What happened to him?"

"Took off the day of his high school commencement. Course, Reggie wasn't going to march with no tassel and cap."

"He failed to graduate?"

"I recall talk to that effect."

"Where is Reggie now?"

"Could be the mayor of Milwaukee for all I know. More likely he's dead. Never heard another word of him."

So much for querying Reggie about Spider's sense of haute dentition.

"Did you ever notice gold decoration on Spider Lowery's teeth?"

"You mean like crowns or something?"

I explained dental sparkles. "Maybe later, after Spider joined the army? Perhaps in snapshots he mailed home from Nam? Maybe Plato or Harriet showed some to you? Or sent one to the paper? Or posted some online?" I knew I was reaching.

"Nah. What's so important about Spider's teeth? I thought you were all set with Harriet's DNA."

"The sparkle may prove helpful in identifying the body I disinterred. Assuming it's not Spider. Besides, Harriet's hospital slides are five years old. I'm exploring backup options, in case the samples are too degraded for sequencing."

"Don't know what to tell you, miss. Spider was"—Beasley hesitated—"different. But I doubt he'd a done something foolish like ornamenting his teeth with gold."

"What *do* you remember about Spider?"

Beasley blew air through his lips. "I recall back in high school he offered to give his mama a kidney. Harriet was born with bad ones, guess it's what finally killed her. Have to admit, I thought that was mighty generous. Spider wasn't a proper match, wrong blood type or something. His brother, Tom, offered too. Course that was many years later. That didn't work out either. Not sure I'd have done that."

"Spider?"

Beasley didn't answer right away. Then, "I remember he did a science project on spiders. Filled fifteen or twenty of those big white boards with pictures and diagrams and little note cards. Had all kinds of jars lined up with labels and spiders inside. The thing won first prize. Got displayed at the library. They still pull the posters out now and again. Spiders are long gone, of course."

"Anything else?"

"I recall him going off to war. I recall him coming home dead. Sorry."

I could think of nothing further to ask. Thanking Beasley, I disconnected.

Danny's call came while Katy and I were underwater eyeballing butterflies, tangs, and one particularly doleful-looking trumpet fish.

While digging a towel from my bag, I noticed my BlackBerry's message light blinking.

Danny's message was short. *Call me.*

I did.

"What's up?"

"Thought you'd want to know. I researched Xander Lapasa's family. His parents, Alexander senior and Theresa-Sophia, are both dead."

I heard paper rustle.

"Alexander Emanuel, Xander, was the first-born of six kids, four boys, two girls. One sister, Mamie Waite, lives in Maui, is divorced, and has one daughter. The other sister, Hesta Grogan, lives in Nevada, is widowed, and has two sons.

"One of the brothers, Marvin, was mentally handicapped and died young, in the seventies. The other two, Nicholas and Kenneth, still live in the Honolulu area. Each is married, Kenneth to his first wife, Nicholas to his fourth. Between them, they have eleven kids and eighteen grand-kids."

I did some quick math. If Xander Lapasa was twenty-nine when he disappeared in 1968, that meant he was born in 1939.

Danny must have read my thoughts.

"The surviving siblings are all in their sixties."

"Tell me about Daddy." I wasn't sure why all this family history was relevant, but Danny seemed eager to share what he'd learned.

"Alex Lapasa made his way to Oahu in 1956 and got a job at an East Honolulu gas station. Two years later, the station owner died. A hit-and-run. A handwritten will transferred owner-ship of the station to Lapasa."

"Sounds kinky."

"The cops found nothing linking Lapasa to the accident. The victim had no family scream-ing for justice, so who knows how thorough the investigation was."

I made no comment.

"A hurricane blew the station off the map nine months after Lapasa took possession. Having no source of income and, apparently, no enduring love of petrol, Lapasa turned to selling real estate. And saw potential. Recognizing that a lot of baby-boomer parents would be needing a lot of cheap housing, Lapasa shifted into low-end home construction. He'd put up a bungalow, sell it, put up two more.

"When Hawaii gained statehood in 1959, the building industry exploded. Lapasa leveraged everything, expanded, made millions. From the sixties to the nineties he diversified. Today the Lapasa empire has more tentacles than an anemone."

"Sounds like old Alex was one smart cookie."

"Yes."

I noted a hitch in Danny's breathing.

"What?" I asked.

"Lapasa was always, shall we say, controversial. Some said he had the Midas touch. Others said he was just lucky. All agreed he was ruthless as hell."

"When did he die?"

"In 2002."

"Who runs the business today?"

"Number two son, Nicholas."

A big clapper went *gong!* in my head. I'd seen the name in the *Honolulu Advertiser* many times, occasionally preceded by a descriptor such as Slick or Tricky. Yeah, like Nixon.

"*That* Nickie Lapasa?"

"That Nickie Lapasa."

I vaguely remembered Alex Lapasa's passing from news coverage during one of my visits to the CIL. The funeral was a five-ring circus.

"Wasn't Lapasa under investigation for RICO

violations at the time of his death?" I referred to the Racketeer Influenced and Corrupt Organizations Act passed by Congress in 1970.

"Yeah. And it wasn't the first time. Rumor had it Alex had ties to the Mafia. Nothing ever stuck."

I thought a moment.

"Isn't Kenny Lapasa a member of the Honolulu City Council?"

"He is."

Xander had vanished. Marvin had died. Nickie and Kenny were alive and thriving. I wondered about the sisters.

"Are Mamie and Hesta involved in the family business?"

Danny snorted. "Definitely not the Lapasa style."

"Meaning?"

"No girls allowed."

"Yet it was Theresa-Sophia who corresponded with the army concerning Xander's disappearance."

"The old man probably viewed letter writing as beneath him."

"Why do you suppose Xander went to Nam?"

"There were rumors about Lapasa's involvement in drug trafficking. Maybe he sent his kid to Southeast Asia to scout postwar possibilities. You know, drug sources, transport options."

"Who did you talk to?" I asked.

"Tricky Nickie. It was like getting through to Obama."

"How did he react?"

"At first he was skeptical. I told him that the dental ID, though unofficial, was solid, and asked if Xander had ever broken any bones. He said Xander busted his jaw and collarbone in a car wreck the summer after his junior year in high school. I described the healed fractures we'd spotted on the bones and X-rays."

"Did that convince him?"

"Not totally. I said that, to reassure the family, a DNA comparison could be done if he or one of his siblings would provide a sample. The guy went ballistic, said no way was any government toady sticking a probe into any member of his family. I explained that the process was painless, just a cheek swab. He grew even more agitated, I'll spare you the verbiage, finally hung up on me."

"If some of Alex Lapasa's business dealings were as shady as rumor has it, maybe Nickie's worried about privacy issues. Felons tend to be protective of their DNA."

"Maybe. But Nickie's never been linked to anything illegal. Anyway, an hour later he rang back, irate, ranting about incompetence, stupidity, professional misconduct. He threatened to phone his congressman, his senator, the ACLU, the Joint Chiefs of Staff, the president, CNN, Jesse Jackson, Rush Limbaugh, maybe even Nelson Mandela."

"He didn't say that."

"Maybe not Mandela."

"Why so angry?"

"We kept his brother on our shelves for over four decades."

Good point, I thought.

"Again, I offered to do comparative testing, said DNA had been successfully sequenced from the remains in two thousand one. He demanded that that information be destroyed, said he didn't want his family in"—Danny's voice went gruff—"no bullshit government database."

"Anything else?"

"He said heads would roll."

"First Plato Lowery, now Nickie Lapasa. Weird."

"I've dealt with weirder."

Changing gears, I shared my theory concerning the gold duck-mushroom thing buried in Lumberton with 2010-37, and described my conversation with Sheriff Beasley.

"He'd never heard of dental sparkles?"

"No."

"You'd think Beasley would have encountered at least one if they occurred with any frequency in his jurisdiction," Danny said.

"The sparkle craze may have bypassed Robeson County." I thought a moment. "It may go nowhere, but we could try locating Reggie Cumbo."

"The cousin," Danny said.

"Yes."

"The guy you exhumed in Lumberton has to be Luis Alvarez," Danny said. "Alvarez is still missing. His bioprofile is identical to Lowery's and fits the remains. Alvarez is Mexican-American. Sparkles are big with Mexican-Americans."

"Now," I said. "But was that the case back in the sixties?"

"I'm not sure, but I think so." Danny was silent a beat. "We should recheck the photos in Alvarez's file."

"We should," I agreed.

"First thing tomorrow."

"First thing."

We had another date.

24

SUNDAY EVENING WE ENJOYED, OR ENDURED, A "battle of the ringtones." Our musical choices were the stuff of psych dissertations.

Lily's current pick was "Super Freak" by Rick James. Katy was using Cab Calloway's "Minnie the Moocher." Ever the optimist, I'd switched to the *Happy Days* theme. Ryan was still featuring Big Bird and his pals.

Dinner was once again cooked on the grill. While we were clearing the dishes, Cab announced an incoming call. Katy excused herself, returned minutes later, pensive, but face basically arranged in a grin.

One query from me brought full disclosure.

Katy's caller had been Coop's older brother, Jed. Jed had been exceedingly apologetic about the manner in which Katy had been treated. Because Coop's death had received so much publicity, the Cooperton home had been inundated with contact from journalists, well-wishing strangers, and citizen wackos opposed to the war. As self-appointed protector of the family's privacy, Jed's uncle Abner had assumed phone responsibility. His strategy: rebuff any caller unknown to himself personally.

Jed told Katy that he had something he believed Coop would want her to have. Though perplexed, Katy clearly was pleased. And more relaxed than I'd seen her since Coop's murder.

Ryan was next. Despite the sunny ringtone, his news came from the other end of the spectrum. His voice was grim as he updated me later, alone in the kitchen.

Lutetia was leaving Montreal for her home in Nova Scotia. Until further notice Lily would be Ryan's responsibility. Bye-bye. Adios.

My reaction was mixed. While I knew Lutetia's departure would hurt Lily and cause Ryan untold complications, I can't say I was sorry to bid Ryan's ex adieu. Metaphorically, of course. We'd never once spoken.

My first caller was Hadley Perry. She told me three things.

One, she'd gotten no hits with the MP families. Two, Honolulu PD Detectives Lô and Hung would begin canvassing hospitals first thing in the morning. Three, she was taking heat from the mayor and city council for closing Halona Cove.

Again in hushed tones, I shared Perry's report with Ryan, this time on the lanai.

Ryan's mouth corners twitched as his mind performed the same transposal mine had.

"Lô is Vietnamese, puts a little cap over the o. Hung is Chinese. The two have partnered for nine years, and are no longer receptive to comments concerning their names."

Anticipating the usual reaction, Perry had

diverted any witticism I might have offered. I did the same with Ryan.

"I thought you were here for some dude who died in the sixties," Katy said.

Ryan and I swiveled in surprise. Neither of us had heard Katy come through the sliding door.

"I am. Several dudes, actually," I said. "And the local ME asked my advice on a recent local case. I assumed you wouldn't want to hear about it." Given Coop's death. I didn't say that.

Katy looked from me to Ryan then back again. "Sure I do."

Ryan rose. "If you'll excuse me, ladies, I haven't checked my e-mail in days." Lame, but Ryan sensed Katy was feeling excluded.

Katy settled into the lounge chair Ryan had vacated. I told her about Hadley Perry, the body parts, the tooth marks, the surgical pin, and the partial tattoo.

"Live every week like Shark Week."

Huh?

"Tracy Jordan? *30 Rock*?"

Still, I was lost.

"The NBC sitcom? Tracy Morgan's character was referring to a series on the Discovery Channel? Lampooning motivational quotes? Never mind. My remark was stupid. It's wrong to joke about victims."

I patted her hand.

"No offense taken."

For a moment we both listened to the tick of palm fronds and the shush of gently breaking waves. Katy spoke first.

"I've been spending a lot of time on my blog."

"Commenting on what?"

"The stupidity of war."

"Sounds worthwhile."

"I'm going to write about the insensitivity of what I just said." She thought a moment. "About how we sometimes lose sight of the fact that every death is tragic."

"I'd very much like to read your thoughts."

"You have to say that." Shooting to her feet, she buzzed my cheek. "You're my mother."

Before I could protest, she hurried inside.

My second caller was Tim Larabee, the ME in Charlotte. A decomposed body had been found in a sandpit off a rural highway in Cabarrus County. He'd been on-scene since midnight, suspected the remains were those of a housewife missing since the previous fall. An anthropology consult would be needed. He wondered, no pressure, when I'd return.

Happy Days.

Lily's phone rang at half past ten. Having finished Stephen King, I was on to a Grisham novel. Ryan was watching CNN. Katy was in her room blogging or tweeting or whatever it was she'd said.

After checking caller ID, Lily clicked on and hurried upstairs.

I looked over at Ryan, recognized the changed jawline, the tensed shoulders. Understood. Suspecting Lily's caller was Lutetia, he was steeling himself for his daughter's tears.

A half hour later Lily returned. She was calm, almost smiling. Curling on the sofa, she offered no explanation.

My eyes met Ryan's. He raised questioning brows.

I nodded toward Lily.

Ryan didn't grimace, but he came close.

I nodded again, harder.

"That your mom?" Ryan asked his daughter, casual as hell.

"No."

I feigned total absorption in my book.

Seconds passed. A full minute.

"Anderson Cooper's got really great hair." Lily's eyes stayed glued to the TV. "But I hear he's short."

Monday, Ryan agreed to drive Lily up to the North Shore. She wanted to visit the Turtle Bay resort where scenes from *Forgetting Sarah Marshall* were shot. He wanted time alone with his daughter.

Katy stayed home to work on her blog.

Traffic in the city was one giant snarl. By the time I reached Hickam it was almost eight.

No problem. Danny entered the JPAC lot two cars ahead of me. He waited as I parked and climbed from my Cobalt.

"Aloha."

"Aloha."

"Primo wheels," he needled.

"Very funny."

"You could call Avis, try to upgrade."

"It's not worth the effort. I've got a case back in North Carolina, so I'll probably head out in a day or two."

"You just arrived."

"I've been here ten days."

"What about the case you're working with Perry?"

"Cases."

While we walked, I told him about the second shark vic, the traction pinhole, and the partial ankle tattoo.

"Perry should get a hit on one or the other," Danny said.

"I think so. And with no more remains, there's nothing else I can do."

"Your work here is done."

"My work here is done. After we look at Luis Alvarez's photos."

I noticed Danny was sprouting one of those jawline crawlers so inexplicably popular with the male demographic.

"Growing a beard?" I asked.

"Giving it a shot." His chin hitched up and twisted from side to side. "What do you think?"

"A man's gotta do what a man's gotta do."

The chin dropped.

We were in the corridor leading to the CIL wing when Gus Dimitriadus appeared in the lobby on the far side of the glass, arms hugging a cardboard box to his chest. A potted palm projected from one side, a trophy of some sort from the other.

Dimitriadus was frowning. Shocker.

Danny opened and held the door wide.

Dimitriadus's head came up. His frown morphed to a full-blown scowl.

"Need help?" Danny offered.

"You've done enough."

"Look, this doesn't have to be pers—"

"Really? Doesn't it?"

What a prick, I thought, and immediately felt bad. After all, the guy had just gotten canned from what he'd undoubtedly thought was a career job.

"If you have more boxes, we'd be happy to—"

"I'll bet you would." Dimitriadus cut me off.

I looked into his eyes.

And saw pure hatred directed my way.

Wordlessly, Danny and I stepped aside.

As he moved through the door, Dimitriadus put out one elbow and jabbed my chest. Hard.

Taken off guard, I stumbled backward.

"Jackass," Danny said to Dimitriadus's retreating back. To me, "You OK?"

"I'm fine."

"The jerk did that on purpose."

"He's venting," I said. "I'm an easy target."

"That's no excuse."

"The man just lost his job."

"He'll lose his nuts if he tries another move like that."

Sir Danny, Avenger of Damsels Bashed in the Boobs.

While Danny went for coffee, I settled in his office with the Alvarez file.

The old black-and-whites were as I recalled.

I glanced only briefly at the head and shoulders portrait of Private Alvarez in uniform. No smile. No use.

I picked up the shot of nine sweaty soldiers dressed in sleeve-rolled fatigues and studied the man with the name *Alvarez* scrawled in ink across his chest.

Excitement fizzed through me.

Alvarez's face was turned from the lens, as though he'd been distracted just as the shutter clicked. He wasn't smiling, but, surprised, perhaps curious or frightened, had unconsciously drawn back his lips.

Revealing most of his upper front teeth.

I was searching for a magnifier when Danny appeared.

"Any luck?" He set two steaming mugs on his desk.

"Maybe. Where's your hand lens?"

"Let's use one of the Luxos."

We hurried into the lab.

Danny lit the fluorescent bulb on a round, table-mounted magnifier. I positioned the photo, then manipulated the arm until Alvarez's mouth came into focus under the lens. We both leaned in, Danny's head so close I could feel his ear next to mine.

And there it was. A bunny-shaped shadow on Alvarez's right central incisor. A minute point of light sparked from the bunny's bow tie.

"Hee-haw!"

"Hee-haw!"

We bumped hips like jocks bump chests in an end zone.

"Our computer geeks will magnify the image so that the tooth is one-to-one with the fragment of sparkle you found. Then they can do a superimposition. Given the circumstances of the Huey crash, the fact that the biological profile fits

Alvarez perfectly, and the dental evidence, the ID should be solid."

"And you can try sequencing mitochondrial DNA, assuming a maternal relative can be found."

"We can indeed."

Beyond the glass wall that sealed off the lab I noticed Dimitriadus cross the lobby carrying another cardboard box. This one appeared heavy, probably books. When he'd disappeared from sight, Danny and I returned to his office.

The coffee was now tepid. We sipped it anyway.

"So Alvarez was found shortly after the crash and buried in North Carolina as Spider Lowery," I said. "Lapasa was found eight months later, in the same general area, with Spider Lowery's dog tag. Since Lowery was already ID'd, Lapasa went to Tan Son Nhut as an unknown, then to CIL-THAI, finally here."

"And, thanks to us, Luis and Xander are both going home."

"As is Spider," I said.

"Well done." Danny beamed.

We clinked mugs.

Sipped.

But *was* it? The loose ends bugged me.

"I can understand the mix-up with Alvarez and Lowery. But why was Lapasa wearing Spider's dog tag?"

"Good question."

"And was Lapasa on that chopper? If so, why?"

"Technically that's two questions."

"And how did Spider end up in Quebec?"

"We've got a foursome! But you forget the most intriguing question of all."

I gave Danny a "go on" look.

"How did we let each other slip away?"

"Come on, Danny. This is serious."

"Perhaps I am too."

Whoa!

"You love your wife."

"Madly," he said. "That's a problem."

There was a beat of embarrassed silence. Then, "Just kidding." Big goofy smile. "I keep thinking about my conversation with Nickie Lapasa." Danny slid a pen through his fingers, tapping the tip then the butt to his blotter. "Why was Nickie so opposed to the idea of DNA testing that might positively identify his brother's remains?"

"If the rumors about organized crime are true, my initial hunch was probably dead-on."

"Probably."

Tap. Tap. Tap.

"You know what?" Pointing the pen at me. "I'm going to do it anyway."

"Do what?"

"A DNA comparison."

"Where will you get a family sample for comparison?"

"I'll think of something." One finger tapped a temple, just as it had outside the Lanikai house upon our arrival. "I've got an arrival ceremony this afternoon, but right after that, I'm on it like fat on bacon."

Sunday, Monday, happy days!

I checked my BlackBerry.

Hadley Perry.

Not wanting to dampen Danny's good mood, I optcd to takc thc ME's call in thc lobby.

While worming through stacks of books and papers, I noticed a shadow cross the tile beyond the open office door.

In the corridor, I looked left and right. Empty.

Had someone been eavesdropping? Dimitriadus? If not, who? Why?

Perry's news blew the issue right out of my head.

25

"Lô JUST CALLED. HE FOUND A FIFTEEN-YEAR-old male who broke his left tibia and fibula back in 2003. Francis Kealoha. The kid spent time as an in-patient at The Queen's Medical Center."

"In traction?"

"Yes, ma'am. The pins were removed the following year."

"The guy's quick."

"The Queen's is Hawaii's only designated trauma center, so Lô started there, put the screws to some chick to do a database search using our suggested parameters. Kealoha's record popped right out."

"Did Lô contact the family?"

"The mother died in '07, father's been out of the picture for years. But he managed to track down a sister. Gloria. A real piece of work. Gloria said the last time she talked to or saw her brother was three years back. She thinks."

"Did Lô learn of any associates, anyone who might have noticed that Kealoha had disappeared?"

"Gloria swears she knows none of her brother's friends, has no idea where he's been living for the past few years. Or what he's been doing. Lô's working on it. I'm heading to The Queen's now, thought you might want to meet me."

"Why can't Lô pick up the medical file and drop it by your office?"

"The treating doc's being a prick. Says he can't release anything without permission from a parent or guardian. Or proof of death."

"That's ass backward."

"Yes."

"How old is Gloria?"

"Thirty-two."

"So what's the problem? Lô can get a release from her."

"Gloria's a prossie with no love of cops. Lô's call must have spooked her, because she's stopped answering the phone. He went by, got no response, heard no sounds of activity."

"Is Hung having any luck with the tattoo parlors?"

"Apparently that shark motif is fairly common. The only unusual elements were those little loopy things along the top border. One tattoo artist thought they were probably added later. The tat angle may turn out to be a bust."

"Who's Kealoha's doctor?"

"Sydney Utagawa, an orthopedic surgeon."

"Where are you meeting him?"

"In his office at The Queen's. We can examine the file, but he keeps possession."

"Give me directions."

She did.

"I'll be there in twenty."

* * *

When Captain James Cook stumbled onto the Hawaiian Islands in 1778, the population numbered roughly 350,000. By 1854, when Alexander Liholiho ascended the throne as King Kamehameha IV, that number had dropped to approximately 70,000. Such was the impact of Western microbes.

From the moment of his inauguration, King K and his queen, Emma Naea Rooke, fought for the establishment of health care for native Polynesians. In 1859 the royal couple's dream was realized in the form of a tiny, eighteen-bed, temporary dispensary. The following year, a permanent facility, The Queen's Hospital, was built on a parcel of land called Manamana, at the foot of the Punchbowl.

Over the years, buildings spread outward from the original rock coral and redwood structure championed by his and her highness. Renamed The Queen's Medical Center, the hospital is now a megacomplex of high-rise towers, multilevel parking decks, specialty research and treatment centers, physicians' office buildings, medical libraries, and conference centers.

I got lost leaving Hickam, but eventually blundered onto Vineyard Boulevard. Following Perry's directions, I turned onto Lusitana Street and found the parking area for Physicians Office Building 1. Seems the docs are no more creative than the troops in naming their habitats.

Or maybe someone was making a statement. Physicians Office Building 1 was a nondescript stone block devoid of redeeming architectural detail. Nice tree to one side, though. Baobab? Nawa? An arborist I'm not.

As I walked toward the entrance, I noted the main hospital tower looming beyond, chalk white, its backdrop the glass and steel of downtown skyscrapers.

I rode the elevator with two men and a woman, all in lab coats with stethoscopes looped in their pockets. The woman flipped through a chart. The men watched the floor buttons blink in succession as we ascended. Discreetly, I scanned name tags.

Nussbaum. Wong. Bjornsen.

Cultural diversity. Honolulu rocks.

Utagawa's office was on the third floor. Perry was already there, positioned with her back to the door. The hair spikes were currently a tasteful magenta.

Behind the desk sat a man with wire-rimmed glasses and a hairline holding, for the moment, at midcrown. I assumed this was the intractable Dr. Utagawa.

Utagawa's face was blotchy, suggesting agitation. Or rosacea. Knowing Perry, I guessed the former.

Utagawa rose when I entered. Too quickly, as though glad of rescue. His left hand lingered on a file, palm arched, manicured fingertips spread like spider legs. Other than the folder, the desktop was empty.

We shook hands, exchanged names. Utagawa gestured to a chair beside the ME. I sat. He sat.

Utagawa aligned the file with the edge of the desk. Laced his fingers on it.

"I have been explaining to Dr. Perry, as I did to the detective with whom I first spoke, this case involves a minor. Until I have permission from a parent or guardian, or a court order, I can discuss this file only to the extent that ethics allow."

Utagawa squared his shoulders, prepared for battle.

"It's been years since you treated this kid—"

"Of course." I cut Perry off. "We understand completely, and wouldn't want you to do anything to violate doctor-patient privilege."

Utagawa's frown eased ever so slightly. He nodded, more with his eyelids than with his head.

"Please"—I smiled my most beguiling smile—"tell us what you can."

Utagawa's gaze flicked to Perry, back to me, dropped. Opening the file, he began extracting conscience-friendly facts.

"On August thirteenth, 2003, fifteen-year-old Francis Kealoha arrived by ambulance at the emergency department of The Queen's Medical Center. Kealoha had injured his left leg while surfboarding." Utagawa adjusted his glasses. Skimmed. "The ER attending took X-rays, concluded that an orthopedic consult was indicated. I was the surgeon on call."

Lots of page flipping.

"Following examination, I admitted the patient for reconstructive surgery." Utagawa's lips compressed. He was finished.

"Kealoha had suffered a distal metaphyseal fracture of the tibia?" I prompted.

"Among other injuries."

"The tibial shaft was unstable, so you managed the fracture with calcaneal pin traction, is that correct?"

"And subsequent plaster of Paris casting. There were no pin track problems, and the break progressed to complete union."

"How long did you treat Mr. Kealoha following his discharge?"

"Until removal of the cast. Though advised to continue therapy, the patient kept no appointment after that. During his final visit, he complained of slight residual subtalar joint stiffness."

"Do you have Mr. Kealoha's X-rays?"

Tight nod.

"May we compare Mr. Kealoha's left lower leg films to those taken from our unknown?"

Utagawa rose and strode to a wall-mounted light box. Perry and I followed. A large black square had already been clamped into place.

As Utagawa flipped the switch to illuminate the fluorescents, Perry withdrew her X-ray and popped it beside that which Utagawa had ordered in 2003. Utagawa straightened both.

We all looked from antemortem to postmortem and back, and back again, comparing details of bony architecture and microstructure.

Everything matched. The shape and robusticity of the malleolus. The diameter and contour of the medullary cavity. The density and orientation of the trabeculae. The number and positioning of the foramina.

The size, depth, location, and angulation of the traction pinhole.

"Oh, my." Utagawa spoke for all of us.

Minutes later, Perry and I were wending

through the parking deck. She now carried two large brown envelopes.

"Lô and Hung plan to canvass Gloria Kealoha's neighbors?" I asked. "See if Francis was known in the neighborhood?"

"They're on it as we speak. If someone recalls Kealoha dropping from the radar, maybe they'll remember a pal vanishing at the same time. A twofer would make my job a hell of a lot easier. And God knows I could use a break. My ass is in a sling over the Halona Cove closing."

"Who's unhappy?"

"Everyone."

Wishing Perry luck, I headed to my car.

There seemed little point in returning to the CIL. Ryan and Lily were in Turtle Bay.

I dialed my daughter's cell.

Katy was pumped. Her new blog post had stimulated a lot of response. She wanted to stay with it for a couple more hours, then she'd be up for some beach time.

Oahu's windward shore stretches about forty miles from Kahuku Point in the north to Makapu'u Head in the south. Lanikai lies roughly three-quarters of the way down, between Kaneohe Bay and Waimanalo Bay.

I considered a moment. Decided.

Instead of shooting west on the Pali then down, I'd take the long way home, circling the island's southernmost tip, then looping back north. The views would be spectacular and, with luck, might include whales. Or some buff boy surfers.

But *kohola* and naked *kane* weren't the only draws. The route would also take me past

Halona Cove, the inlet where Francis Kealoha's ankle had been recovered. I'd been there before but taken little note of the landscape. I was curious to view the location in person.

After buckling up, I exited the parking deck and eased into traffic.

Bypassing Waikiki, I pointed the Cobalt toward Diamond Head and slipped through a neighborhood of opulent homes. Kahala. The Lapasa family turf.

Past Kahala, the H-1 dwindles to a narrow two-laner called the Kalanianaole Highway. Highway 72. The day was Hawaiian tropic perfect. I lowered the window and let the wind play with my hair.

I followed the Kalanianaole past Hawaii Kai, Hanauma Bay, and Koko Head, stopping at every scenic marker along the way. Forty minutes out, I pulled into an overlook near Makapu'u Beach Park and got out of my car. Two dozen vehicles crammed the small lot.

To the right, the craggy cliffs of Makapu'u Point rose in the distance. To the left, tourists circled the Halona Blowhole, cameras poised, willing the capricious waterspout to make an appearance.

Far below, off the southernmost railing, lay Halona Cove, a golden crescent cradled in the palm of towering black cliffs. From Here to Eternity Beach.

Not a single greased body lay on the sand. Not a single bronzed boarder rode Halona's waves. Newly erected signs blocked the narrow path snaking down the cliffside. *Kapu!* Forbidden!

I stood a moment, wondering how Francis Kealoha and his unnamed companion had ended up in the cove. Had they picked their way down the rugged trail to swim? To fish? Had they died elsewhere, then their bodies washed in and been trapped among the rocks? Had the sharks attacked when the men were still alive? Had they scavenged following some deadly turn of events?

I had no answers. But, oddly, I felt better having visited the site.

Past Makapu'u Point, I skirted Waimanalo Bay; at three and a half miles, Oahu's longest uninterrupted stretch of sand. *Makai,* oceanward, waves thundered toward a rocky shoreline, sunlight sparking the curves of their backs. *Makau,* inland, the mountains rose cool and green, as though posing to inspire a Monet or Gauguin.

I was stealing peeks at a line of surfers when I felt a bump and the Cobalt lurched.

My foot hit the brake. My eyes jumped to the rearview mirror.

A black SUV was riding my tail. Its windshield was tinted and afternoon sun bounced from the glass.

I squinted, trying to see the vehicle's occupants. Two hulking silhouettes suggested a male driver and companion.

"Well, aloha to you too." Glaring into the rearview, I lowered my speed.

The SUV dropped back.

My eyes returned to the road.

Seconds later, I felt another bump, this one harder than the first.

Through my open window, I heard an engine roar.

Again, my eyes sought the mirror, my foot the brake.

Horrified, I saw the SUV swerve wide, then cut back and smack my driver's-side rear quarter panel.

The taillight shattered.

The Cobalt's back end shot right.

Anger fired through me, swiftly replaced by fear as the right rear tire dropped from the pavement.

Death-gripping the wheel, I fought for control.

No good. The left tire dropped.

The world hitched sideways as I spun.

The SUV was disappearing up the road to my right. A burly arm waved from the passenger-side window.

Though not a precipice, the shoreline at this point was pitched and rocky. There was no guardrail.

Surf pounded behind me.

I eased off the brake and depressed the gas pedal.

The engine whined, but the car didn't budge.

I pressed harder. The wheels spit gravel into the air.

The Cobalt began a slow backward slide.

26

HEART THUMPING, I FUMBLED AT THE SEAT belt.

The clasp slipped from my fingers.

The car continued its backward slide, angling more sharply with each foot.

Frantic, I tried again.

The metal gizmo came up, snapped back into place.

Crap!

Willing calm into my trembling fingers, I carefully raised the faceplate.

The lock clicked and the prongs slipped free.

With a lurch, the rear axle dropped. The car picked up speed.

Flinging the belt aside, I jerked up on the door handle.

Too late!

Metal crunched. The car plunged downward.

Adrenaline shot through me.

One second? Two? A thousand?

The Cobalt's trunk slammed rock, snapping my forehead into the wheel.

The car balanced a moment, front grille pointed skyward.

Thinking back, I remember vehicles pulled to the shoulder. Gawkers, eyes wide, mouths forming little round Os. At the time, none of that registered.

An eon ticked by, then, in slo-mo, the Cobalt toppled sideways into the sea.

Gravity, or the impact, sucked me down. My spine slammed the gearshift, then the passenger-side door. Somehow, I remained conscious.

Water soaked the back of my clothes, my hair. Above, through the driver's-side window, I could see sky and clouds.

Grabbing the steering wheel with my right hand and the seat back with my left, I dragged myself upward over the center console toward the driver's-side door. The car wobbled.

A voice screamed in my head.

Get out!

But how? Lower the half-open window?

No power!

Try to squeeze through?

Get stuck, you'll drown!

Already, six inches of water filled the Cobalt's down side.

Open the door?

Go!

Desperate, I lifted the handle and pushed upward with both palms.

My angle was off. Or my arms were too weak. The door wouldn't budge.

A gurgling sound filled my ears. I looked down.

Eight inches.

Think!

My eyes scanned the small space in which I was trapped. Floating sunglasses. A map. No purse.

Yes!

Yanking the keys from the ignition, I wedged the door handle in the up position. Then, panting from exertion and fear, I arm-wrapped the steering wheel and seat back, flexed my knees, and kicked out with both feet.

The door arced upward, swung back. Moving like lightning, I caught it before the lock could engage.

The passenger seat was now half submerged.

Muscling the door wide, I scrabbled through the opening and launched myself upward and outward.

Free fall, then I hit. Salt water filled my mouth and ears. Closed over my head.

I came up, gulped air. A wave broke, first battering me forward then sucking me back.

Blinking and treading, I gauged the distance to shore. Only a few feet, but the surf was gonzo.

Frantic, I swam a few strokes. Lost ground.

Don't fight the current! Go with it!

Ignoring every instinct commanding me to swim, I rolled to my back. Aware that waves come in sets, I waited for lulls. Tested.

Too deep.

Too deep.

Too deep.

Finally, my feet touched bottom.

I tried to stand, lost my footing on the algae-covered stones. A breaker threw me. Pain fired across one cheek and up one knee.

I tried again.

Again was tossed, this time pinned to a boulder. Waves pounded my body. I couldn't break free. Couldn't breathe.

From nowhere, a hand gripped my arm. Strong.

Another.

With rubber arms and legs, I pushed from the rock. Stood in water up to my waist.

Two strange faces. Male. Young.

"You OK?"

I nodded, gulping air.

"Can you walk?"

I nodded again.

"Man, lady. That was quite a show."

"*Mahalo*," I croaked.

We picked our way shoreward.

Once ashore, my rescuers insisted on calling an ambulance. I told them I was unhurt. They pressed. I refused, requested they phone the cops to report a single-car accident with no injuries.

When the young men had moved off, I sat, willing control over my trembling limbs. My pounding heart. My harried adrenals.

Again and again I asked myself what the hell just happened. How had a chain of events that started with an autoerotic death in Montreal almost gotten me killed on a highway in Hawaii? Was the accident linked to the Hemmingford pond victim? To Plato Lowery in Lumberton, North Carolina? To a case at the CIL? If so, which one? Lowery? Alvarez? Lapasa? To the fired anthropologist, Gus Dimitriadus? To the work I was doing for Hadley Perry? To the Halona Cove victim with the traction pin, Francis Kealoha? To his unknown companion? Or was the collision with the SUV just that, an accident? A case of wrong place, wrong time?

When composure returned, I moved toward the gawkers. A young woman lent me her phone. Susie. Nice hair. Very bad teeth.

Katy had no car. Danny was tied up at his arrival ceremony. Perry was being grilled by the powers that be.

Hating it, I dialed Ryan.

He went apeshit. As anticipated.

"You think these tools forced you off the road on purpose?"

"Probably. I felt three separate hits spaced apart."

"Did you recognize them?"

"No."

"The vehicle?"

"No."

"Did you get a tag number?"

"No."

"Were they drunk?"

"There wasn't time for a Breathalyzer."

"You're sure you're not hurt?"

"I'm fine." For the fourth time. "But the Cobalt is toast."

"Shit. Lily just went out for an SUP lesson."

"SUP?"

"Stand-up paddling. You float on a surf-board-looking thing and propel yourself with a paddle. Don't ask me why. Anyway, she's out of contact for another twenty minutes." Agitated breathing. "Look, I can run down there, take you to Lanikai, shoot back up here—"

"Where are you?"

"Wailea."

"That's at least an hour from here."

"Maybe I could—"

"Ryan, it's no biggie."

Actually, it was a real pain in the ass. I was soaked, my knee hurt like hell, my face was hash from the lava rock, and, obviously, I had no wheels and no wallet.

"How will you get home?"

"The cop probably has reams of forms I have to fill out. Maybe he'll take pity on me. Or order a taxi." If Samaritan Susie has left with her phone.

"Would the rental agency send someone to pick you up?"

"Right. I'm going to be *très* popular with Avis." I was dreading that call.

"The accident wasn't your fault."

"They'll be gratified to know."

"Yo?"

I turned.

The cop was shouting at me from outside his squad car. Older guy, probably fifty. Palenik. I was *très* popular with Officer Palenik, too. No ID. No license. Car resting in ten feet of water.

"Your story checks out," Palenik bellowed, to the interest of the onlookers. "How about we move this along?"

"I'll be right there," I shouted back. To Ryan. "Look, I've got to go. I'll see you at the house."

I was right. Tolstoy devoted less paper to *War and Peace* than the Honolulu PD does to a traffic accident.

I was finishing the last form when a white Ford Crown Victoria made a U-ey and slid to a stop on our side. The shoulder was empty now, save for the cruiser in which Palenik and I sat.

The Crown Vic's driver got out and walked in our direction, hitching his pants. Which were white. His untucked shirt was aloha blue and red. His left hand gripped a gym bag.

Based on size, I wasn't sure if the guy was full grown.

Palenik watched, never budging from behind the wheel.

No alarm. OK. I was cool, too.

Proximity resolved the question of age. Though standing five-three and weighing maybe 120 wet, up close our visitor's face said he was in his forties. High cheekbones and hidden upper lids suggested Asian ancestry. Turquoise eyes and ginger hair suggested input from elsewhere.

The man placed a forearm above the driver's-side window, leaned on it, and spoke to Palenik.

"Aloha, Ralph."

"Aloha, Detective."

Detective?

"How's it hanging?"

"Can't complain."

The turquoise eyes roved to me. "Dr. Brennan, I presume?"

Palenik grinned. A first. "How long you been waiting to deliver that line?"

"It's nice when you can give an old classic your own spin." Detective Nameless also grinned.

My clothes were molded to my body. My makeup was soup on my face. My hair was hanging in salty wet tangles. My car was in the drink. I was not amused.

"So, *Ralph*. We know who I am. We know who you are." My frown slid from Palenik to the face hanging outside his window. "Perhaps an introduction is in order?"

The men exchanged one of those smirky ain't-testosterone-grand glances, then Detective Nameless straightened, rounded the cruiser, and opened my door.

"Ivar Lô." A diminutive hand shot my way.

Surprise made me blurt, "Hung and—"

The hand was withdrawn. "My partner's handling a domestic dispute."

"How did you know—"

"Detective Ryan thought you might need dry clothes." Lô tossed the gym bag onto my lap. "Sorry, no undies."

I should have been grateful. Instead, I felt peeved. And embarrassed.

Lô circled back to Palenik. "Got a call from a guy on the job, homicide, Montreal. He's stuck up on the North Shore. Asked me to deliver the little lady to a rendezvous point."

Deliver the little lady?

"Her lucky day. She gets a little ride-along."

Lô smiled in my direction.

Ride-along? Not only had Ryan kicked into shining knight mode, Lô was treating me like some dimwit TV viewer with cop fantasies. The old anger switch tripped in my brain.

I reined it in. No reason to antagonize the little twerp.

"I am perfectly capable of calling a taxi."

"And paying with what?"

"I'm certain—"

"You done with that form?"

I handed the clipboard to Palenik.

"Ryan says you come with me." Lô was bending in, speaking to me.

"Does he." Tundra cold. "I do not need a ride-along, Detective Lô. I've spent a great deal of time on police investiga—"

"You can change in my car."

"I have no intention—"

"Wrecker's on the way." Palenik cut me off. Why not? Lô was doing it. "I'll deal with the tow."

"I owe you, buddy," Lô said.

Palenik started his engine. Subtle fellow, Ralph.

Clutching Lô's gym bag, I got out of the cruiser and slammed the door. Hard.

Lô pointed at the Crown Victoria. "I'll wait here."

"And where will this little ride-along take me?" Barely civil.

"Your partner's meeting us in Kalihi Valley."

Oh?

"I've got a CI says Francis Kealoha was murdered."

27

THE CROWN VIC'S INTERIOR SMELLED OF SOY sauce and garlic.

Lô drove like Ryan. Gun it. Brake. Gun it. Brake.

Or maybe it was the gallon of ocean sloshing in my gut.

Ten miles out, I felt queasy.

I suspected I was wearing Lô's clothes. The parrot shirt and waistband fit reasonably well, but the pants legs stopped three inches short of my soggy sandals.

My cheek was raw and my forehead had a lump the size of a peach pit. My hair was knotted atop my head. Poorly. I had no comb. And only tissues to remove my smeared mascara.

Fetching.

The radio hissed and spit the usual cop stuff.

Lô had donned John Lennon shades. Now and then I peeked his way.

Apparently, my curiosity wasn't all that subtle.

"Norwegian mother, Vietnamese father."

My eyes snapped front and center.

"A blessing I got the old man's height."

I glanced back at Lô.

"Scares the crap out of people." Deadpan.

"I'd have guessed it was the shirt."

"Icing on the cake."

Silence filled the car for another mile. Then, "Ryan seems like good people."

"He's a prince."

"He explained how you two roll."

I didn't reply.

"He says you're OK."

Though incapable of arranging my own transport home. I bit back a pithy retort.

Truth be told, I was more annoyed with myself for contacting Ryan than I was with Ryan for taking over. I knew the man's style. I called anyway. My bad. But what the hell? Though hiding it, I was actually pretty shaken up.

"You disappointed me," Lô said.

"I disappointed you?"

"Ryan swore the 'little lady' tag would bring a boatload of feces down on my head."

"Did he."

"The 'ride-along' bit was strictly mine."

"Icing on the cake."

"As it were."

"You should go into comedy, Detective Lô. Maybe get a job writing for Tina Fey."

"Yeah, that could work." Lô nodded slowly, as though seriously considering the suggestion. "First I'll nail the dogball who sent your car into orbit."

"You think it was deliberate?"

"I intend to find out." Lô flicked a glance my way. "You want, I could take you up to Lanikai."

"I feel much better than I look." Not true, but I'd have eaten pigeon droppings rather than admit to weakness.

Lô shrugged. "Your call."

"Tell me about Francis Kealoha."

"The kid's sister lives over by Kalihi Valley. KPT. A lovely chunk of real estate."

Kuhio Park Terrace is the largest of Hawaii's public housing projects. Kalihi Valley Homes, another big gorilla, isn't far away. Small wonder that most of the state's new immigrants start out near Kalihi Valley. I'd read that upward of eighty percent of the area's population is Asian and Pacific Islander, that probably half is under the age of twenty.

"Gloria. A fine young lady." Lô killed the radio with a jab of his thumb. "We'll drop in on Sis, then have a chat with my CI. Ryan will hook up with us there."

"Your CI will be cool with outsiders present?"

"He'll do what I tell him."

"What if Gloria's not home?"

"She's home. And by the way, you're a potted palm when I talk to these wits."

Thirty minutes later Lô parked near a high-rise complex that looked like a nightmare straight out of the seventies. Built in an era when the goal in public housing was to isolate and stack, KPT has all the warmth and charm of a barracks in the gulag.

Following a ten-minute wait, during which Lô stood calmly, arms crossed, and I paced, mourning the loss of my BlackBerry, we rode an over-crowded freight elevator to the fifteenth floor. A concrete balcony led past trash chutes jammed with ruptured supermarket and pharmacy bags. Insects swarmed the overflow—aluminum cans, bottles, soiled diapers, chicken bones, rotten produce, bunched tissues.

Lô stopped at unit 1522 and pounded with the heel of one hand.

No sound but the buzzing of flies.

He banged again, louder. "Honolulu PD. We know you're in there, Gloria."

"Go away." The muffled voice was female and faintly accented.

"That's not going to happen."

"I'm not dressed."

"We'll wait."

Seconds passed, then locks rattled, and the door swung in.

Gloria Kealoha was big. Very big. She had nutmeg skin and bottle-blond hair, and wore enough maquillage for an entire village makeover.

Pocketing his shades, Lô badged her. "Detective Lô. We spoke earlier concerning your brother."

"And I told you what I know."

"Francis is dead, Ms. Kealoha. I'm sorry for your loss."

"Life's a bitch." Gloria drew deeply on a half-smoked Camel jutting from her fingers.

"Questions remain."

"So, what? I'm going on *Jeopardy!*?" The smoke-cured laugh was completely joyless.

"I need the names of Francis's friends."

"Sorry, toots, can't do it now."

"This isn't a social call, Gloria. We talk here or we talk downtown."

"Jesus, who died and made you God?"

"My uncle."

"Fuck you."

"No thanks."

Gloria's eyes slid to me.

"Who's the haole?"

"Dr. Brennan identified your brother."

"What the fuck, girl? You stop a train with that face?"

"I'm sorry for your loss," I said.

"You some kinda coroner?" Gloria yanked on the bustier. A rosebud tattoo that had once winked from low-cut necklines appeared above the spandex as a stretched and wilted blossom.

"I need the names of your brother's friends." Lô brought the interview back on track.

"I told you. I got jack."

"Where was Francis living?"

Gloria drew on the Camel, exhaled, waved the smoke from her face with a once-manicured hand.

"I heard he went to California a couple years back. Last I knew he was still there."

"You were unaware that Francis had returned to Honolulu?"

"We weren't exactly on each other's mailing lists."

"What *can* you tell us?" Lô's voice had a "don't screw with me" edge.

"Look." Gloria took a drag, tossed, then crushed the cigarette butt with the ball of one flip-flop. "I got nothing. The kid was ten years younger than me. Growing up we lived in different worlds. By the time Frankie was six, I was off on my own. I really honest to God never knew him."

"Dig deep. Give me something."

Gloria picked a speck of tobacco from her lip, inspected then flicked it. "OK. The story of my life. When I was fourteen and Frankie was four my ma left my pa for a guy she met working as a hotel maid. Two months after, our old man bought it in a boating accident."

Gloria stopped. Lô waited, hoping she'd feel compelled to elaborate. She did.

"Ma married the creep. We got adopted. Eighteen months later the asshole split. Guess a ready-made family wasn't his thing after all."

"Who was the guy?"

"Sammy Kealoha."

Lô studied Gloria as she spoke. I studied Lô.

"Where is he now?"

"You're the detective, you tell me."

"How did your brother feel about him?"

"Hated the guy's guts."

"Why?"

"Frankie blamed Sammy for screwing up his life."

"How so?"

"Shit, you name it. For busting up the family, for us living in the projects, for Pa drowning, for Ma going freako, for the rash on his ass."

Gloria crooked a hand to her face, registered surprise at the absence of the Camel.

"After Sammy left, Ma worked when she could, drank when she couldn't. Soon as I turned sixteen I boogied for Kona to do my own thing."

"Your thing?"

Gloria crossed her arms. "Massage therapy."

"Uh-huh. Do you recall if your brother had any tattoos?"

"Sure. A fluffy French poodle right on his dick. He called it—"

"Tell me, Gloria. This massage therapy. You licensed for that?"

Lô slid a photo from one pocket. As he passed it to Gloria I recognized a close-up of the shark motif tattooed on the Halona Cove ankle.

Barely glancing at the image, Gloria handed it back.

"I'm going with Picasso."

"Did Francis ever break a leg?"

"Yeah. He did." Gloria's surprise sounded genuine. "I forgot about that."

Lô rotated one hand in a "give me more" gesture.

"He was in high school."

Again, the hand.

"Not much to tell. Frankie got drunk, went boarding, wiped out. He ended up at The Queen's. My mother whined about it in a couple of letters. She was so pissed I felt sorry for the kid and sent him a card."

For a quick moment some internal turmoil flashed in Gloria's eyes. Was gone.

"That's when Ma was still writing to me." Shoulder shrug. "Then she died."

"I'm sorry," Lô said.

"What the fuck. Bottom line, I got to thank the old gal." A meaty arm swept an arc, indicating the squalid surroundings. "Thanks to Ma I'm living the American dream."

Lô drew a card from his pocket and handed it to Gloria.

"If you think of anything, call me."

Ignoring the card, Gloria stepped back.

"And, until we get this resolved, don't travel without letting us know," Lô added.

"Well, shit busters. There goes yachting in Monte Carlo."

Gloria closed the door.

The locks reengaged.

As we drove off, I looked back.

The towers of Kuhio Park Terrace loomed bleak and hopeless against the perfect blue sky.

Like the occupants trapped in them, I thought sadly.

28

As we drove from Kuhio Park Terrace to a McDonald's across from the Kapalama Shopping Center, Lô sketched some background on the man we were about to meet. I didn't ask, wasn't sure why he felt compelled to share the information.

The CI, Fitch, was a street rat that Lô had once saved from arrest. A junkie who threatened no one, Fitch moved invisibly among the bangers, base heads, pimps, pushers, hookers, and stoners inhabiting Honolulu's underbelly. In exchange for food and money, he provided Lô with the occasional tip or insider perspective.

At four in the afternoon, the McDonald's lot held only a handful of cars.

As we crossed the asphalt, a figure in a faded yellow tee and LL Cool J rolled-up sweats crossed our path and pushed through the door before us. The brim of a way-too-large cap hid the person's face, but hairy calves suggested male gender.

My instincts told me we'd connected with Fitch.

Glancing left, then right, the CI disappeared

into a booth at the rear of the restaurant. Like Lô, he was short and wiry. I guessed his age at midtwenties.

Lô went to the counter. I followed.

Lô ordered a Big Mac, fries, and two Cokes.

I ordered a Diet Coke. The girl looked at me oddly, but said nothing.

Lô paid. As we waited, the smell of frying fat kicked my nausea up a notch.

When our food was ready, Lô carried the tray to the rear booth. I sat down and slid to the wall. Lô dropped into the space beside me.

The CI's eyes rolled up below their bill, checked the restaurant, me, then settled on Lô. The irises were brown-black, the whites the same dull yellow as the tee.

"Who's the chick?"

"Myrna Loy."

"What's she doing here?"

"Don't worry about it, Fitch."

"What the fuck happened to her?"

"Ninjas."

Lô removed two drinks, gave me one, then pushed the tray forward. Using both hands, Fitch yanked it to his chest.

"I don't like it." The table edge started tapping the wall. Under it, Fitch's left knee was bouncing like a piston.

"Tough," Lô said.

"This isn't our deal." Fitch's eyes did another sweep. He ran a hand along his jawline.

"My party." Lô pointed to the wall. "Move over. I'm expecting more guests."

Fitch opened his mouth, reconsidered, lurched

left. All the man's movements were quick and jerky, like those of a crab caught in a net.

Lô and I sipped.

Fitch dived into his burger.

Lô pulled a small spiral from his pocket and flipped the cover. Clicked a ballpoint to readiness.

As Fitch ate, wilted shreds of lettuce dropped to the burger's discarded wrapper. A hunk of tomato. A glob of cheese.

"It's my health we're risking here." As Fitch spoke, chewed hunks of beef tumbled in his mouth.

"You're the one eats that garbage," Lô said.

"You know what I mean." Grease coated the CI's lips and chin.

"How about finishing that? Watching you's not doing my gut no favors."

Fitch was squeezing a third packet of ketchup onto his fries when something caught his attention behind our backs.

Lô and I turned.

Ryan was walking in our direction.

"Who the hell's this?" Fitch hissed.

"William Powell."

"He a cop?" Fitch either missed or ignored Lô's second Walk of Fame joke.

"Yeah, Fitch. He's a cop."

"A narc?" The left knee was pumping gangbusters.

"Aloha," Ryan said.

"Aloha," Lô and I answered.

Ryan tensed on seeing my face. He made no comment.

Scowling, Fitch shrank farther left.

Ryan slid into the booth.

Eyes down, Fitch jerked the tray sideways and continued shoving fries into his mouth.

Lô tested the ballpoint with sharp, quick strokes.

"So what have you got?" he asked.

Fitch swallowed, sucked his soda, snatched up and bunched a paper napkin. His eyes crawled to Ryan, to me, to Lô.

"This is fucked-up, man."

Lô didn't answer.

"Word gets out—"

"It won't."

Fitch jabbed his chest. "It's my ass—"

"If this is too much for you, I've got things to do."

"I know how cops work." Fitch's tone had gone high and whiny. "Use people and leave 'em on the street like gum."

The balled napkin hit the tray and bounced toward Lô.

"Calm the fuck down, Fitch."

The CI slumped back and crossed his arms. "Shit."

A woman nosed a stroller to the table beside our booth. She looked about sixty. I couldn't see the baby, wondered if it was hers. Weird, but I did.

Fitch's eyes jumped to the woman. Again circled the restaurant.

"I don't want to be celebrating a birthday here." Lô made no effort to mask his impatience. "You got something for me or not?"

"Cash?" Fitch asked.

Lô nodded.

Leaning forward, the CI placed both forearms on the tabletop and began worrying the sides of the tray with his thumbs.

"OK. About six months back your guy shows up—"

"Francis Kealoha?"

"Yeah, yeah."

"Shows up from where?"

"California. San Fran, I think. Maybe LA. That part I'm not sure."

"This better be solid."

"Yeah, yeah. Kealoha shows up with this dude called Logo."

"You know Logo's real name?"

Fitch shook his head.

Lô made a note in his spiral. Then, "You're sure this was Francis Kealoha?"

"Yeah, yeah. We grew up together at KPT. It was him."

"Go on."

Fitch's thumbs flipped up, dropped. "That's it. Frankie and Logo show up together. A few months later both drop off the radar."

"Give me some dates."

"I look like their travel agent?"

Lô's glare could have reversed global warming.

"OK. I'm thinking I stopped seeing them maybe three, four weeks ago."

Lô turned to me. The time frame worked, given the condition of the remains from Halona Cove. I nodded.

"Where was Kealoha living?"

"I heard up at Waipahu."

Lô made a note on his pad. Then, "Go on."

"That's it."

"Then your bony ass pays for that burger."

Seconds passed. A full minute.

Fitch's thumbs made soft, scratchy sounds against the edge of the tray.

"What I got's worth more than a nifty."

"Don't you read the papers? It's a bad year for bonuses."

Fitch cocked his chin at me, then Ryan.

"I got risk here."

Lô considered a moment. Then, "If it's good, we'll see."

Beside us, the baby began to cry.

Fitch's eyes again danced his surroundings.

"Word is Kealoha was doing business where he shouldn't have."

"Dealing what?"

"Coke, weed. The usual."

"Who'd he cut in on?"

"L'il Bud."

Lô's nod indicated familiarity with the name. "Go on."

Fitch inhaled. Exhaled. Pulled his nose. Leaned even closer to Lô.

"Street says L'il Bud ordered a hit."

"Street naming a doer?"

"Pinky Atoa. Ted Pukui."

Lô scribbled the names. Again, his demeanor suggested knowledge of the players.

"How'd it go down?"

"I heard they got shot up at Makapu'u Point."

I pictured the craggy outcrop. The shark-ravaged flesh recovered from Halona Cove.

I remembered Perry's tale of the suicidal poet from Perth.

Cold fingers tickled my spine.

"You got questions, Doc?"

I realized Lô was addressing me. For the first time, I spoke to his CI.

"How old was Logo?"

Fitch regarded me blankly.

"Roughly. Twenty? Forty? Sixty?"

"Shit, I don't know. Maybe a little older than Kcaloha."

"Describe him."

"Dark hair, dark eyes. Body by beluga."

"Meaning?"

"The guy was big."

"How big?"

"Six feet, maybe three hundred pounds. Typical Hamo. That's why they hung together. Those guys are thick."

It took a minute for the comment to register.

"Kealoha is a Hawaiian name," I said.

"That got changed."

"Changed?" An idea began to materialize in my mind.

"When Kealoha's old lady come here."

"Came here from where?"

"Tafuna."

I remembered Gloria's crack about the American dream. I thought she'd been referring to Honolulu. She'd meant the United States.

"Before that it was something else," Fitch said.

I looked from one detective to the other.

Lô's expression suggested his brain was connecting the same dots as mine.

A subtle angling of the brows told me Ryan was not. To his credit, he asked no questions.

"May I see Perry's autopsy photo?" I managed to keep my voice calm.

Lô pulled the five-by-seven from his pocket and laid it on the table.

I studied the image.

There were the black and red swirls within the half-sickle form. There were the filigreed strips extending outward from the sickle's two sides, converting the whole into a *tapuvae*, an ankle bracelet tattoo.

And there were the three loopy things riding the bracelet's upper edge. The elements possibly added later. The two backward Cs flanking a U.

I knew what they were.

"Paper and pen?" I felt totally jazzed.

Lô passed me his ballpoint and a page from his notebook.

Positioning the paper's lower edge along the truncated upper border of the little loopy things, I continued the line of each C upward and to the left, then swooped each right, converting the backward Cs to Ss.

Lô watched without comment.

I closed the top of the U, converting it to an O. SOS.

Lô regarded my handiwork a moment, then reached for his phone.

I rotated the photo and drawing so Ryan could see.

"*Tabarnac*," he said.

29

PHONE TO HIS EAR, LÔ HURRIED OUTSIDE. Fitch tracked him like a puppy hoping for a treat.

We waited.

I sensed Ryan assessing my injuries.

Three middle school girls giggled and elbow-shoved their way to the bathroom, each carrying a shoulder-slung pack.

The woman beside us finished eating and rolled off with her baby.

Fitch watched in fidgety silence.

Finally, Ryan nodded to someone over my shoulder.

"He's back."

We rose and joined Lô in the parking lot.

"My partner's going to contact California, see what they've got on Kealoha, have them run the street name Logo through their database on gangs."

"Remember, no blowback on me."

Lô ignored his CI.

"Later Hung and I will haul Atoa and Pukui to the bag."

"Look, I gotta go." Fitch was shifting his

weight from foot to foot. There wasn't much to shift.

Yanking his wallet from a back pocket, Lô counted out five twenties.

Fitch grabbed for the bills.

Lô pulled them back. "Keep in touch?"

"Yeah, yeah."

Lô extended his hand.

Fitch snatched the money and skittered out of sight.

"Weird dude," Ryan said.

"Guy's a tweaker."

"It's all about the intel."

"Yeah." Lô bounced a glance off me. "SOS. Sons of Samoa." The faintest smile played his mouth. "You're right. The little lady's not bad."

"She has her moments," Ryan said.

No way the little lady was getting sucked into that. I said nothing.

"A gang tat." Lô slowly wagged his head. "I missed it."

"Honolulu having problems?" Ryan asked.

"Until recently I'd have said no. We've got gangs, sure. The Samoans run together, sure. Everyone acts bad-ass, sure. But mostly the violence is Jets and Sharks type of crap." Lô slid the John Lennons onto his nose. "Lately things have escalated."

"How?" I asked.

"Not long ago a street tough named Lingo got capped in Chinatown. A week later, there's a stabbing."

"Retaliation?"

Lô nodded. "Both vics were Samoan. A witness to the stabbing claimed one of the doers shouted 'KPT SOS.'"

"Kuhio Park Terrace. Sons of Samoa," I translated for Ryan.

"Could be a turf war," Ryan said.

"Two punks from Oakland are going down for the shooting," Lô said. "We suspect West Coast traffickers are heading this way."

"And the locals are opposed," Ryan said.

"And not rolling over."

"If that's the case, Fitch's intel skews pretty good."

"Yeah," Lô said. "It does."

At six, Ryan and I were still threading through traffic. Slogging, really.

I'd used Ryan's phone to call Katy, explained about the accident, and told her that we were on our way home.

She'd demanded details. Sidestepping most questions, I'd assured her that I was fine. She'd offered to throw something together for dinner.

I'd then given Ryan an overview of Lô's conversation with Gloria Kealoha.

"But, until Fitch, you never made the Samoa connection," he said.

"No."

"What pulled the trigger?"

"Hamo. Tafuna. Waipahu," I said.

"Klaatu. Barada. Nikto," he said.

"What?"

"*The Day the Earth Stood Still*?"

I was lost.

"Buttercup." Feigned disappointment. "Nineteen fifty-one? Michael Rennie and Patricia Neal? Neal said those three words to Gort and the Earth was saved. Never mind. You're probably distracted by my good looks and charm. How'd you get Sons of Samoa out of Fitch's account?"

"Three things. First, he used the term *Hamo*. That's slang for Samoan."

"I thought it was a lunch meat that paired well with cheese."

I ignored that.

"Samoan is a member of the Polynesian language family. Some of the other dialects substitute the letter *h* for the Samoan *s*. So Samoa becomes Hamoa."

"Thus Hamo. I didn't know that."

"Second, Tafuna is a city in American Samoa. Fitch said that's where the Kealohas came from."

"Except back home they weren't the Kealohas." Ryan was quiet a moment. "How was a woman with two minor dependents and no job or job skills allowed to immigrate to the U.S.?"

"Though not citizens, people born in American Samoa are American nationals, free to travel throughout the United States and its territories."

"OK. Third?"

"Waipahu. There are a couple of fairly good-sized Samoan communities on Oahu, one near Kalihi Valley, another up at Waipahu."

"Kealoha lived at Waipahu."

"Voilà."

"But how'd you make the leap to Sons of Samoa?"

"Remember that kid I ID'd about a year and a

half back? The one with the full-body tattoos?"

"The Latin King stabbed outside the bar in Sainte-Anne-de-Bellevuc?"

"Yes. I spent hours researching gang tattoos for that case."

"Gold star, Brennan."

Before I could say thanks, Ryan executed one of his head-spinning topic swaps.

"Tell me about the crash."

"I did that."

"Do it again."

"A car pulled to my bumper, tapped me once, tapped me a second time, went to pass, and swerved into my left rear. I cut the wheel—"

"What kind of car?"

"A black SUV."

"Year? Make?"

"It happened too fast."

"How many occupants?"

"Two. I think. The glass was tinted. I couldn't really see."

"Male or female?"

"Yes."

Ryan gave me a look that said he wasn't amused.

"The passenger was definitely male," I said.

"How do you know?"

"He waved."

Ryan let a few beats pass. Then, "Lô doesn't think it was an accident."

Nor did I. But I hadn't wanted to consider the implications.

"What's his thinking?" I asked.

"That it was done on purpose." Sarcastic.

"Fine," I said. "Devil's advocate. Who would want to hurt me or at least frighten me?"

"Let's start with the improbable and work our way in."

Ryan drummed agitated fingers on the wheel.

"Here's one. You angered a local mafioso by insisting he submit a sample of his DNA."

"Nickie Lapasa? That's ridiculous."

"Really? How did Lapasa's old man kick-start his career?"

"No one ever proved the hit-and-run—"

"OK. How about this one? A wacko anthropologist thinks you cost him his job."

"Dimitriadus may be nuts but I doubt he's violent."

"He threw an elbow at you."

Remembering the scene at JPAC, I had to admit, Dimitriadus was upset.

"And, call me crazy, but you're about to ID two people murdered in a drug war."

"Allegedly murdered."

Again, Ryan's look was withering.

"Besides, no one knows that," I added.

"Right. Street gangs are notorious for their lousy communication networks."

"Here's one." It came out more snappish than I'd intended. Or not. "I crossed paths with a couple of drunks."

"Uh-huh," Ryan said.

I expected the usual snarkfest from our daughters. To my surprise, Katy and Lily were together in the kitchen. Tool was blasting from the sound system and both were singing "Vicarious" into wooden spoon mikes.

On seeing us, Katy rushed mc.

"Oh my God!"

Lily stared, mouth open, spoon frozen before it.

"You should see the other guy," I said, disengaging from my daughter's embrace.

No one laughed.

"What's for dinner?" I asked, perky as Gidget.

"You said it was a glorified fender bender." Katy's tone was stern. "A fluke that the car got wrecked."

"I'm fine," I said. For the umpteenth time that day.

"If you were fine you wouldn't be wearing that shirt."

"I like birds."

"Your hair is wet. Your face is a train wreck."

"What's that fabulous smell?"

"We made marinara sauce," Lily said. "And shrimp."

"Allow me to change, feed me pasta, and I'll tell you anything." I raised both hands like a spy ready to crack.

Katy watched with suspicion as I climbed the stairs.

Minutes later I was back in a clean shirt and shorts.

I provided the bare essentials. Sans mention of Lô's theory. Swerve. Bump. Plunge. Rescue. In this version the water was two feet deep.

When I finished, Katy commenced one of her typical cross-examinations.

"I thought you were going to JPAC."

"I did. Happily, everything's wrapped up there. What did you do today?"

"What were you doing on the southern end of the island?"

"After JPAC I met with the medical examiner."

"About the guys eaten by sharks?"

"Sharks?" Lily's eyes went wide.

I glanced a question at Ryan.

"Oh, yeah," he said. "Definitely tell her."

"A few days back, body parts were recovered from a cove on the southern end of the island. The ME asked me for help. I think we've established who the two men were."

"You can share a little more detail than that." Ryan's eyes were hard on his daughter.

"The victims were probably members of a gang called Sons of Samoa. They may have been murdered and thrown off a cliff."

"For dealing drugs," Ryan added.

"Who were they?" Katy asked, tone a bit gentler.

"Sorry, sweetie. I can't tell you that."

"How old were these men?" Now and then Lily's island childhood sounds in the lilt of her speech. It did so in that question.

"Your age." Again, Ryan spoke straight to his daughter.

"It happened at the southern end of the island?" Katy guessed.

"Makapu'u Point. I finished early with the ME, and decided to take the scenic route home." Rueful smile. It hurt. "Bad choice."

Katy's eyes met Lily's. I was clueless as to the message that passed between them.

"Hey, this sauce is great," I said. "Whose recipe?"

"It came from a jar," Lily said.

"Then, hats off to the shoppers." I raised my glass.

Only Ryan tapped my drink with his.

"Listen," I said. "Look at the upside. We'll get a better set of wheels."

Katy opined that the Cobalt was a piece of crap. Lily agreed.

Lily said I should soak in a hot bath. Katy seconded her suggestion.

Katy volunteered to do the dishes. Lily said she'd help.

Lily offered to drive Katy to her surfing lesson in the morning. Katy accepted.

Ryan and I exchanged glances. Huh?

I did take the bath.

While submerged in wisteria-scented bubbles up to my chin, I reviewed my efforts since arriving in Honolulu.

I'd wrecked a car. Fine. Point against me.

I'd determined that Spider Lowery hadn't been killed in Vietnam. The news would shatter Plato Lowery's world, but a wrong would be righted.

I'd identified the man buried in Lumberton, North Carolina. Forty years after dying in a chopper crash, Luis Alvarez would finally go home.

I'd located the remains of Xander Lapasa. Though not exactly gracious, the Lapasa family would also get closure.

I'd helped Hadley Perry close the Halona Cove

cases. And open a beach. Perhaps Logo's and Kealoha's killers would be brought to justice.

And Lily and Katy were getting along.

Lily was right. The hydroaromatherapy relaxed my muscles and calmed my nerves. I emerged from the tub feeling pretty damn good.

30

I AWOKE TO THE FEELING I WAS BEING WATCHED.

Opened my eyes.

The room was shadowy gray. Through the balcony door I saw pewter clouds skimming the ocean.

The clock said 8:40.

"That's going to be one sick scab."

I rolled to my back.

Katy was standing beside my bed.

Scooching to my bum, I stuck a pillow behind my head and patted the mattress.

Katy dropped down beside me. I noticed she was holding a paper.

"You're awake early," I said.

"I may have screwed up."

"Oh?"

"You know I started a blog last winter, right?"

"Right."

"Somehow it got linked over to some biggies, like BuzzFeed and BlogBlast, even the Huffington Post. I can't believe the number of hits I'm getting and the number of people posting comments."

"That's great."

Katy sighed.

"Isn't it?"

"Lately I've been blogging for Coop. I wanted to talk about the stupidity of war, of young people dying far from home, in foreign countries, you know."

"OK." I had no idea where she was going.

"It went totally viral. But people were all over the map, talking about kids getting killed by drunk drivers, shot in drive-bys, shot by cops." Katy twisted a strand of hair as she spoke. "Then, two days ago, this whole new thread started. About gangs."

Uh-oh.

"I mean, there must have been two hundred posts about kids dying as a result of gang violence."

Katy ran the strand of hair across her upper lip. Drew it back. Repeated the gesture.

"Do you know how many gangs there are in Los Angeles alone?" Her tone reflected shock and dismay.

"Tell me you didn't write about the case I discussed last night."

Nothing.

"Did you?"

"You never said not to." Defensive. "And I didn't use any names. I couldn't. I didn't know any."

"Oh, Katy."

"They were young, someone killed them. It's sad, Mom. Even if they were drug dealers."

"Did you mention me?"

"No." Quick. "But I did say the murder happened here."

"Did you identify the gang?"

Katy nodded.

Shit!

"This morning I found this posted to my site."

She handed me a printout of the entry.

> YOU TELL CRASY LADY DOC SHE FUCC MIGHTY GANG MIGHTY GANG FUCC HER. AND ALL ENEMIES. MIGHTY GANG SOS. SONS OF SAMOA CRIP. FUCC W SOS YOU DIE!!!

My heart threw in extra beats. I forced myself to keep smiling, willed myself to stay calm for Katy's sake.

"Lady doc. Could that be you?" Katy asked.

I put an arm around her shoulders. "The Internet's full of loons."

Some of whom kill, I thought.

"Could it be a threat?"

"More of a rant."

"How could they know? About you, I mean."

"Relax." I decided to low-key it for now. The posting was obscure and almost illitcrate. What wcre the chances it was related to yesterday's collision?

"I feel awful. I never thought—"

"Hey."

We both looked up. Lily was in the doorway wearing a bikini top and cutoff jeans. Exceptionally short ones.

"So." I patted Katy's leg. "You have a surf lesson. Then what do you ladies have planned for today?"

"Miss Priss has agreed to a day at the beach. Going to risk burning her skinny black butt."

"At least mine doesn't go all freckly-ass red."

Katy gave a thumbs-up. Lily returned it. Both were smiling.

Whoa.

"Where's your dad?" I asked Lily.

"In the kitchen."

"Serving breakfast?"

She nodded.

"Let's eat," I said.

We were finishing Ryan's coconut-mango pancakes when the landline rang.

"I'll get it." Lily fired from her chair.

"Who's taken possession of Lily?" I asked.

"What? She's decided she likes it here," Katy said.

I looked at Ryan. His eyes were fixed on his daughter. In them I saw love. And something else. Hope? Suspicion? Fear?

"It's some guy named LaManche." Lily held the handset pressed to her chest.

"I'll take it," I said, surprised.

Ryan raised questioning brows. Why would the chief be calling from Montreal? I raised mine in reply. No idea.

"Thanks for breakfast. Before you take off, there's something I'd like to ask you about."

"I'm not taking off," Ryan said.

Lily handed me the phone.

"*Bonjour.*" I rose and moved outside to the lanai. "*Comment ça va?*"

"*Sacrifice,* she lives. Temperance, you no longer return my calls?"

"I lost my BlackBerry."

I told LaManche about the wreck.

"You are unharmed?"

"I'm good."

"*Bon*. Then you have learned a valuable lesson."

"Don't drive too close to shoulders hugging the sea?"

"An SUV trumps a Cobalt every time."

"Noted. What's up?"

"Bad news."

"I hate it when people open a conversation with that."

"I did not. I complained about you going incommunicado."

"What's the bad news?"

"I received results from the DNA section on the gentleman found floating in the Hemmingford pond."

"John Lowery. Spider."

"Apparently not."

"What?"

"According to the report, it is not Monsieur Lowery."

"What?" I was hearing LaManche's words, but their meaning was not sinking in.

"The sequencing did not match."

"The sample was too degraded?"

"The sample was degraded, but the technicians were able to amplify. The results were exclusionary."

"How did the LSJML get a comparative sample? Plato Lowery refused to submit a swab."

"Local law enforcement in North Carolina

was very cooperative. A sheriff whose name eludes me was particularly accommodating."

"Beasley?" Of course. I knew this. I was in denial.

"*Oui. C'est ça.* Sheriff Beasley recalled that John Lowery's mother was hospitalized for a short period before her death. He found that the hospital had retained pathology slides. One specimen was sent to AFDIL. At our request, another was sent to the LSJML DNA section. Extraction was successful, and testing shows that the Hemmingford victim is not Harriet Lowery's son."

"But the sample was degraded."

"Temperance, they have confidence in the results. The sequencing does not match."

The naughty-nurse floater was not Spider Lowery? How was that possible? Then who was he?

Did the exclusion mean I was wrong about the man buried in the Gardens of Faith Cemetery in Lumberton in 1968? Was that man Spider Lowery and not Luis Alvarez, after all?

And what about Xander Lapasa? We still didn't know why Lapasa was found wearing Spider Lowery's dog tag.

"—sorry. I know this is not what you hoped to hear."

"No, sir. It's not. But thanks for letting me know."

I was standing with the phone in my hand when Ryan came up behind me.

"Bad news?"

I shared LaManche's news on the DNA exclusion.

"What about the FBI fingerprint match?"

"Yeah."

"*Tabarnac.*"

"Yeah."

I was about to tell Ryan about Katy's blog when his cell phone sounded.

Katy and Lily chimed in from the kitchen.

Sunny day. Keeping the clouds away.

"Ryan here." Waving down the giggles.

"Uh-huh."

Ryan patted the front of his golf shirt. Found no pocket. Pantomimed writing.

I delivered pen and paper from the counter.

"OK. Shoot."

He scribbled what looked like two names. A long pause followed.

"When?"

Pause.

"What's the address?"

Ryan jotted something else.

"We'll be there.

"That was Lô." Jamming the phone onto his belt. "For the past three years Francis Kealoha has been running with an SOS gang operating out of Oakland. Went by Francis Olopoto."

"Probably his original Samoan name."

"Logo's a guy named George Faalogo."

"Also a Samoan name."

"Ted Pukui's in the wind, but they've bagged Pinky Atoa. They'll let him cool his heels awhile, then grill him. Hadley Perry is otherwise engaged. Since you're her rep on the case, Lô invited us to observe."

"Is that standard here?"

"How would I know?" Ryan lowered his voice. "Maybe the little fellow has designs on your awesome little ass."

I narrowed my eyes and cocked my head in the direction of our daughters.

"Then why would he invite you?" I whispered.

"He knows I have first dibs."

My eye roll was of Olympic quality.

"Is Atoa being charged?" I asked.

"No. The guy owns a pit bull that's supposed to be mean as a snake. Gata."

"I think *gata* means snake."

"Apparently Gata killed some neighbor's Chihuahua. Atoa thinks he's being hauled in because of that. Lô and Hung will focus on the dog for a while, then spring Kealoha and Faalogo."

"I'll be ready in ten."

We took Ryan's rental car, a Pontiac G6. As he drove, I used his cell to phone Danny. First off, I told him about the crash.

"Why didn't you call right away?"

"You were at your arrival ceremony."

Next I told him about LaManche's report. He was as shocked as I was.

"You've got to be kidding."

"Wish I were. Have you heard from AFDIL concerning the remains I exhumed in Lumberton?"

"They said no way on nuclear DNA, doubted they'd even get mitochondrial. Besides, there's no Alvarez maternal to provide a sample for comparison. Looks like we can kiss that avenue good-bye."

"LaManche said Harriet Lowery's specimens

were pretty degraded. I think it's worth trying to locate another source."

"Will your lab foot the bill for a second round of tests?"

"Leave that to me."

"Should I ask Plato one more time?"

"Got any other ideas?"

"I'll make the call," Danny said.

"What a mess," I said.

"A real conundrum."

Within the hour things would really hit the slag heap.

31

Mist coated the windshield as Ryan and I drove into town. All the way, he flicked the wipers on, then off. On. Off.

The Honolulu PD is headquartered in a white stone building parked on Beretania Street like a big square ship. Though mere blocks from the Botox, designer labels, and brightly striped umbrellas of Waikiki Beach, its denizens hail from a different world.

Lô's directions sent us to the third floor. We rode an elevator packed tight with the usual assortment of clerks, detectives, and uniformed cops checking in or out, carrying sealed evidence bags, or sneaking off to wherever it is they cloister to smoke.

The homicide squad was a large open room filled with desks shoved into clusters of twos, threes, and fours. Lô and his partner occupied a solo pair at the back.

Like Lô, Hung was a surprise. Tall and muscular, she had bone white skin and glossy black hair chopped off at the ears. Her chestnut eyes contained colored flecks that sparked like chips of glass from the sea. Only a subtly humped nose kept the woman from being a stunner. I liked that she hadn't changed it.

Lô made introductions. Hung's first name was Leila.

We all shook hands. Lô dragged over chairs and we sat.

Hung went straight to the point. I liked that, too.

"Back in the eighties the Sons of Samoa was mostly a social group. Later it became a full-fledged gang in Hawaii. SOS died down for a while, then revived around 1998 as a prison gang called USO Family or USO, United Samoan Organization. It's complicated, but *uso* can mean brother in Samoan."

"If you're male, referring to a male sibling," I said. "It can also mean sister, if you're female referring to a female sibling."

Hung looked at me. Behind us, a phone rang. Someone answered.

"She's an anthropologist," Ryan said.

"Sure she is." Hung continued. "At one time USO was only Samoan, but intel says the group is now mixed race and has approximately two hundred members in Hawaii."

"USO is pretty much restricted to our correctional facilities," Lô added.

"Kealoha and Faalogo were SOS," Ryan said.

"Right. SOS spread from Hawaii to California, Utah, and Washington State. On the mainland SOS are usually Crips."

Though I didn't interrupt, I must have looked confused.

"The Crips aren't one gang, but an identity which other gangs adopt. Crip gangs in other cities can actually fashion themselves by regional cultural indicators that have nothing to do with Los Angeles."

"I didn't know that," I said, trying to make up for my earlier smarty-pants offering.

Hung consulted a notepad.

"According to L.A. County Probation Department statistics, in 1972 there were about eight Crip gangs. By 1978 that number had risen to forty-five. By '82 there were one hundred and nine, and by the late nineties, according to Streetgangs-dot-com, there were one hundred and ninety-nine individual Crip gangs active in L.A. County."

"Jesus," I said.

"Crip growth seems to have stabilized in Los Angeles, even declined in certain areas undergoing demographic change. But copycat Crip gangs are springing up in other parts of California, the U.S., and abroad."

"*Tabarnac.*" Ryan shook his head.

Hung looked at me, this time in question.

"It means 'Oh, my,'" I said.

"Stateside, SOS are known as bad actors," Lô said. "Intimidation, extortion, drug rip-offs, even murder."

I heard a door open, voices behind us.

Hung took in the room with a quick sweep. Then the sea-glass eyes returned to us.

"What we're seeing is mainland Samoans making a move for Hawaiian distribution."

"Of?" Ryan asked.

"Mostly coke and weed. Some meth."

"Who's the local majordomo?"

"A guy named Gilbert T'eo."

"Street name L'il Bud," Lô added.

Hung's desk phone rang. She picked up, turned a shoulder to speak to the caller.

"Where's T'eo's home base?" Ryan asked Lô.

"Right now, Halawa. That's a medium security prison here on Oahu."

"Atoa and Pukui work for T'eo?" I asked.

Lô waggled a hand. "Close enough."

Hung cradled the receiver. "The system's up. Shall we see what Mr. Atoa has to say?"

The interview room was what I expected, a gloomy little box devoid of whimsy or warmth. The walls were noxious green, the tile scuffed and scratched by generations of nervous feet.

A gray metal desk occupied the center of the small space. One straight-back wooden chair faced two others across the battered desktop. A wall-mounted phone and camera were the room's only other embellishments.

Ryan and I observed via a video screen and speaker down the hall. The image was grainy black-and-white, the sound tinny, the dialogue occasionally overridden by background noise.

Pinky Atoa looked like a tall, skinny twelve-year-old. He wore the usual gangsta costume of crotch-hanging jeans, enormous athletic tee, and oversize cap. His high-top red sneakers beat a steady tattoo on the floor.

Obviously, Hung and Lô had done casting before our arrival. Lô played bad cop, Hung played good.

Hung introduced herself, her partner. Atoa kept his gaze on his hands.

"This interview will be recorded for your protection as well as ours."

Hung next spoke for the benefit of the record, stating the date, time, and place, and identifying herself, her partner, and the interviewee. Throughout, Atoa alternated between chewing a thumbnail and drumming the desktop.

"You nervous about something, Pinky?" Lô asked.

"I want my dog."

"That pit's one nasty piece of work."

"It was self-defense."

"The Chihuahua weighed three pounds."

"The thing came at him."

"Must have been terrifying."

"Shit." Exaggerated head wag. "Don't you guys ever give up?"

"Your neighbor filed a complaint."

"The whore needs to get laid."

"We just want the facts, Mr. Atoa." Hung, the voice of reason.

For several minutes Hung asked questions about the dog attack. Atoa seemed to relax slightly.

"So, what? I gotta pay a fine? No biggie. I got cash."

"It's not that easy. Things look bad for Gata."

"What the hell's that mean?"

Both detectives gazed at him sadly.

"Get the fuck outta here."

The bony fingers recommenced dancing.

"Honolulu has laws to protect citizens against dangerous pets," Lô said.

"That little shit dog's been dead a month. Why's the bitch coming at me now?"

"Perhaps she's been moving through the stages of grief."

Another head wag. "That's good. You're funny, Mr. Policeman."

"I try."

"So, what? The cunt wants a new pup?"

Lô shrugged.

"What the fuck?" Atoa spread his hands. Smiled. "I'll buy her a puppy."

"Doesn't really solve the problem with Gata, now, does it?" Lô.

"Meaning?"

"Start picking out an urn."

Atoa exploded from the table. His chair hit the floor with a crack.

Lô shot to his feet.

"No way you're killing my dog, you bastard." Atoa's hands were bunched into fists.

Hung spoke in a tone meant to be soothing. "Let's all calm down. Mr. Atoa, would you like something to drink?"

Atoa's eyes went shrewd. "What? So you can take my DNA? I'm not stupid."

"Why would we want your DNA, Pinky?" Lô's voice was deadly.

"Fuck you."

"Please, Mr. Atoa." Hung circled the table and righted the chair. "Sit."

Atoa held a moment, then, "This is so fucked."

Atoa dropped into the seat and thrust out both legs. The red sneakers started winging from side to side.

Lô and Hung exchanged a look above Atoa's head.

"Here we go," I said to Ryan.

Hung spoke as she returned to her seat.

"Perhaps something can be worked out concerning Gata."

Lô shot his partner a look.

Hung gestured "hold on" with one hand.

Lô crossed his arms in annoyance.

"Quid pro quo. That means you help us, we help you."

"I know what it means," Atoa snapped.

"Good. You can help Gata. Who knows? Maybe yourself."

"I'm listening." Atoa was working the thumbnail, avoiding eye contact.

Another look passed between Lô and Hung.

"George Faalogo." Lô paused. "Frankie Kealoha."

No reaction.

"You know those guys, Pinky?"

Atoa shook his head.

"How about Ted Pukui?"

"Who?" Mumbled.

"Look at me." Lô's tone was sharp.

Atoa didn't budge.

"Look at me!"

Atoa's head snapped up. For the first time I saw fear in his eyes.

"How about Gilbert T'eo?"

"Everyone knows L'il Bud."

"Word is you and Pukui assisted T'eo with a business problem."

Atoa's gaze flicked to Hung. Found no support.

"Faalogo and Kealoha." Lô hammered on. "Makapu'u Point."

"What the fuck are you talking about?"

"Wasn't much left when the sharks finished, but we got enough."

"This is bullshit."

"Is it?"

Atoa licked his lips.

"How much you love that dog, Pinky?"

Atoa regarded Lô with a look of undiluted hatred.

"You claim to be smart. Know all about DNA. I'm sure you watch *CSI* and *Law and Order.* Maybe *Bones,* but that may be over your head. Surprising you and your pal got sloppy with things like prints and bullets. You know. Clues?"

A typical cop bluff. Lô wasn't actually saying the police had fingerprints or ballistics evidence.

"We're providing a chance here, Pinky. Work with us, we'll try to help you out."

"I ain't messing with L'il Bud. You think I'm nuts?"

"How old are you, kid?"

Atoa didn't reply.

"How old are you?" Lô barked.

"Eighteen."

"I'm thinking your buddy is a wee bit older."

"Pukui's twenty-nine," Hung said. "Been in the box four times."

"I'm going to describe a hypothetical, then ask you something," Lô said. "You know what a hypothetical is?"

"I ain't stupid."

"We'll see." Lô paused, as though framing his

thoughts. "We got a kid who knows nothing and we got a guy who's been through the system. We offer both the same opportunity. The catch is, only the first taker gets the deal."

Another bluff, implying Pukui was also in custody.

"Here's the question. A two-parter. Can you handle that?"

Atoa said nothing.

"Who rolls over? Who takes the fall?"

Atoa squeezed his lids shut and shook his head.

Lô waited.

Opening his eyes, Atoa leaned forward. "What you're asking can get me killed."

"Bad news for the dog," Lô said.

Atoa ran a hand across his face and threw back his head. His windpipe bulged like a corrugated tube.

Lô and Hung looked at each other, expressions tense. The kid's first utterance would indicate if they'd won or lost.

At last Atoa sat forward. He looked at Hung a long moment, then, "I talk to you, not him."

"No problem. But he stays here."

"All I did was drive."

"If true, that will work in your favor." Hung kept her voice neutral.

"You'll look out for my dog?"

"I'm going to read you your rights now, Pinky."

"Shit. Shit. Shit."

Hung read from a small card. When she'd finished, "Do you understand what I just told you?"

"Yeah," Atoa said. "I'm fucked."

"Do you still want to talk to us?"

"Like I got a choice?"

"Yes, Pinky. You do. And you have the right to counsel."

"What the fuck. Let's go."

"Tell me about Kealoha and Faalogo," Hung said.

"Guys were sleeved." Atoa used the prison term for tattoo-covered arms.

"Why the hit?"

"All I know is shit I overheard."

Hung gestured "give it to me" with one hand.

"L'il Bud told Ted he wanted to lay it on hard."

"Ted Pukui."

Atoa nodded.

"You're saying T'eo was sending a message?"

"You deaf or something? Yeah, that's what I'm saying I heard."

"What message?"

"It ain't healthy dealing in another man's mix."

"Who was this message for?"

"The guy sent Kealoha and Logo here."

"And that would be?"

Atoa appeared as though he were undergoing a change of mind about cooperating. Hung repeated her question.

"Some guy in California."

"Got a name?"

I was certain static distorted Atoa's answer. But Lô and Hung's shock was obvious.

"Spell that, please," Hung said.

Atoa did.

My face went hot as the room shrank around me.

32

I FELT A HAND ON MY SHOULDER.

Looked up.

Two blue eyes mirrored the confusion in mine.

"Did he say Al Lapasa?" Ryan asked.

"That's what I heard."

Voices continued buzzing through the speaker.

"Wasn't the guy in the box at JPAC named Alexander Lapasa?"

I nodded glumly.

"The guy wearing Spider Lowery's dog tag."

"It has to be a coincidence."

"A coincidence the size of Sierra Leone."

"There must be dozens of Al Lapasas," I said. "Besides, Atoa is talking about a Samoan from California. Lapasa was Italian, and from Honolulu."

Ryan and I refocused on the interview. Hung was now asking about L'il Bud T'eo.

"L'il Bud's one bad dog." Atoa shifted in his seat. "People cross him, they pay."

"People cross me, they pay." Even with poor

transmission, Lô's voice sounded cold. "But I don't have them shot."

"This is bullshit." Atoa again rubbed his face.

"Talk about Al Lapasa," Hung said.

"All I know is what I heard."

"What did you hear?"

"Lapasa's an OG. Owns a bar in Oakland."

I felt my stomach clench. OG. Original gangsta. Did that mean Lapasa was older than your average banger?

"SOS?" Hung asked.

Atoa nodded. Two vertical lines now burrowed up the bridge of his nose.

"Go on," Hung said.

"Kealoha and Faalogo were tipped up with Lapasa."

"And?"

"That's all I heard."

"You've got what I'd call selective hearing."

Atoa's gaze slid to Lô. Held. The detective stared back, face and body perfectly still.

Atoa's mouth drew sideways in a half smile that suggested not a hint of humor. "I thought cops had height requirements."

"I'm an exception."

"Yeah? Why's that?"

"Because I'm such a mean sonofabitch."

Atoa slumped back and crossed his arms. "I got nothing more to say."

"Here's something to think about." Lô leaned forward and laced his fingers on the tabletop. "Ever hear of Nickie Lapasa?"

Atoa pushed out his lips and looked at the ceiling.

"Nickie Lapasa's connected, Pinky. I'm not talking Facebook or My fucking Space. I'm talking real mean men with real bad attitude. And you know what you did, you dumb shit? You messed with Nickie's life."

Atoa's eyes stayed up, but the jittery feet belied his fear.

Lô cut a glance to his partner, then tipped his head toward the door.

Hung reached over and flicked a switch.

The screen went blank.

Ryan and I met Hung and Lô in the hall.

"Well played," Ryan said.

Lô and Hung both smiled.

"You think there's a link between Al Lapasa in Oakland and Nickie Lapasa in Honolulu?" Ryan asked.

Lô shrugged. "Maybe yes, maybe no. Can't hurt to let Pinky think about it."

"Is he aware who Nickie is?"

"Who knows?"

"Now what?" Ryan asked.

"Now we let the little bastard sweat for a while," Lô said.

"Will it take long to background Al Lapasa?" I asked.

Hung checked her watch.

"You guys get coffee. I'll call Oakland."

When we got to her desk Hung was drawing stick figures and shoulder-cradling the phone, obviously on hold. Lô placed a Styrofoam cup on her blotter. She started to say thanks, instead spoke into the mouthpiece.

"Yeah, I'm here." She readied her pen. "Shoot."

Lô, Ryan, and I sat and removed the lids from our containers.

I sipped. The swill tasted like mud puddle run-off. Or at least how I imagined mud puddle run-off would taste.

Hung said "Uh-huh" and "OK," asked a few questions. Finally, "That's it?"

Pause.

Hung thanked the person on the other end and disconnected.

"This is what I got." Clicking and reclicking the pen. "The guy's full name is Alexander Emanuel Lapasa."

Again, the world receded. This couldn't be happening. First Spider. Now Lapasa.

"—U.S. citizen, born twelve fourteen, '39, right here in the lovely metropolis of Honolulu."

I blinked. Blinked again.

"Lapasa's got no sheet, but the Oakland cops have been watching him for several years. He owns a dive called the Savaii. An SOS hangout. They think he runs drugs out of the bar."

"The locals can't nail him?" Lô sounded disgusted.

"Lapasa maintains a low profile, keeps layers between himself and the street."

"How long has he been in Oakland?" My voice sounded wrong, high and strained.

"Lapasa's name started popping up in the mid-nineties, when he bought the bar. But they think by then he'd been in the area awhile."

"Did you get a Social Security number?"

Hung looked at me oddly, but read from her notes. I jotted the digits.

"He's SOS?" Ryan asked.

"Yeah, but the guy's in his sixties now."

Lô snorted. "A model citizen with a schnauzer and a lawn."

"Don't know about the dog," Hung said. "But Lapasa paid cash for both the bar and his condo."

"Now what?" Ryan asked.

"Now we get Al hauled across the ocean and booked in a cage," Hung said.

"Based on the statement of an eighteen-year-old junkie looking to save his ass?" Lô tipped back in his chair and planted one foot on an open desk drawer. "We won't get a warrant and there's no way Lapasa's going to budge."

"I may have an idea," I said.

All eyes turned to me.

"May I use your phone?" I asked Ryan.

I called Danny from the hall. Speaking in hushed tones, I explained where I was and what had happened.

"Son of a friggin' gun. Do you have a DOB and SSN?"

I read them off, waited while Danny checked Xander Lapasa's file. It didn't take long.

"It's him."

Then who was 1968-979, the corpse found wearing Spider Lowery's dog tag? Neither Danny nor I posed the question aloud.

One thing troubled me. I'd laid it on Ryan, but where had I gotten the notion?

"Wasn't Xander Lapasa Italian?" I asked.

"What made you think that?"

"You said there were rumors Alex Senior was mobbed up."

"I meant that in a general sense. Organized crime. Not the Italian Mafia."

"You said he looked like some guy on *The Sopranos*."

"In that snapshot he did."

I'd been guilty of buying into an ethnic stereotype. I'd made an assumption based on Xander's looks, the sound of his name, and rumors of Mafia ties.

"Remember the story about old Alex coming to Hawaii, inheriting the gas station, going into real estate?"

"Yes," I said.

"He came to Honolulu from Samoa."

I took a moment to let the new reality sink in. Then, "May I tell the cops what we know about Xander Lapasa and the remains at JPAC?"

"You trust them to keep it confidential?"

"Yes."

"Then I don't see a problem. Why? What are you thinking?"

I outlined my plan.

"Could work," Danny said.

"We may need your help in securing Nickie's cooperation," I said.

"Oh, yeah. I'm Mr. Persuasive. I was just shot down again by Plato Lowery."

"Does he know about the path slides Beasley found and submitted?"

"No."

"Anyway, will you phone Nickie?"

"Yeah. Why not."

"It's all gone to hell, hasn't it, Danny?"

"Yeah. It has."

"Does Merkel know?"

"Not yet. I'll keep you in the loop. And, Tempe."

"Yes."

"Be careful."

The others were as I'd left them. So were the cups. I'm convinced no one drinks squad room coffee. You pour the stuff, let it cool, then toss it out.

I explained the situation at JPAC. The unidentified bones in the box. The ID of 1968-979 as Xander Lapasa. Nickie Lapasa's refusal to allow family members to submit DNA. The detectives listened without interrupting.

When I'd finished Lô spoke first.

"So you think Al Lapasa could be this guy who went missing in Vietnam forty years ago?"

"His date of birth and Social Security number match those on file for Xander Lapasa."

"How'd he get from Nam to California?"

"I don't know. But that's usually where the planes landed."

"What do you propose?" Hung asked.

"We all want Al Lapasa in Honolulu, right?"

Nods all around.

"You can't get a warrant for extradition based solely on Atoa's statement, and it's unlikely he'll make the trip voluntarily."

More nods.

"So we trick him."

"The guy's shrewd." Hung sounded skeptical. "If he is expanding his distribution into Hawaii, why would he come here and place himself at risk?"

"Double that if he's been living quasi-under-cover for forty years." Lô sounded as dubious as his partner.

"Could Lapasa know Kealoha and Faalogo are dead?" Ryan asked.

"Unlikely," I said. "The media reported nothing about the remains. And Perry hasn't verified the IDs."

"But if Lô's CI knew, wouldn't SOS?" Ryan pressed.

"L'il Bud T'eo and his buddies are USO," Lô said. "Lapasa and his crew are SOS Crips. Word might not travel across gang lines all that fast."

"What's your plan?" Hung asked.

"We have Nickie Lapasa's lawyer call Al Lapasa and say he has a client who's been searching for him for years. He'll say that Al is mentioned in Theresa-Sophia's will."

"Why would Nickie go along with something like that?"

"We tell him Al could be his long-lost brother."

"You just told him his long-lost brother is lying on a shelf at the CIL."

"We say that since Danny talked to him, researchers at the CIL discovered they could be wrong, that Xander could be this man living in Oakland. We play to Nickie's ego. Tell him he was probably right all along."

"What makes you think Nickie isn't already hip? If he does have drug connections, and Al Lapasa is in the game, why wouldn't Nickie be aware of who Al really is?" Lô asked.

"Because Xander didn't want Nickie to

know. For whatever reason, he's been lying low for forty years. JPAC queries spanning that entire time have obtained not a single hint to suggest any family member suspected Xander was alive. And I doubt Nickie knows the story on every drug dealer up and down the West Coast."

"In this little fantasy, how'd Nickie finally track Al down?" Lô.

"The administrator of Theresa-Sophia's estate has had lost heirs investigators searching off and on for years. They finally found him. Look, it's worth a shot. Al may believe that he has to come to Honolulu, meet with the executor of the will, and prove his identity in person. I'm sure the attorney can come up with legal jargon that sounds convincing."

A few moments passed while everyone considered my idea.

"Al was born in Honolulu," Hung said. "Even if he's not your long-lost Xander, he might figure he's got relatives here he knows nothing about."

"He'll hit the Internet, learn the Honolulu Lapasas are loaded, get greedy, get sloppy." Lô was coming around.

"And if he is Xander Lapasa, it's even more likely he'll buy into the story," I said.

Lô and Hung exchanged glances. I knew what they were thinking.

"If you want to try selling this guy a line, we've got no objection," Lô said. "But we can't compromise the Kealoha-Faalogo investigation. If this falls apart without Al ever leaving Oakland, this is strictly a CIL inquiry. My partner and I never heard any of this."

"Any of what?" I asked.

"So," Ryan said. "Who calls Nickie?"

"I'll be right back."

I retraced my steps to the hall.

33

DANNY INSISTED ON RECIPROCITY. THOUGH he doubted the scheme would succeed, he'd call Nickie if I'd take one more run at Plato.

I agreed.

Back in the squad room, I gave Lô and Hung a thumbs-up.

We chatted a moment, then Ryan and I left. Everyone said they'd keep in touch.

Little did we know how quickly we'd reconvene.

Ryan and I stopped for dim sum at the Chinatown Cultural Plaza Shopping Center. As Ryan made selections from an armada of carts, I called Plato Lowery.

"When will you people give up? I told that French guy and I told that army guy. No. N. O. This is harassment."

"I'm sorry you feel that way, sir."

"I do."

"We don't mean to offend. We're just puzzled by your refusal to cooperate in a small way."

"You're barking up the wrong tree."

"My colleagues and I want to get it right."

"Then send my boy home and leave us be."

Conversation hummed around me. Glassware clinked.

"Mr. Lowery, may I ask *why* you won't submit a sample for DNA testing?"

"No. You may not."

Through a window I looked across at the statue of Sun Yat-sen. He looked as unbending as Plato sounded.

"The process isn't painful," I said.

"Painful? I'll tell you what's painful. Having someone tell you your boy ain't your boy. That's painful. That's painful as hell."

"Sir, that's not—"

"You people got no idea the hurt you can cause."

Lowery was growing more strident with every word.

"All these years I've been telling myself the past is past. Those doctors and nurses with their needles and probes and fancy words. It was crazy. *They* were crazy. Those fools and their tests nearly cost me my family."

The old man's voice sizzled through the handset pressed to my ear.

"And the damndest part? They all died anyway. Spider. Tom. Harriet. In the end, all that science didn't make one spit of difference."

I looked over to see Ryan studying my face.

"Now the army comes along wanting to churn the whole mess up again. I didn't believe nothing then, and I don't believe nothing now. It's done. Spider was my boy. He died in the war. That's it. Done. You got it?"

I found myself listening to empty air.

"He sounded a bit overwrought." Ryan placed a dumpling on my plate.

"A bit. That's the largest number of words I've ever heard him connect."

"Why so distressed?"

"I'm not really sure." I set Ryan's phone on the table. "Half of what he said didn't make sense."

"Like what?"

I tried to reconstruct Plato's outburst in my mind.

"Basically, he doesn't trust doctors or science."

"I gather he won't be submitting a swab."

"Definitely not."

"Now what?"

I raised frustrated hands. "We work with what we've got."

Danny rang as Ryan was paying the bill.

His task had gone far better than mine.

Nickie Lapasa wanted answers concerning his brother. He and his attorney would concoct a convincing scenario. The attorney would contact Al Lapasa. Nickie would phone when he had news.

I was pleased. But stunned.

So was Ryan. Did Nickie have reasons other than closure on Xander?

That night the clouds and mist gave way to rain. Rivulets ran down the glass doors opening onto my balcony. Now and then a gust snuck in and rattled the frame.

Danny phoned at nine.

"Al Lapasa bit."

"You're kidding."

"He'll arrive in Honolulu tomorrow afternoon."

"Get out!"

"Avarice is a wonderful thing."

"You think that's it?" I asked.

"Who knows," Danny said.

I told Ryan, then called Lô.

He reacted as I had, though in somewhat more colorful prose. He'd talk to Hung, let me know when they had a plan.

Finally, I brought Hadley Perry up to speed.

Her surprise was delivered in hues as vivid as Lô's. As we spoke, I also detected a note of annoyance. Because I was in and she was out of the loop on *her* case? Because I was with Ryan and she was not? Because the court testimony in which she was engaged was not yet finished and she would remain on the sidelines? Answering Perry's questions, I felt a smug sense of satisfaction. Petty, but there you have it.

That night sleep refused to come. My mind kept chewing on the two recent shockers.

Harriet Lowery's DNA was not a match for the Hemmingford floater.

Xander Lapasa might be alive.

Had Danny and I made too great a leap when comparing the antemortem and postmortem dental X-rays? The partial filling? The mandibular fractures?

Why had Nickie Lapasa gone along with my

plan? What did he hope to gain from Al Lapasa's presence in Honolulu? Did he actually believe the man was his brother?

Xander Lapasa went missing in Vietnam in 1968. Had he survived? Lived all those years as Al Lapasa? If so, why had he never contacted his family?

Or had he?

What had Xander been doing in Vietnam?

When did Al Lapasa surface in Oakland? Where was he prior to that?

What did Nickie know?

What did Nickie want?

Why did Nickie refuse to allow a DNA comparison between a Lapasa family member and JPAC's 1968-979, presumably his brother, Xander?

Ditto for Plato Lowery. Why did he refuse to submit a sample?

Plato's rant suggested that his wife's death had been wrenching. Had Harriet's illness scarred the old man so deeply it destroyed his faith in medicine and hospitals?

What had Plato said? *In the end, doctors and science didn't make one spit of difference.*

I replayed Plato's words in my mind, trying to better understand his thinking.

One comment seemed a disconnect. *Those fools and their fancy test nearly cost me my family.*

What fools? What test?

Cost his family? How?

Now the army comes along wanting to churn the whole mess up again.

I'd assumed the reference was to Spider's death. If not, what mess?

I organized what little I knew about the Lowerys.

Harriet had passed away five years earlier. She'd suffered from kidney disease all her life, eventually received a transplant. Sheriff Beasley had said that neither son was the donor.

I pictured Plato clutching his album in my car. Thumping his chest so hard I flinched. *My boy!*

Again, on the phone today. *Spider was my boy!*

Both sons had offered their mother a kidney. Spider in the sixties, Tom years later.

Why could neither donate an organ?

Harriet's twins were obviously not matches for her. Was that what had Plato so upset? Had testing turned up something the old man didn't like?

The thought hit me like a bullet.

Paternity.

Had Plato discovered he was not the father of Harriet's twins? Was he desperate to keep that fact hidden?

The digits on my clock said 2:18.

Rain still swished softly in the gutter overhanging my balcony.

I was twisting the notion this way and that when a scream shattered the silence.

Heart banging, I threw back the covers and shot from my bed.

Ryan was barreling up the stairs two at a time.

Katy was flying through her door.

The three of us met in the hall.

"I saw someone!" Katy's face was adrenaline white. "Rain was coming in. I got up to close the door and there he was."

"Where?" Ryan and I spoke as one.

"Out on the lawn."

"A man? A woman?" Ryan asked.

"A man. I think. He looked pretty big."

"What was he doing?"

"Just standing there. Under a tree. When I screamed, he ran off."

"Lily!" Ryan rushed toward his daughter's room.

The TV was tinting the walls and furniture an eerie blue. Colors danced on the glass of the open balcony door, blurry reflections of movement on the screen.

Lily stood in shadow between the bed and a highboy dresser. In the dimness, her eyes looked way too large.

Ryan rushed forward. Stopped at arm's length from his daughter, uncertain.

"Are you all right?" Ryan's voice sounded taut and gentle at the same time.

Lily nodded.

Ryan scanned the room, assessing. Though the bedding was tangled, Lily was fully dressed.

Katy and I watched from the doorway.

Lily stood with her back pressed to the wall.

Ryan strode onto the balcony and surveyed the landscape below.

"Who screamed?" Lily asked.

"I saw someone down by the pool," Katy said.

Ryan stepped in and slid the door sideways. Water plumed from the track.

"Holy hell!" Katy sounded scared. "That posting. Could this be related?"

Ryan snicked the lock into place, turned, frowned at me.

Crap!

I hadn't told him about the threatening message on Katy's blog.

"What posting?" he asked.

I gave a condensed version.

"And you didn't mention this little incident because . . . ?"

"I got distracted."

"Distracted?"

"First LaManche called with his bombshell about Harriet Lowery's DNA." As the excuse left my lips I knew it was lame. "Then there was the news about Al Lapasa."

Ryan spoke to Katy.

"Was the man alone?"

"I think so."

"Which way did he go?"

"I didn't see. I— I'm sorry. I acted like some B-grade Hollywood heroine."

"Can you describe him?" I recognized the altered tone. Ryan had kicked into cop mode.

Katy shook her head. "It was dark."

Ryan walked over and placed a hand on each of his daughter's shoulders.

"Look at me."

Lily's eyes rolled up.

"Why are you dressed at two in the morning?"

"I fell asleep watching TV."

"Watching what?"

Lily shrugged. "Nothing special. Just stuff."

"Do you have any idea who this intruder might be?"

"I didn't see the guy."

A few beats passed.

"I'll double-check the gates and the house." Ryan shot a look my way. Angry? Troubled? Disappointed? "Let's all get some sleep."

34

WHEN I AWOKE, DAWN WAS JUST A PALE HINT along the horizon.

Instantly my thoughts circled to where they'd been just prior to Katy's scream.

Had I stumbled upon Plato's unstated motive for stonewalling use of his DNA? Did he fear another man had fathered his sons?

Throwing back the covers, I crossed the floor and opened my balcony door. Breathed deeply.

Overnight, the rain had stopped. The air smelled of salt, damp foliage, and wet sand.

It was six thirty-seven.

Late morning East Coast time.

Anxious for answers, I didn't bother with coffee, just grabbed a Diet Coke from the kitchen and returned to my room.

Checked a number.

Dialed.

Sheriff Beasley was in his office and took my call.

I minced no words.

"Plato still refuses to give DNA. I find that baffling."

"What's his reason?"

"He won't give one."

"Plato's an odd duck."

"From time to time, I encounter people who won't submit bodily fluids for testing. Sometimes for religious reasons. Sometimes out of ignorance. Sometimes because they're guilty as hell. With Plato, I sense that it's none of those."

No reply.

"Sheriff Beasley, is there something you're holding back?"

"What are you talking about?" Guarded.

"You tell me."

"You'll need to be more specific, miss."

Beasley was wasting my time. Those who do so fail to enjoy the sunny side of my disposition.

"How about this? If I made an inquiry into Harriet Lowery's kidney transplant, would I dig up some curious facts?"

Beasley was silent a long moment before speaking.

"If you're wanting medical information, you'll have to speak to Harriet's doctor."

"Might you know who that is?" Icy.

More hesitation, then, "Patricia Macken."

"Might you have contact information for Dr. Macken?"

Beasley exhaled loudly.

"Hang on."

The sheriff put me on hold for almost five minutes.

"OK." He read off a number.

"Thank you." Dickhead. I didn't say it, but the good sheriff heard it in my tone.

I was about to disconnect when Beasley spoke again.

"Plato may be stubborn and uneducated, but he's honest, works hard when given the chance."

"I believe he is."

"This is Lumberton." In case I'd forgotten. "Let's keep this as low-profile as possible."

Excitement fizzed in my chest. Beasley's comment was a tell that I was on the right track.

"Of course."

I disconnected and dialed Macken.

A woman answered, said the doctor was in an examination room and could not be disturbed.

I explained that I was calling about a former patient. Stated that my business was urgent.

The woman promised to deliver my message.

I sat back, satisfied I'd soon have an answer.

Twenty minutes later I was pacing the room. Didn't physicians have to hustle these days? Eight minutes per patient? Two? A heartbeat? How long could Macken spend with one person?

I dressed. Brushed my teeth. Tied back my hair. Let it down. Checked the phone to be sure the line was working. Ran through some e-mail. Checked again.

At eight forty the damn thing finally rang.

I snatched up the receiver.

"This is Patricia Macken." Though firm, the voice was clearly that of an older person. One born in Dixie. "I have a message to call this number. My nurse indicated it might be a medical emergency."

"Not exactly. But thanks for getting back to me. I'm Dr. Temperance Brennan. I work for the medical examiner in Charlotte." KISS. Keep it simple, stupid. And local. If needed, I'd elaborate, add detail. "I'm calling about a woman named Harriet Lowery."

"Yes." Suspicious.

"I believe you treated Mrs. Lowery for kidney disease until her death five years ago."

"Who did you say you are?"

I repeated my name and affiliation.

"Why is the Charlotte ME interested in a patient who died under a physician's care in a hospital in Lumberton?"

"Actually, it's the coroner in Montreal, Canada, who is interested. I consult to that office as well."

"I'm confused. What does this have to do with Harriet Lowery?"

"In fact, the interest is in her son, John."

"Spider?"

"Yes."

"Spider died in Vietnam."

"Perhaps not."

An intake of breath told me Macken hadn't seen that coming.

"Please explain."

I gave her the basics. The Hemmingford floater, Jean Laurier, identified by fingerprints as John Lowery. JPAC. The Huey crash in Vietnam in 1968. The exhumation in Lumberton. The suspected mix-up of John Lowery and Luis Alvarez.

"My colleagues and I thought we had the confusion sorted out, then DNA sequencing excluded Harriet Lowery as the mother of the Quebec victim."

Macken said nothing, so I continued.

"Harriet's DNA was obtained from pathology slides stored at Southeastern Regional Medical Center. As you can imagine, the material was somewhat degraded. We'd like to run another comparison using a sample from Spider Lowery's father. Plato refuses to submit a swab."

I paused, allowing Macken the chance to speak. She offered nothing.

"We're wondering why, Dr. Macken."

"Perhaps Mr. Lowery knows you are wrong."

"Everything else indicates that the man who died in Quebec is Spider Lowery. If we're wrong, DNA from Mr. Lowery could establish that."

"Why are you calling me?"

Why was I?

"If I could understand Plato's opposition, I might have a chance at changing his mind."

"I doubt that."

"It's a question of paternity, isn't it?"

"What do you mean?"

"Neither Spider nor Tom was a suitable donor for Harriet. We both know that happens all the time in families. It means nothing. But in the course of testing for tissue compatibility, I suspect something unexpected turned up. Something devastating for Plato."

"Meaning?"

"I suspect tests showed Plato was not the father of Harriet's children."

Macken took a very long time to answer.

"You're right, Dr. Brennan. And wrong. The experience almost destroyed Mr. Lowery. But the issue wasn't paternity."

"If the—"

"It was maternity."

"What? Wait. I don't understand. Harriet wasn't the mother?"

"Could you hold, please?"

I heard a clunk, footsteps, then the sound of a closing door. The air thickened on the other end of the line.

A scrape, then Macken was back.

"I am going to speak with you further, even though I really should not without authorization from Harriet's family. I will do it because Harriet has been deceased a good while and because you seem to know many facts already. Mostly, I am going to speak to you further to keep you from going off on a tangent not supported by the facts.

"Testing was less sophisticated in the sixties when Spider offered to donate his kidney. Thirty years later, it was a different world. Not only was Tom ruled out as a donor, DNA sequencing showed that he could not be Harriet's son."

I was lost for words.

"Plato and Harriet swore it was nonsense. But the conclusion was undeniable. I had no choice but to speak to the sheriff."

"Beasley."

"Yes. He tried to learn what he could. But Harriet and Plato totally shut down. And almost fifty years had passed. Records showed the twins were home-birthed. A midwife assisted, but the sheriff was never able to track her down.

"Though both boys were grown, and Spider was long dead, Sheriff Beasley had to consider the possibilities. After the boys' birth, the Lowerys spent a long time on government support. Had they perpetrated some sort of welfare fraud? Had they kidnapped one son? Both? Had they been involved in some sort of illegal surrogacy or adoption scheme?

"In the end, Sheriff Beasley decided Spider and Tom had been loved and well cared for. They'd had decent childhoods. What was past was past. He let the matter drop."

Macken went silent for so long I thought maybe we'd been cut off.

"Hello?"

"I'm here. Five years later Tom was dead. Two years after that it was Harriet. Plato never recovered. I find the whole thing very, very sad, don't you, Dr. Brennan?"

I nodded, realized she couldn't see me do it.

"Yes," I said. And meant it.

While I'd been phoning and pacing and phoning, Ryan had also been busy. When I met him in the kitchen he'd already talked to Lô.

"Lô wants the text from Katy's blog posting."

"I'll get it."

I ran upstairs, slipped into Katy's room, and retrieved the printout.

"Given the hostile nature of this"—Ryan flicked the paper I'd handed him—"the guy in the yard, and your little incident down by Waimanalo Bay, Lô thinks we should keep the girls close for a while."

"He thinks Katy and Lily are in danger?"

"Probably not, but he prefers to play it safe. He'll send a patrol car past here once every hour."

"Danger from whom?"

"Obviously, he doesn't know. Calm down. It's a courtesy. I'd do the same for visiting law enforcement in Montreal. But you should have showed this to me." Again, Ryan flicked the printout.

"Agreed."

Ryan inhaled. Exhaled. Rubbed his hands up and down his face.

"I hope my lamebrain kid wasn't planning to sneak out last night."

"With the guy in the yard?"

Ryan nodded. It was clear his parental patience was stretched to the snapping point.

"Do you think Lily might be backsliding?"

"I don't know."

"Have you searched her room? Questioned her?"

"If I do that and I'm wrong, I could be destroying what little trust I've built."

"If you do that and you're right you could be saving her life."

"Yeah," he said. "I know."

"Is there anything I can do to help?"

Ryan shook his head.

A beat passed.

"Heroin's a mean bastard," he said.

I reached out and stroked Ryan's cheek, saddened by his obvious distress.

Danny called at ten.

"Lapasa's plane lands at two fifteen. Nickie's driver will meet the flight and take Al from the airport to his attorney's office."

"Why not headquarters?"

"Nickie won't go for that. Lô's good with the

arrangement. He thinks being dragged to a cop shop might cause Lapasa to shut down. Or bolt. Besides, Lô has insufficient grounds for arrest."

"OK."

"You're to be present to scope the guy out."

"Why me?"

"You've seen Xander Lapasa's file and photos."

"So have you."

"You're an anthropologist. And you live more than fifty miles away."

I smiled at our old definition of an expert. Someone coming from afar and carrying a brief-case.

"You'll be in the reception area so you can observe Al up close and personal when he arrives," Danny continued. "Can you look litigious?"

"I'll get coaching."

"Al will be taken to a conference room and told that Nickie wants the meeting recorded. You and Lô will actually be observing."

"Will Nickie be watching the interview?"

"No. He wants nothing to do with it. Think you can handle the part?"

"They'll give me an Emmy."

Lô called shortly thereafter, repeated the instructions, and invited Ryan to tag along.

The attorney, Simon Schoon, was a partner in a firm whose offices occupied the third floor of a modern brick building on Bishop Street, halfway between the Aloha Tower and Hawaii Pacific University.

Ryan and I got there at two. A receptionist greeted us in a marble-floored foyer, indicated chairs, nodded conspiratorially. She had gray eyes, overplucked brows, and the tightest French twist I've ever seen. A nameplate on her desk said Tina Frieboldt.

I picked up and pretended to read a copy of *National Geographic*. Ryan chose *Sports Illustrated*.

Lô arrived twenty minutes after we did. He waited on the far side of the room, fingers laced, staring at nothing.

At five past three, the elevator dinged. Seconds later, the door opened. A man entered and walked straight to Tina. He was short and stocky with thinning red hair. I guessed from the black jacket and tie that this was the driver.

"Mr. Lapasa is here."

"Please show him in."

I flipped a page in my magazine, totally disinterested.

"The gentleman prefers to remain in the hall. It's a flu thing. He doesn't want to be around people."

Damn!

Feigning impatience, I checked my watch. Flipped another page. Shifted in my seat.

Through the open door I could see a man in the corridor.

My heart dropped.

The man had thick black hair and stood at least six feet tall.

35

THE MAN'S BACK WAS TO ME. HE WORE A navy suit. The edge of a frayed white collar circled his neck.

Very tall. Dark hair.

Like Xander Lapasa.

Nickie's driver recrossed the marble, exited to the corridor, and spoke to his passenger.

"I'll take you straight to the conference room, Mr. Lapasa."

Navy Suit turned and stepped sideways. Another man came into view.

The second man was of average height, with wispy gray hair and pasty skin. Covering his nose and mouth was a surgical mask, the kind sold in drugstores to ward off germs.

Navy Suit gripped his companion's arm, then the trio turned left down the hall.

"What the hell?" Lô was on his feet. "Which one's Lapasa?"

Tina remained serene, her updo flawless.

"I wouldn't know, sir. Shall I take you to your observation post?"

"Yeah," Lô growled. "Do that." Then, to

me, "You know which one of these turds is Lapasa?"

I shook my head.

"Let's go," Lô said.

We left the reception area and turned right.

"Observation post?" Ryan whispered from one side of his mouth.

"Sshh," I warned.

"The chick thinks she's Moneypenny."

Tina led us to a glass-sided room with a long, gleaming table and twelve swivel chairs. As we settled in she picked up a remote and hit several buttons.

An image sparked on a large flat-screen monitor wall-mounted at one end of the room. Voices piped from its speakers, clear and static free.

Handing Lô the remote, Tina withdrew.

"This puppy definitely beats your setup," Ryan said.

"We don't get to charge three fifty an hour," Lô replied.

"Good point."

Ignoring the banter, I watched Navy Suit ease Face Mask into a chair. The man moved gingerly, as though ill or fearful of injury. Once seated he kept his eyes on his hands.

The table on the screen was round and smaller than ours. Seated at it was a man with a bow tie and tortoiseshell glasses. In front of him lay a yellow legal pad and a silver Cross pen.

I assumed this was Nickie's attorney, Simon Schoon. Behind the lenses Schoon's eyes looked dark and sharp.

Navy Suit took the chair beside his companion.

I studied the two men from California. Which was Al Lapasa?

Schoon spoke first.

"My client appreciates your willingness to appear in person."

"My client has his reasons for agreeing to do so." Navy Suit.

Yes! The tall guy was a lawyer.

I focused on Lapasa, the man in the mask.

"And you would be?" Schoon asked.

"Jordan Epstein." Epstein slid a card across the table. "I represent Mr. Lapasa."

Schoon glanced at but did not touch Epstein's card.

"Before proceeding, we'd like the courtesy of knowing who *you* represent," Epstein said.

"My client prefers to remain anonymous," Schoon said.

"I'm afraid we must insist."

"I'm afraid I must decline."

Epstein pushed back his chair. "Then this interview is over."

Throughout the exchange, Lapasa had not raised his head. He did so now.

"It's Nickie Lapasa, isn't it?" Muffled by the pharmacy mask.

Schoon's face betrayed nothing.

Lapasa raised his voice and spoke to the room. "You out there, Nickie? You getting this?"

Epstein laid a hand on his client's arm. Lapasa shook it off.

"I got people know the Internet as well as yours do, Nickie. You find me, I find you." The words were overly precise and paced, like those of a drunk trying hard to sound sober.

"Mr. Lapasa, I advise you to remain silent."

Lapasa ignored his lawyer.

"You looking for your brother, Nickie? Might be I could help you out with that. First you tell this douche bag to quit dicking us around."

"Very well." Schoon licked his lips. "Let's work with the assumption Nickie Lapasa is seeking information on the death of his brother."

"What makes you think he's dead?"

"Let me rephrase. Do you know anything about the whereabouts of Xander Lapasa?"

Epstein swiveled to face his client. "Don't answer that."

"Why not?"

"Remember our discussion."

"It's the reason I dragged my sick ass onto that goddam plane."

Epstein's eyebrows plunged into a downward V. He was losing control of his client.

My attention stayed riveted on Lapasa's face. Above the mask, his eyes looked jaundiced and dull.

And something else.

An alarm pinged softly deep in my brainpan.

Epstein returned his attention to Schoon. "Please tell us about Theresa-Sophia Lapasa's will."

"I can't do that without proof of your client's identity."

"I'm the fucking Wizard of Oz." Lapasa's laugh morphed into a cough.

Epstein plucked a hanky from his pocket and handed it to his client.

Schoon's lips formed a thin hard line as he waited out the hacking.

Recovering, Lapasa jammed his fingers and danced his thumbnails against each other. The action traveled through the speakers as a series of clicks.

I studied Lapasa's eyes.

Again the ping.

What was my subconscious noticing that I was not?

Lapasa broke the silence. "It's a scam, right?"

"Excuse me?" Schoon asked.

"I can smell a scam at fifty yards out. There's no goddamn will."

"Sir?"

"Enough of this horseshit." One thumb flicked at Epstein. "Tell him what I got."

"Mr. Lapasa, I can't help you if you won't follow my advice."

"What the fuck. I'm dying."

"You're certain about this?"

Lapasa nodded.

Epstein paused a moment, clearly disapproving. Then he began.

"Mr. Lapasa has cancer. His prognosis is not good. He is willing to provide information in exchange for amnesty concerning his involvement in certain events."

"I have no authority to negotiate criminal charges."

Epstein glanced at his client.

Lapasa signaled for him to continue.

"These events took place over forty years ago."

I drew in my breath.

Epstein's client was the right age but far too short to be Xander Lapasa. Who was he? Where was this going?

Schoon undoubtedly knew that no such warning was needed for an interrogation that was neither custodial nor conducted by law enforcement, but knowing that Lô was listening, he thought he would gild the lily. He spoke directly to Epstein. "If your client plans to admit to criminal activity, I must insist on a Miranda reading."

"I am present as Mr. Lapasa's attorney. My client understands his rights and the implications of his actions."

"Is that correct, Mr. Lapasa? You've discussed your statement with counsel and are making it freely and without pressure or promise of gain?"

"Yeah, yeah. Whatever. I'll be dead in three months."

"Let me remind you that this interview is being recorded." Schoon picked up his pen. "Proceed, Mr. Lapasa. I'd like to hear this directly from you."

"I killed him."

"Killed who?"

"A guy named Alexander Lapasa."

My eyes shot to Ryan. To Lô.

Their brows were floating an inch up their foreheads.

"When was this?" Schoon's voice revealed nothing, no surprise, no censure, no jubilation. It was completely neutral.

"In 1968."

"Where?"

"Vietnam."

"Go on."

"That's it. I killed the guy, stole his wallet and passport, and headed up-country."

"Your motive?"

"I wanted out."

"Out of what?"

"The army, Nam, the whole fucking war."

"Why was that?"

"You for real?"

"Please answer the question."

"I was eighteen, liked my ass in one piece."

"Why Xander Lapasa?"

"He wasn't military. I figured having civvy ID would buy me freedom." Lapasa turned to Epstein. "These fucking meds are kicking the shit out of me. I gotta take another leak."

Lapasa shuffled out, supported by his lawyer.

My mind pinwheeled with questions.

Neither of the men was Xander Lapasa. Epstein was a lawyer. Face Mask was far too short. Who was he? Where in Vietnam had he crossed paths with Xander?

Face Mask had been living as Al Lapasa since the sixties. Where was he prior to arriving in Oakland? What was he doing?

I chewed a cuticle, too agitated for speech. Behind me, Ryan and Lô were also silent.

An eon passed. Another.

The cuticle turned raw.

Finally, Epstein and his client returned.

Schoon picked up where he'd left off.

"How did you kill Mr. Lapasa?"

"Shot him with my M16."

"You then stole his identity papers, went AWOL, and lived as Al Lapasa."

"That's what I'm saying."

"Why Al?"

"What?"

"Why not Xander?"

Lapasa shrugged. "The guy's passport said Alexander. I figured Al."

"What is your actual name?"

"That ain't important."

"We'll come back to that." Schoon made a note on his tablet. "Where did you meet Mr. Lapasa?"

"I wouldn't exactly say we met."

"Very well." Prim. "Where did you kill Mr. Lapasa?"

Face Mask slowly wagged his head, eyes steady on Schoon.

"Sir?"

"I give you that, you squash me like a Napa grape."

"I beg your pardon?"

"This is where you give me something, Mr. Lawyer."

Schoon's eyes held steady behind their lenses.

"You think I'm scum."

Schoon started to object. Face Mask stopped him with a raised hand.

"Kids today talk about something called a bucket list. You ever hear of that?"

"No."

"It's shit you want to do before they plant you in the ground. You know, before you kick the bucket."

Schoon said nothing.

"I did some things when I was young don't make me proud. I spent most of my life looking over one shoulder. Now they tell me my insides is hash. My list says I gotta put things to rest."

Face Mask drew a long, deep breath.

"Here's the deal. Take it or leave it. You get what you need on Lapasa. I go home to die at peace in my bed."

Schoon thought it over.

"I'll have to clear this with the DA."

"Knock yourself out."

Face Mask slouched back in his chair.

36

SCHOON JOINED US SECONDS LATER.

"How do I proceed?" he asked Lô.

"I've got no objection to you dealing on Xander Lapasa. He's talking forty years ago. A murder in Vietnam. Jurisdiction would be a nightmare. Besides, the guy may have zilch. Maybe he's trying to cash in on some rumor he heard."

I'd thought of that, too.

"But stay away from Kealoha and Faalogo," Lô said. "If the scumbag's moving drugs into my city he's going down. Cancer or no cancer."

"This may take a while," Schoon said.

It didn't. Ten minutes later he was back.

"The DA agrees. We give Lapasa rope, hope he hangs himself on something else. A prosecutor will join us shortly, but the DA said to proceed since we're recording and Lapasa has counsel present. Besides, he doesn't think we have jurisdiction since the alleged crime took place in Vietnam and the perp was active-duty military."

Schoon left. A minute later he reappeared on the screen and took his seat.

"All right," he said. "You have immunity on anything you say regarding Xander Lapasa."

Face Mask looked at his lawyer.

"We'd like that in writing," Epstein said.

"You shall have it," Schoon replied.

Epstein nodded.

Schoon picked up his pen. "Tell me about the death of Alexander Lapasa."

The pharmacy mask shrank inward, puffed out. Then, "Lapasa and I are waiting for a chopper to take us up-country."

"Where was this?" Schoon asked.

"Long Binh."

My heart began beating so loud I thought the others might hear it.

"To pass the time we start chewing the fat. I ask why he's out of uni. He says he's civvy, in-country looking for business ops once the war wraps up.

"We finally lift off. The chopper's barely in the air when we take a hit, go down hard. The pilot, copilot, and crew chief buy it. Same for a kid riding in back. I walk away. So does Lapasa." Face Mask shrugged. "Seemed like a perfect business op for me."

Sweet Mother Mary!

I shot a hand out to Ryan. "Give me your cell."

"What?"

"Just give me your cell." Sharp.

Ryan did.

I punched buttons, my eyes jumping between the phone and the man on the screen. Schoon was now asking about dates.

"January, 1968."

"The day?"

"I don't know."

Danny answered on the first ring.

"The maintenance worker who witnessed the Huey crash at Long Binh. Did you ever track him down?"

"Harlan Kramer?"

"Whatever."

"I talked to him. He's retired and living in Killeen, Texas. Didn't learn anything new—"

"Did you ask how many men boarded the Huey?"

"The manifest listed five. Four crew members and Spider Lowery."

"But did you ask him how many boarded?"

"No."

"Call him back. Ask him."

"Now?"

"Yes."

"What's going on—"

"Just do it. Let me know what he says."

I got up. Paced. Gnawed flesh from my thumb.

Ryan and Lô looked at me like I'd gone over the edge.

On the monitor, Schoon was asking Face Mask to describe Xander Lapasa. The weapon.

Finally the phone rang.

"Kramer saw six men board—four crew, a recently released prisoner, and a civilian." Danny sounded embarrassed. "He said no one ever asked him that question. All they wanted to know was how the chopper went down."

"And he never mentioned it because he figured they had a manifest."

"Yeah."

"Thanks, Danny. I'll explain later."

I refocused on the man on the screen.

"How far did you and Mr. Lapasa travel from the scene of the crash?"

Face Mask shrugged. "Hell, I don't know. Maybe a quarter mile."

"On foot."

"No. We called a fucking cab."

"And you shot him."

"How many times I gotta keep saying it?"

The dark pupils. The Al Pacino brows.

Of course.

That was the message my subconscious was pinging.

"Then what?"

"I put one of my tags on his body and split."

"What was your reason for being in Long Binh at that time?"

"I was getting out of jail."

"It's Spider," I whispered.

"What?" Ryan asked.

"Who?" Lô asked.

"John Lowery. People called him Spider."

"*Tabarnac.*"

"Who?" Lô repeated.

"Ssshh." I hushed them both, wanting to hear the rest of Spider's account.

"—you go after shooting Mr. Lapasa?"

"Saigon for a few years. Then Thailand. Bangkok. Chiang Mai. Chumphon. Back to Bangkok. Stayed there until '86."

"Then?"

"Got homesick."

"You returned to the United States?"

Spider nodded.

"Using an eighteen-year-old passport." Schoon sounded dubious.

"I got a new one."

"How was that possible?"

"This dipshit crawl out from under some rock?" Spider asked Epstein, voice oozing scorn.

"Continue," Schoon said.

"That's it." Spider shrugged. "I been here ever since."

"Living as Al Lapasa."

"Keeping clean. Paying taxes. Even got a pooch."

"Your real identity, sir?"

Face Mask looked at Epstein.

Epstein nodded.

"John Charles Lowery. Born March twenty-first, 1950, in Lumberton, North Carolina. Father Plato. Mother Harriet."

I knew. Still, hearing it sent an electric charge through me.

"Look, I gotta eat," Spider said. "How about you scare up some sandwiches, maybe a couple sodas."

Schoon looked momentarily undecided. Then, "Perhaps we do need another break."

Nickie's lawyer rose and walked off camera. I suspected he'd decided it was time to phone his client.

I turned to face Ryan and Lô.

For a full thirty seconds no one ventured an opinion. Lô went first.

"My gut says this asshole's full of shit."

"It has to be Spider," I said. "Who else would

know about Long Binh? The Huey crash? Xander's reason for traveling to Vietnam?"

"How could Xander have been on a military chopper?" Lô asked.

"Civilians hitched rides all the time," I said.

"He look right for it?"

I pulled two pictures from my purse. The snapshot I'd found in Jean Laurier's desk drawer. The team photo Plato had taken from his album.

The three of us studied the face of young Spider. That of the man on the screen.

Both had the same dark eyes and heavy curved brows.

"Hard to tell with the mask," Lô said. "Plus this guy's circling the drain."

"The eyes seem right," Ryan said.

"If the man's lying, what's his motive?" I asked.

No one had a theory on that.

"One thing bothers me," Lô said. "How'd this Spider, not being Samoan, hook up with SOS?"

Or a theory on that.

"If he is legit, that would explain Spider's dog tag turning up with Xander Lapasa's body," I said.

"It *wouldn't* explain us rolling Spider's prints off the Hemmingford vic," Ryan countered.

"No," I agreed. "But it would explain why DNA showed that that man could not be Harriet's son."

"Anyone thirsty?" Lô rose.

"Diet Coke," I said.

"Coffee."

"Don't start without me." Lô disappeared through the door.

To pass the time, I looked again at the photos. There was Spider leaning on the Chevy. There he was, a scrolly number 12 on his chest.

I wondered what position Spider had played. If he'd enjoyed baseball. How often the coach had sent him into a game.

Plato said a cousin got Spider to join the team, that his son mostly rode the bench.

What was the cousin's name?

Reggie. Reggie Cumbo.

I looked at Reggie, down on one knee, unsmiling. The resemblance to Spider really was uncanny.

Plato said the boys were related through Harriet.

I pictured the old man as he spoke of his wife. Again felt his grief.

What had Plato said? Harriet had pretty eyes, one brown, one green as a loblolly pine.

A minute particle popped into being in my brain.

Fingerprints said the man who died in Hemmingford was Spider Lowery.

DNA said he wasn't.

Army records said Spider Lowery died in Vietnam.

The man talking to Schoon said he didn't.

I remembered the snapshot of Harriet Lowery standing on a pier. Her sun-fried chest. Her mismatched eyes.

The lone particle was joined by others.

I remembered my conversation with Harriet's transplant physician. Macken admitted that irregularities had surfaced during testing for tissue compatibility. DNA showed that Harriet could not be Tom's mother.

Plato and Harriet rejected that.

Tom was Spider's twin.

I recalled a court case. An article.

The particles coalesced into a full-blown theory.

I stared at the monitor, hardly breathing, willing the man in the mask to look into the camera.

The door opened.

Come on!

Footsteps crossed the room.

Come on!

Lô set a Coke in front of me.

Come on!

On the screen, Schoon entered and placed a white paper bag on the table. The duo from California withdrew sodas, sandwiches, paper napkins. Popped cans. Opened and squeezed packets of mayo and mustard.

Do it, you bastard! Look at me!

Finally, he did.

And I knew who he was.

And what had happened.

37

I SHOT TO MY FEET.

"I need to get online."

Ryan and Lô looked at me like I'd said I was joining Al Qaeda.

"Tell Schoon to stall."

"Why?"

"Just keep this guy talking."

I hurried to reception and made my request.

Unruffled, Tina led me to an empty office, typed a few keystrokes, and withdrew without query.

Moneypenny was all right.

Logging on, I went to the *New England Journal of Medicine,* called up an article, and speed-read. Scribbled notes. Moved through link after link until satisfied my understanding was adequate.

Next I entered a name and followed those loops.

A second name.

More loops.

I practically danced my way back to the conference room.

A woman had joined Ryan and Lô. She was tall, with short brown hair and acne-scarred cheeks. I placed her age at midthirties.

Lô made introductions. He didn't look happy. The newcomer was Maya Cotton, an ADA with the Honolulu prosecutor's office.

Cotton and I shook hands.

"Anyway, sorry to spoil your day," Cotton said.

"Sonofabitch." Lô whacked a table leg with one foot.

"What?" I asked, not really interested, anxious to share my breakthrough.

"They kicked Pinky Atoa this morning."

That surprised me. "He admitted to being involved in the Kealoha-Faalogo murders."

Snorting in disgust, Lô gestured to Cotton.

"It turned out Atoa was actually only sixteen. The confession's out. Since there's really nothing else, he couldn't be held."

Down the hall, Schoon was still questioning Face Mask.

"Did I miss much?" I asked, gesturing at the screen.

"Spider's reborn," Ryan said. "Plans to join the Jesuits."

"I know what happened." I was so jazzed I showed no empathy for Lô's frustration. "Spider. Xander. Lapasa. I just needed some medical info."

"Lecture alert," Ryan whispered to Lô and Cotton.

"I'll keep it brief." I was too pumped to take offense.

"And intelligible."

"Yeah, yeah. No jargon."

Deep breath.

"In 2002 a pregnant woman named Lydia Fairchild applied for welfare in the UK. In addition to her unborn infant, she had two children by a man named Jamie Townsend. As part of the application process, Fairchild had to provide DNA evidence that Townsend was the father. Results showed that he was, but indicated that she wasn't the mother."

"Bummer," Ryan said.

"No kidding. Fairchild was accused of fraud and her kids were taken into care. A judge ordered that a witness be present when she delivered, and that blood samples be taken from Fairchild and the baby. DNA indicated she was not the mother of that child either, even though it was a witnessed birth. A breakthrough came when lawyers discovered a similar case in Boston."

"Thank the Lord for defense attorneys." Lô, the king of sarcasm.

"In fact, it was the prosecutor." I smiled at Cotton. "In 1998 a woman named Karen Keegan needed a kidney transplant. Her adult sons were tested for suitability as donors. Two of the three failed to match her DNA to the extent a biological child should. More sophisticated testing showed that Keegan was a chimera, a combination of two separate sets of cell lines with two separate sets of chromosomes."

"How'd they figure that?" Ryan asked.

"Different DNA sequencing was found in tissues other than the ones originally taken from

Keegan. Fairchild's prosecutors suggested this possibility to her lawyers, and DNA samples were collected from members of the extended family. The DNA for Fairchild's children matched that of her mother to the extent expected for a grandmother."

"Showing she *was* the mother." Cotton looked confused.

"Further tests showed that while DNA obtained from Fairchild's skin and hair didn't match her children's, DNA obtained from a cervical smear was different and did match them."

"Fairchild was carrying two different sets of genes." Ryan simplified, but basically got it right.

"Yep."

"That's what this chimera thing is?" Lô.

"Yep." I glanced at my notes.

"This is where she tells us all about it," Ryan warned the other two.

"Two types of chimerism occur in humans. With microchimerism only a small portion of the body has a distinct cell line. Typically that arises because foreign cells have managed to stabilize inside a host."

"Foreign?" Cotton asked.

"Could be cells originating from maternal-fetal exchange during pregnancy. For example, the fetus may pass on its stem and progenitor cells to the mother via the placenta. Because they're undifferentiated, these cells may be able to survive and proliferate in the mother's system. Maternal stem cells may be transferred to the fetus in the same way."

No one said anything, so I continued.

"Microchimerism can also occur between twins. Actually, the most common form of human chimera is called a blood chimera. That results when fraternal twins share some portion of the same placenta. Blood is exchanged and takes up residence in the bone marrow. Each twin is genetically distinct except for their blood, which has two distinct sets of genes, maybe even two distinct blood types."

"How common is it?" Ryan.

"It's estimated that up to eight percent of fraternal twins are blood chimeras." I thought a moment. "Things like blood transfusions or organ transplants can also produce microchimerism in a recipient."

"That what happened to these ladies you're talking about?" Lô asked.

"No. What Fairchild and Keegan had is a much rarer type, tetragametic chimerism. This occurs when two separate ova are fertilized by two separate sperm and produce two zygotes."

Ryan raised a cautioning finger. "Embryos."

"Yes, sorry. It occurs with fraternal or nonidentical twins. The embryos fuse very early in development, creating a single baby with two distinct cell lines. One set of DNA may appear in the kidney and another set may appear in the pancreas."

Cotton summarized. "So these women, Fairchild and Keegan, each merged with her twin to form one baby with a hodgepodge of genes from both twins."

"Yes."

"Holy crap," Lô said. "These people must look weird."

"Many chimeras exhibit no overt signs of their condition. Or there may be minor peculiarities, differences in eye color, differential hair growth, that sort of thing. Others aren't so lucky. Doctors at the University of Edinburgh treated a man who complained of an undescended testicle. When they examined him, they found he had an ovary and a fallopian tube."

On-screen, Schoon was asking why Face Mask had been sent to Long Binh Jail.

Ryan cocked his chin toward the monitor. "What's this got to do with Lowery?"

"He's not Lowery."

"Where's Lowery?"

"Dead in Quebec."

"The DNA says no."

"Harriet Lowery was a chimera. She had one brown eye and one green eye. And Blaschko lines,"

No one asked, so I surged on.

"Blaschko lines appear as Vs or Ss or loops on the skin in specific parts of the body. They're invisible under normal conditions, but certain diseases of the skin and mucosa manifest themselves according to these patterns."

"Making them visible," Ryan guessed.

"Yes."

"They're like, what? Stripes?" Lô asked.

"Blaschko lines are thought to represent pathways of epidermal cell migration during fetal development. The point is, chimeras often have them, and in one picture in Plato's album, I could see them on Harriet Lowery's chest."

"Was she sick?"

"That I don't know. But she had Blaschko lines. And according to Plato, Harriet also had mismatched eyes."

"If she was a chimera, that would explain why her DNA didn't match that of her sons." Ryan was clicking.

"Exactly."

"Meaning the guy in the pond was Spider after all." Again, he indicated the screen. "Meaning this turkey isn't."

"Bingo."

"So who is he?" Lô asked.

I rotated the team photo.

All three bunched close.

I tapped a boy standing in the back row. "This is Spider Lowery."

"Agreed," Ryan said.

I tapped a boy kneeling in the front row. "This is his cousin."

"Sonofabitch," Lô said.

"They could be twins," Cotton said.

"Who is he?" Ryan asked.

"Reggie Cumbo," I said. "Look at the man talking to Schoon."

Three heads swiveled up.

"What color are his eyes?"

"Brown."

"According to Plato, Spider's eyes were green."

Ryan worked it over in his mind. Then, "You're thinking the cousins traded places back in sixty-eight. Spider went to Canada. Reggie went to Nam."

I nodded. "The physical resemblance was good enough to fool anyone who didn't really know them. They either swapped dental records or somehow Reggie removed them from his file."

"I'm lost," Cotton said.

"I'll fill you in later," Lô said.

"Why?" Ryan asked me.

"I don't know. Probably Spider got drafted and didn't want to go. Reggie was always the more aggressive and assertive of the two, according to Plato. He may have wanted to join but couldn't get in. He'd been arrested several times, hadn't graduated high school. Unless Reggie tells us, we may never learn precisely why they did it."

Ryan straightened. "How do you want to play this?" he asked Lô.

"Let me question him," I said.

"No way."

"I'm an anthropologist," I pressed. "You're a cop."

"You weren't kidding," Lô said to Ryan. "The chick is good."

"I told you."

"What I mean is, Reggie may view me as less threatening than you."

"I do have a badge," Lô said.

"And a gun," Ryan added.

"And I'm wearing this shirt." Lô flipped the hem of yet another aloha delight.

"You two are hilarious," I said. "But Cumbo has been granted limited immunity. Right now, he can walk anytime he wants. I can come at him from the JPAC angle. He claims he wants to die with a clear conscience. I can work that, talk about Plato, talk about getting Spider properly buried."

"How sure are you on this chimera thing?" Lô asked.

"To be absolutely certain, I'll need more of Harriet's DNA. But right now, it's the only theory that makes sense."

Lô looked at Cotton.

"I lost Atoa. I'd like to hang something on this guy."

"I don't see a downside," she said. "He's been Mirandized. He's got counsel. The army has a legitimate interest. Dr. Brennan's their rep on this Spider thing."

Lô hesitated.

Sighed.

"What the hell."

I started toward the door.

"And, hey," Lô said.

I turned, hand on the knob.

"Hit him with everything."

38

CUMBO DIDN'T GLANCE UP WHEN I ENTERED the room.

Schoon and Epstein did. The lawyers watched in silence as I walked toward the table.

Up close I could see that Cumbo was sweating big-time. The collar of his hoodie was soaked with perspiration pumping from his face and neck. His eyes were underhung with flabby half-moon plums. His skin was the color of dun.

"I'm Dr. Temperance Brennan." Taking a seat.

"Doctor?" Epstein looked from me to Schoon.

"ADA Cotton suggested that I participate in this interrogation."

"Doctor?" Epstein repeated.

"I'm a forensic anthropologist."

"I don't see the relevance."

"I work for JPAC." I spoke directly to Cumbo. "The Joint POW/MIA Accounting Command. Perhaps you've heard of it?"

Cumbo didn't raise his head or acknowledge my question.

"JPAC's mission is to locate American war

dead and bring them home. And they do a fine job of it."

Epstein started to object. I continued to ignore him.

"I'm involved in the case of a soldier who was killed in Vietnam, eventually buried in his home state of North Carolina."

Nothing.

"That soldier's friends and family called him Spider."

The half-moon plums pinched up ever so slightly.

"Recently an odd thing happened. A man died in Canada. Fingerprints identified that man as Spider. But Spider was buried in Lumberton, North Carolina."

Cumbo began working his thumbnails. I noticed they were yellow and ridged.

"As you can imagine, this situation created considerable confusion. The army doesn't like confusion. They opened an investigation to determine how the same man could be dead in two places."

I paused for effect.

"But I think you know."

"This is ridiculous," Epstein said.

Still I ignored him.

"Spider's real name was John Charles Lowery."

Epstein and Schoon both looked surprised. Epstein regretted it. Forced his face blank.

"But you claim *you* are John Charles Lowery. You say you killed Xander Lapasa in Long Binh forty years ago and assumed his identity."

Placing my forearms on the table, I leaned in.

"But John Charles Lowery never went to Vietnam. Did he, Reggie?"

Still Cumbo avoided my eyes.

"You remember Spider. You were cousins. You went to school together. Played baseball together. Wasn't it you who encouraged Spider to join the team?"

Cumbo's thumbnails were clicking double-time.

"Want to know how Spider died? He tied a rock to his ankle and drowned himself. His body's lying in a morgue in Montreal. The tag on his toe says John Doe."

A bit loose with the facts, but close enough.

Epstein flapped a hand, dismissive. "We're finished here. This woman is clearly misinformed." He gripped the arms of his chair and began to push back.

"You're right and you're wrong." Cumbo's eyes bore into mine.

"Mr. Lapasa, I strongly advise—"

Without turning, Cumbo raised a finger, a teacher demanding silence.

Epstein frowned disapproval.

Unhooking the elastic loops from his ears, Cumbo removed the mask.

I forced myself still.

Cumbo hadn't worn protection out of fear of infection. The lower half of his face was grotesquely disfigured. His chin skewed right at an unnatural angle, and his lower jaw appeared way too small. I guessed most of his mandible had been surgically removed. His neck had a cavernous indentation, and a scar jagged diagonally across his throat.

"That make us even? Your face is shit too."

I kept my eyes steady on Cumbo's.

"You nailed it," he said. "I'm not Al Lapasa. And I'm not Spider."

"You're Reggie Cumbo."

"Haven't been Reggie Cumbo for over forty years."

"You reported for military service in Spider's place."

"He didn't want to go. I did."

"Spider went to Canada."

Cumbo shrugged. "He liked snow."

"Did you keep in touch?"

"For a while. I forwarded his mama's letters. Quit when I headed to Nam." Cumbo's mouth executed a slippery sideways maneuver. "Still got some of her crap in a box."

"The army wasn't what you expected."

Cumbo's eyes narrowed.

"Combat. Hot, stinking jungle. You wanted out."

"That war was stupid." Defensive.

"So you murdered Xander Lapasa."

"What? Am I watching a rerun?" Cumbo tossed the mask. It did a lopsided roll across the table, then dropped to the floor.

I switched topics.

"You own a bar in Oakland called the Savaii."

"That a crime?"

"Savaii is a town in Samoa."

"Now we all get an A in geography."

"The Savaii is a hangout for members of a street gang called Sons of Samoa."

Cumbo raised then dropped his hands back on the table. *So?*

"How does someone from Lumberton, North Carolina, end up SOS?"

"I got dark good looks so I fit the part. Indian, you know." Cumbo's mouth and chin tucked sideways in an attempt at an ironic grin. It was repellent. "Crips heard the name Lapasa, figured I was Samoan. Being a cuz worked for me, so I rolled with it."

Schoon cleared his throat.

Epstein listened, quiet but vigilant.

"Tell me about Francis Kealoha."

"Who the fuck's Francis Kealoha?"

"Perhaps you know him as Frankie Olopoto."

Below the scar Cumbo's Adam's apple rose then fell.

"How about George Faalogo? That name ring a bell?"

Cumbo said nothing.

"Let's talk about Nickie Lapasa."

No response.

"Xander's brother. Xander Lapasa. The poor chump you murdered. I'm sure you're aware that Nickie Lapasa is a powerful man. A rich man. I'm sure you know the Lapasa family has financial interests that extend far beyond the state of Hawaii. Maybe even to California. You told us you looked Nickie up online. Was that a little fib, Reggie? Are you and Nickie acquainted through, shall we say, professional ties?"

Schoon came to life.

"We will not discuss Nicholas Lapasa's personal or professional affairs at any time during this interview."

"Is that why you sent Frankie and Logo out here?" I pressed on.

Cumbo's eyes narrowed even further, but he said nothing.

I pulled another topic switch.

"I understand you're under investigation for selling illegal drugs. You deal out of your bar, Reggie?"

Now it was Epstein's turn to object. "You're crossing a line, miss."

"You looking to expand distribution?" I continued drilling Cumbo. "Is that why you sent Kealoha and Faalogo to Hawaii? They your front men for new projects?"

"Enough!" Epstein was on his feet.

"You screwed up, Reggie. You sent Frankie and Logo onto another man's turf. Ever hear of L'il Bud T'eo? You sent them into T'eo's house."

"This is outrageous." A flush was spreading upward from Epstein's collar.

"You got them killed, Reggie."

"What the fuck?" Cumbo's lips parted, revealing a tongue that looked like a shriveled eel.

"The sharks didn't leave much to ID."

Cumbo's mouth closed, made another oily loop.

"Your line of questioning is completely out of order."

For the first time I looked at Epstein. I had to credit the guy. He was tenacious as crabgrass.

"For this interview to continue you must focus exclusively on circumstances surrounding Xander Lapasa's death."

"Fine. Let's focus on Xander. Your client says he wants to come clean about the murder. Still he lies about his real identity." I turned to Cumbo. "Why is that, Reggie?"

"I told you. I have regrets."

"You're seeking peace? Forgiveness? Or are you just looking to save your ass?"

Cumbo snorted in derision.

"You know what I think, Reggie? Maybe the cops are closing in on your little operation. Maybe you're taking heat from SOS for getting Frankie and Logo killed. Maybe you found out T'eo's put a price on your head. Whatever. I doubt you give a rat's ass about clearing your conscience. I think you're looking to boogie again."

I was on a roll, making it up as I went along.

"I think you see the clock ticking on Al Lapasa. I think you're hoping John Lowery is your new get-out-of-jail-free card. That's your MO, right? Steal someone else's name and disappear? Reggie Cumbo becomes Spider Lowery. Spider Lowery becomes Al Lapasa. Now it's time to go back to being Lowery. To disappear."

Cumbo thrust his head forward so his nose was inches from mine. I smelled his sweat, felt his rancid breath on my face.

Locking his eyes on mine, Cumbo curled, then exploded his fingers.

"Poof!"

Droplets of saliva sprayed my face.

Revolted, I drew back and reached for my

purse. I was searching for a tissue when the door opened.

I swiveled.

Lô's face told me something was very wrong.

"May I help you?" Schoon asked.

Lô pointed at me, then hooked a thumb over his shoulder.

I rose and hurried into the hall.

Ryan was standing outside the conference room from which we'd observed the interview. His body looked tense. The ADA wasn't with him.

"Where's Cotton?" I asked.

"Gone."

Lô said nothing further until we joined Ryan. Then, "Pinky Atoa is dead."

"Dear God." I was stunned.

Ryan's expression told me he already knew.

"A bum found him ninety minutes ago behind a 7-Eleven on Nuuanu. He'd taken one slug to the head, three to the chest."

I felt sick. Atoa was sixteen years old. Yesterday he'd been worried about his dog.

"His body was lying beside a Dumpster." Lô swallowed. "His tongue was cut out and nailed to one side."

Sweet Jesus.

"When was he killed?"

"Perry's putting time of death at somewhere between nine and eleven this morning."

"The kid had hardly hit the street." I wasn't believing this.

"Yeah. Someone was waiting for him."

Lô's eyes showed both pain and resolve. He knew what had happened, what lay ahead.

Ryan and I had lived through a gang war. Seen the bloodshed, the senseless death. We knew too.

"I don't know if this prick Cumbo is involved, but deal or no deal, his ass stays put until I find out."

"He acted genuinely surprised when I said Kealoha and Faalogo are dead."

"Yeah, he's innocent as Bambi."

Lô glanced at his watch.

"Hung's on her way here. She'll deal with Cumbo. I've asked Fitch to see what he can scratch up on the Atoa hit. In the meantime, I'm heading to the scene."

Lô's heels squeaked softly as he strode across the marble.

Ryan and I rode the elevator and left the building in silence.

Walking toward his car we shared the sidewalk with tourists checking maps, mothers pushing strollers, shoppers carrying brightly colored bags.

Early-evening sun bathed the city in warm saffron tones. The air smelled of sea and warm stone, with hints of hibiscus and grilling meat.

The day is too beautiful for death, I thought. Death at sixteen.

Ryan was unlocking the car when tires squealed behind us.

We both whipped around.

Blue lights flashed from the front grille and back window of Lô's Crown Vic.

I looked at Ryan. His face told me he shared my apprehension.

We hurried toward Lô.

"I'm glad I caught you." He spoke through his open window. "Fitch called. Word is Atoa was T'eo's hit."

"He ordered one of his own killed?" I was shocked and appalled.

"Someone must have seen Atoa entering or leaving the station, dimed T'eo. T'eo decided to make an example."

"Christ," Ryan said.

"Word is Ted Pukui got twenty thousand to take the kid out."

We waited.

"Fitch heard Atoa's only the warm-up. T'eo plans to send a message, not just here but to all the cuz on the mainland." Lô snorted his disgust. "Grow his legend."

Lô's eyes shifted from Ryan to me and back.

"Where are your daughters?"

"At home." A cold fist grabbed my heart. "Why?"

"Call them."

Ryan dialed the house. Got no answer. Lily's mobile. Voice mail. He handed me the phone. I dialed Katy. Voice mail.

"Why are you asking about Katy and Lily?" I demanded.

"Word is T'eo's offered another twenty thousand for you or one of your kids."

The cold fist expanded to fill my chest.

"He was behind the incident at Waimanalo Bay. Cost him a case of rum to have those punks force you off the road."

"Why?"

"To discourage you from helping Perry. Didn't

work, and now you're causing serious inconvenience. This time he's offering big money."

I saw fury enter Ryan's eyes. Felt it in mine.

"But his intel's off on your kids. According to Fitch, T'eo's order was to take out either white or brown sugar."

39

When overwhelmed by emotion, my mother closed the door. I do the same.

Though rage and fear battled inside me, outwardly I remained icy calm.

"Follow me." Lô flicked a button. A pulsing wail split the afternoon calm.

Pedestrians craned their necks. Or froze. Or continued with their day. Cars nosed toward the curbs.

Ryan sprinted, yanked his door open, threw himself behind the wheel. I was right with him.

Palm-smacking the gearshift, he slammed his foot on the gas. The car jerked forward.

"Try again." Ryan tossed me his cell as we zigzagged through the wormhole created by Lô's siren.

I braced on the dash and punched digits one-handed.

Still no one picked up.

"They were told to stay at the house." Ryan kept two hands on the wheel, two eyes on the road.

"Maybe they're at the pool," I said.

It was lame. We both knew they'd have taken their phones with them.

Traffic was heavy, but thanks to the lights and siren we made it to Kailua in twenty-three minutes.

Over the bridge, a wend through Lanikai, then a fishtail turn up the drive.

Ryan and I flew from the car and raced into the house.

"Katy?"

"Lily?"

Our calls were answered by silence.

I pumped up the stairs. Ryan rushed outside. Seconds later we met in the kitchen. Lô was already there. Our faces told the story.

"Where the hell are they?" Fear added a tremor to my voice.

Ryan laid a hand on my shoulder. "I'm sure they're fine."

Lô was punching buttons on his cell when a sliding door whurped across its track.

Six eyes flew toward the dining room.

"Finally." Katy managed to sound both petulant and anxious at the same time.

"Where's Lily?" I barked.

"That's what *I'd* like to know. She went off with some skanky-looking loser. I got worried, went out looking for her. First the mall, now tonight. One more and technically she's on a spree."

"Why didn't you call me?"

"I *have* been calling you. Over and over." Sudden realization. "Oh, crap. I'm an idiot. Your BlackBerry's in the ocean."

"How long since they left?" Lô asked.

"Maybe thirty minutes."

"What did the guy look like?"

"Who are you?"

"He's a detective," I snapped. "Answer his questions."

"Is Lily in danger?" Panic filled Katy's eyes. "I told her not to go."

"What did he look like?" Lô repeated.

"Dreads, chains, the whole banger thing."

Lô slanted a look at Ryan.

"Do you know where they went?" I worked to hide the dread building inside me.

"Up some trail. Skank-boy told her the view was primo."

"Kaiwa Ridge." Lô was already moving.

"You two stay here." Ryan bolted after Lô.

I spun to face Katy. "Give me your sneakers."

"What?"

"Just do it."

She unlaced and handed them to me. I kicked off my sandals and yanked them on.

"Jacket."

She tossed it.

"Lock every door, arm the security system, then go to your room and stay there. If an alarm sounds, don't wait. Call nine-one-one."

"But—"

"Do it! We're all in danger. Be alert."

Pulling the jacket over my head, I bounded out the door.

The sun was low, throwing long ink houses and hedges across the lawn and street. Soon it would be full dark.

I looked left, right.

A block south Ryan was turning from Moku-lua onto Kaelepulu, running with strong, steady strides. I knew Lô was somewhere ahead.

I sprinted through fingers of sunlight and shadow. I had no idea where Lô was going. If I lost sight of Ryan I was done.

I rounded the corner. Several blocks up on the right was the entrance to the Mid-Pacific Country Club. Just beyond it, Ryan cut left.

I kicked hard, reached the spot, saw a drive-way joining the road. Veered onto it.

Just ahead, Ryan was disappearing into a black hole in vegetation beside a chain-link fence.

I raced toward the opening.

A narrow path snaked uphill at an impossible angle.

Lily may need you!

Grabbing the fence with one hand and a tree branch with the other, I planted a foot and hauled myself onto the trailhead.

Loose soil and pebbles cascaded downward.

My sneaker lost traction.

I fell.

Pain exploded in my already bruised kneecap.

I rose. Tested.

Go!

Advancing from tree to tree, I dragged myself upward.

A hundred yards? Two hundred? At the time it seemed like a climb up Everest.

Finally the trail leveled off. The trees gave way to low-lying scrub, grass, and lava rock.

Ryan and Lô were visible far up the ridgeline, dark figures moving fast through the murky dusk.

Dear God!

The trail crawled the edge of a precipice. No guardrail. No tree trunks. Nothing to the left but yawning space.

I stood panting, heart thudding in my chest.

Far below I could see Kailua Bay to the north and Waimanalo Bay to the south. Lilliputian houses. Lanikai Beach. The two little Mokulua Islands, tiny black bumps in a pumpkin-slashed sea.

Wind danced through my jacket and whipped my hair into a banshee tangle. Loose gravel slithered below the way-too-smooth rubber on the soles of my sneakers.

The height. The treacherous footing. Fear for Lily.

Adrenaline had me wired to hell and back.

I pushed on.

Ten minutes scrabbling upward, then I rounded a curve.

A black cutout rose from the ridgeline above, roughly twenty-five yards from me. Square. Concrete. A leftover from World War II.

I could see a figure on the near side of the pillbox. Ryan, crouched, ready to spring.

At that distance, I couldn't tell what held his attention. Lô was nowhere to be seen.

I took a moment to assess.

The pillbox faced the sea. My approach would be invisible to anyone in it. The wind would mask any sounds I might make.

Gingerly placing each foot, I crept forward.

I was ten feet out when Ryan whipped around, ready to attack.

His eyes widened, then tensed in anger. His upraised arms relaxed a hair. A downward move of one hand gestured me behind his back.

I scurried to him and dropped to a squat.

And noticed the boy.

He lay hidden in shadow cast by the pillbox, dreadlocks haloing his head like snakes around Medusa. His eyes were closed. His chest looked still.

I placed shaky fingers on the boy's throat. Felt no pulse.

I was trying again when his lids fluttered. Half-opened.

I found and squeezed his hand. Bent close. Heard breath rattling in his chest.

"Sarah?" His words barely carried above the wind. "It's so cold."

I whipped my jacket off and spread it across him.

He frowned, puzzled, a faraway look in his eyes.

"It's so cold. I'm freezing." His limbs shivered uncontrollably.

"You're going to be fine," I whispered close to his ear. "We'll get you to a hospital. You're young. You'll make it."

"I can't see, Sarah."

"Hold on." I tightened my grip, felt slight pressure in return.

"Everything's black." Mumbled. "Sarah, I'm dying."

I trembled from cold or fear. Goose bumps puckered my flesh.

The boy coughed wetly. His mouth looked dark. Too dark.

I pressed my chest to his, willing my warmth and strength into his body.

Please, God!

"I'm scared." His lips were right at my ear. "Shit. I don't want to d—"

His words were cut off.

By death?

No! No!

Hot tears streamed my cheeks.

Beside me, I felt Ryan coil.

I raised my head.

Followed Ryan's sight line.

Every muscle in my body went rigid.

A man was dragging Lily through one of the pillbox's doorless openings. One beefy hand wrapped her throat. The other held a gun tight to her temple.

Pukui? It had to be. Out to collect his twenty grand.

Ryan tensed to spring.

Pukui forced Lily toward the seaward side of the pillbox. I could see that the path at that point was less than a foot wide.

Lily's eyes looked like those of a terrified dog, the whites huge, and distorted with fear.

I craned over Ryan's shoulder, terrified to watch, terrified not to.

In the gloom, Lô materialized atop the pillbox, hunched, Glock held two-handed and pointed at Pukui. He inched forward, feeling with his feet, not daring to glance down. One step. Two.

Lô was almost to the front edge of the pillbox

when Pukui shoved his gun under Lily's jaw and forced her chin up. She yelped in pain.

Lô froze.

Ryan braced with one hand against the concrete.

Pukui's head swiveled from side to side.

"We got company?" Pukui shouted. "Do yourself a favor, bro. Get the hell out of here."

Silence.

"Don't fuck with me, man." There was true venom in Pukui's voice.

The next sixty seconds seemed to last an hour.

Lô tensed. Fired.

The shot and a scream exploded as one sound.

Pukui's upper body twisted left. His gun flew from his hand and cartwheeled into shadow.

Lily broke free.

Pukui yanked her back by the hood of her jacket.

Lily went down hard on her bum, struggled for traction with her hands and feet.

Ryan sprang. Drove the heel of his hand into Pukui's Adam's apple.

Pukui staggered back.

Ryan grabbed Lily. Dragged her away from the edge.

Pukui doubled over, gasping. His face was just a mouth hole gaping in the deepening dusk.

Another shot rang out.

Pukui spun. Dropped to his back.

Blood foamed from his mouth and oozed from his chest.

One leg flexed in spasm. His hips bucked.

Before Ryan could move, Pukui rolled and dropped over the cliff.

40

A JET FLEW HIGH OVERHEAD, LEAVING A WHITE cotton-candy trail to mark its passing. Hot breezes swayed the tops of the loblolly pines and rippled the grass like a bright green sea.

The grave at our feet smelled of freshly turned earth. A bouquet lay on the patchwork sod, the supermarket carnations brown and wilted. Beside it, a tiny American flag drooped on its balsa wood stick.

The old headstone was gone. Its replacement gleamed speckled pink in the sun. The inscription was sharp and bone white, a raw wound in the granite.

Spec 2 Luis Alvarez, United States Army
February 28, 1948–January 23, 1968
He died a hero

When JPAC failed to locate an Alvarez family member, Plato offered the grave at Gardens of Faith Cemetery. Said the spot belonged to Alvarez, that he'd be more at peace in familiar soil than elsewhere. Purchased the marker.

Behind us, beside a smaller stand of pines,

another pair of headstones threw shadows on the lawn. Katy and I had placed flowers on the one marking a second new grave.

John Charles "Spider" Lowery
March 21, 1950–May 5, 2010
He loved all living things

The other stone waited above unbroken lawn.

Plato Maximus Lowery
Loving husband of Harriet Cumbo Lowery
Father of John and Thomas
December 14, 1928–

Sheriff Beasley was right. Plato Lowery was a good man.

Ironically, it was the science that Plato distrusted so fiercely that vindicated his faith in wife and family. DNA had confirmed my suspicion that Harriet was a chimera.

At my request, Reggie Cumbo turned over letters Harriet had mailed to her son following his departure for the army. Saliva on the stamps and envelopes yielded a testable sample. The DNA sequencing differed from that obtained from Harriet's pathology slides, and matched the sequencing found in samples taken from the Hemmingford pond victim, Spider Lowery.

Providing the letters was perhaps Reggie Cumbo's final redemption. Shortly after that, he'd gone into hospice care.

Pinky Atoa had gotten it wrong about Cumbo's status with the Sons of Samoa. Cumbo was an OG, yeah, but not an "original gangsta," just an "old guy" who owned an SOS hangout.

Cumbo had probably turned a blind eye at the Savaii, maybe taken kickbacks, but it was unlikely he'd sent Kealoha and Faalogo to Hawaii. Expansion into the islands was apparently their own brainchild.

Cumbo wouldn't be charged with any crime. He'd soon be dead. We'd probably never know his full culpability.

I still wondered about Cumbo's motivation for coming forward after so many years. Was it a Lee Atwater moment? A change in heart—and priorities—as his life drew to a close? Remorse for killing Xander Lapasa, as he claimed? Or the vision of a new business op, a score with Theresa-Sophia's will? We'd probably never know that either.

I never quite understood Cumbo's speech to an unseen Nickie Lapasa in Schoon's conference room. There was no evidence they'd ever met. Perhaps Cumbo felt it was important as he faced death to make his confession to Xander's brother. He'd researched the Lapasas on the Internet and taken the opportunity to go to Hawaii, probably expecting to see Nickie.

Nickie Lapasa had finally agreed to allow his sister to submit a DNA sample. I had no doubt Xander would soon be returned to his family.

I suspected my first guess about Nickie's initial reluctance was right. Even if he now ran a clean business, Nickie, schooled at Alex's knee, saw his father's troubles, probably absorbed the old man's distrust of cops and government.

Hadley Perry survived the political storm created by her closure of Halona Cove, once again ruled her kingdom of death. I never learned if she and Ryan had history. Never would ask.

The boy at the pillbox also survived. His name was Barry Byrd. He was nineteen, played sax in a jazz band, attended university part-time with his sister Sarah.

Lily met Byrd during her visit to the Ala Moana mall that had so irritated Katy. The two kept in contact by phone. They had plans to meet the night Katy saw Byrd by our pool.

Pukui's bullet took out a piece of Byrd's shoulder and fractured his clavicle. He'd lost a lot of blood, but medics brought by helicopter got to him in time. He was released from The Queen's Medical Center two days after his admission.

To date, Ted Pukui's body hadn't been found. Perhaps he'd fallen into a crevice or been wedged between rocks. Perhaps he'd been washed out to sea. Somehow the latter seemed fitting, poetic justice for Kealoha and Faalogo.

L'il Bud T'eo was claiming Pukui acted alone. Could think of no reason why he'd do such a thing. So far the cops had nothing but rumors to tie him to the Atoa hit. Or to the murders of Kealoha and Faalogo. Lô and Hung weren't giving up. They'd nail him one day.

So much deception. So many secrets. Is that how we live our lives?

Lily deceived us about her relationship with Barry Byrd. Reggie deceived the world by living first as John Lowery, later as Al Lapasa. Spider did the same by going underground as Jean Laurier, by concealing his addiction to plastic, proctoscopes, and pink panties. Plato hid the painful possibility that his family might not be what it seemed, though in fairness he never believed the allegations he was suppressing.

Who knew what Nickie Lapasa kept out of sight?

So questions remained.

And Katy had questions of her own.

Why couldn't Coop have left a day earlier? Or later? Why was he on that road at that precise moment?

Why do any of us make the decisions we do?

Charlie Hunt phoned the day I got back to Charlotte. I was friendly but noncommittal. Why?

Was it because of Ryan? If so, why did I keep Ryan outside the emotional guardrail?

Why does Ryan blame himself for Lily's addiction? Why does Lily poison her body with drugs?

I watched my daughter as she considered Alvarez's epitaph. I knew the pain she was feeling. Alvarez was twenty when he died. Coop was twenty-five.

Katy, with the characteristic droop to her shoulders, upper teeth on lower lip, hair draping the sides of her face.

Looking at my daughter, I felt almost giddy with love. Knew I would do anything for her. Risk my life to protect her.

But I knew I couldn't shield her from all pain.

Ryan had returned with his daughter to Montreal. His fears about her using heroin again seemed unfounded. For now. I hoped with all my heart that Lily would stay straight.

Lutetia wouldn't be there to welcome her

daughter. She'd returned to Nova Scotia. Another irony. Lutetia's call to Lily was the spark that had caused Katy to thaw.

I'd asked about the sudden bonding, been surprised by Katy's answer. By the compassion and maturity it revealed.

Lily grew up without a father, Katy said, and is desperate for approval, especially from men. She found her crying in her room. She complimented her shoes.

I smiled at the memory of that conversation.

Katy turned. Ear-tucked her hair.

"Why are you grinning?"

"No reason," I said. "On to Charleston?"

She nodded.

We took a gravel path that curved through gravestones and manicured shrubs.

"It's such a waste," Katy said. "Coop. Luis Alvarez. That Xander guy. They were all so young and full of life. Now they're dead."

I let her talk. We'd been over this, but I understood her need to vent.

"I even wonder about the two guys thrown off Makapu'u Point. And the guys who threw them."

"That's totally different. Those men made life choices, to both harm others and put themselves at risk. They hardly deserve pity."

Katy's face clouded. "But, at some level, there is a similarity. Decisions are made by young people that cause them to die."

"It's unfair to equate soldiers or cops or firemen with people who cause harm and place themselves in danger for personal gain."

"Of course it is. That's not what I'm saying.

Soldiers like Luis Alvarez are selfless heroes. Bangers like Kealoha and Faalogo are self-serving scum."

"I guess I'm missing the point," I said.

"I don't know." Katy sighed. "I keep asking myself why one person takes risks to do something meaningful, while another takes risks to cause harm."

"And why on both sides of the equation some live and some die."

"And that."

"People have been asking those questions since they started painting pictures on the walls of caves." I reminded myself to get her a copy of the *The Bridge of San Luis Rey*.

As we exited through the big wrought-iron gates, I turned for one last look at John Lowery's grave.

What a spider's web you and Reggie wove, I thought. So much grief and deceit. So many people tangled in the threads.

Aloha, Spider.

Gracias, Luis.

Find peace here, Plato.

My Mazda was in the same place I'd parked on the day of the exhumation.

"Got your game on, tough stuff?"

"Ready for the play-offs." Katy grinned. Bleakly.

"What do you suppose Coop left you?"

"I have no idea."

"Let's find out."

FROM THE FORENSIC FILES OF DR. KATHY REICHS

UNTIL THEY ARE HOME

The mission of the Joint POW/MIA Accounting Command, JPAC, is to locate Americans held as prisoners of war and to recover those who have died in past conflicts. JPAC was created in 2003 by merging CILHI, the U.S. Army Central Identification Laboratory, Hawaii, and JTF-FA, the Joint Task Force–Full Accounting. To date, the United States government has found no evidence of any POW still in captivity, so JPAC's day-to-day focus is on the investigation of leads and the recovery and identification of remains.

On average, JPAC identifies six sets of human remains each month. The process is complicated, requiring substantial forensic expertise and multiple levels of review.

That's where I came in. Back in the CILHI day, I served as an external consultant. My duties included analyzing the dossiers of soldiers, sailors, airmen, and marines for whom positive IDs had tentatively been established, and visiting the Honolulu lab twice yearly for oversight and briefing.

Hawaii. Midwinter. Think that was an easy sell to my department chair at University of North Carolina at Charlotte, where I was on faculty with a full-time teaching load?

As Ryan complained to Tempe, the military loves its alphabet soup. At CILHI, I was issued a glossary of acronyms as thick as my arm. KIA/BNR: killed in action, body not recovered. DADCAP: dawn and dusk combat air patrol; AACP: advance airborne command post; TRF: tuned radio frequency. Or trident refit facility. I guess context is important for that one. But you get the idea. It makes a civilian want to join the AAAAAA: the Association for the Abolition of Abused Abbreviations and Asinine Acronyms.

While I've tried to provide a peek into some of the operations at JPAC, much goes on that I've not described in *Spider Bones*. JPAC representatives engage in constant negotiation with governments around the globe, and they work closely with various U.S. agencies, to pursue all leads that might bring missing Americans home.

Each year JPAC recovery teams travel by horseback, boat, train, and helicopter to recover the bodies of U.S. troops missing from World War II, Korea, the Cold War, and Southeast Asia. They slash through jungles, rappel cliffs, scuba dive into trenches, and climb up mountains, toting their weight in survival and excavation equipment. In comparison, my job was a stroll through the park. Physically, at least. Emotionally, it was gripping.

Through Tempe, I've tried to convey the feelings I experienced while examining the files of men and women killed long ago and far from home while serving their country. The maps, photographs, correspondence, unit histories, and medical and personnel records made each case painfully real.

But my time with CILHI wasn't all sad. When not focused on work my colleagues and I had fun. I remember when Hugh Berryman, P. Willey, and I splashed in the Waikiki surf, giggling like kids. And the trip Jack Kenney blew multiple traffic signals and earned the enduring nickname "Red Light." Or when Mike Finnegan and team posed as my undercover security unit and literary manager at a book signing. Through both work and play, I forged bonds that will last a lifetime.

JPAC wasn't always as I describe it today. When headquarters moved to Hickam Air Force Base in the early nineties, the staff included only a handful of anthropologists. Today there are more than two dozen.

And the scope of operation has expanded. In 2008, the CIL opened the Forensic Science Academy, an advanced forensic anthropology program taught under the auspices of the DoD. Department of Defense. (Yep. There's another one.). In 2009 a U.S. Navy hydrographic survey vessel, the USNS *Bruce C. Heezen*, conducted underwater investigation operations in Vietnam's territorial waters, a historic first, marking a strengthening of cooperation between JPAC and the Vietnamese government.

Change was afoot even as *Spider Bones* went to press. On January 29, 2010, U.S. Navy Rear Admiral Donna L. Crisp relinquished command of JPAC to Army Major General Stephen Tom. (Had to scramble to include that update.)

JPAC's mission is daunting. Approximately 78,000 Americans remain missing from World War II, 8,100 from the Korean War, 120 from the Cold War, and 1,800 from the Vietnam War. Tirelessly, personnel continue to interview, search, dig, analyze, measure, and test.

A commemorative board hangs in the lobby of JPAC headquarters, engraved with words similar to those found on POW/MIA flags: *Not To Be Forgotten*. Tiny brass plaques bear the names of those identified since 1973. Happily, there are many plaques.

JPAC's motto appears at the front of this book: "Until They Are Home."

JPAC staff close their meetings and events by repeating the words aloud. In 2009, recovery teams deployed to sixteen countries on sixty-nine missions. JPAC scientists identified the remains of ninety-five men and women.

And they will identify many more.

Until They Are Home.

For information on the Joint POW/MIA Accounting Command visit their website: www.jpac.pacom.mil.

For specific information on a missing American, call or write:

Department of the Army
U.S. Army Human Resources Command
Attn: AHRC-PDC-R
200 Stovall Street
Alexandria, VA 22332-0482
800-892-2490

Headquarters U.S. Marine Corps
Manpower and Reserve Affairs (MRA)
Personal and Family Readiness Division
3280 Russell Road
Quantico, VA 22134-5103
800-847-1597

Department of the Navy
Casualty Assistance Division (OPNAV N135C)
POW/MIA Branch
5720 Integrity Drive
Millington, TN 38055-6210
800-443-9298

Department of the Air Force
HQ Air Force/Mortuary Affairs
116 Purple Heart Drive
Dover Air Force Base, DE 19902
800-531-5803

Department of State
U.S. Department of State
CA/OCS/ACS/EAP/SA29
2201 C Street NW
Washington, DC 20520-2818
202-647-5470